Ways to Kiss a Marquess This Winter

WEDDING FEVER, BOOK 4

SARA ADRIEN &
TANYA WILDE

ARE YOU SIGNED UP FOR DRAGONBLADE'S BLOG?

You'll get the latest news and information on exclusive giveaways, exclusive excerpts, coming releases, sales, free books, cover reveals and more.

Check out our complete list of authors, too!

No spam, no junk. That's a promise!

Sign Up Here

www.dragonbladepublishing.com

Dearest Reader;

Thank you for your support of a small press. At Dragonblade Publishing, we strive to bring you the highest quality Historical Romance from some of the best authors in the business. Without your support, there is no 'us', so we sincerely hope you adore these stories and find some new favorite authors along the way.

Happy Reading!

CEO, Dragonblade Publishing

ADDITIONAL DRAGONBLADE BOOKS BY
AUTHOR TANYA WILDE

Wedding Fever Series (with Sara Adrien)
Dare to Tempt an Earl This Spring (Book 1)
How to Lose a Prince This Summer (Book 2)
How to Seduce a Duke this Autumn (Book 3)
Ways to Kiss a Marquess This Winter (Book 4)

Ladies Who Dare Series
Almost a Scoundrel (Book 1)
By No Means a Gentleman (Book 2)
A Knave By Any Other Name (Book 3)
A Little Bit of Hellion (Book 4)
Just About a Rake (Book 5)
Only a Duke (Book 6)

The Lyon's Den Series
Beauty and the Lyon

Chapter One

M ISS MADELEINE HUNT, known by her confidants as Maddie, and daughter of Viscount Tisdale, bit into a lemon cake while bathing in the warmth of the hearth fire. Before her, she enjoyed the sight of two handsome men playing bridge, their host and the "esteemed" Duke of Paisley. Well, esteemed for his title but certainly not for his personality, integrity, or heart—none of which, she was quite sure, he possessed. She hadn't forgotten his part in almost ending her friend's engagement because of a wager. And when he laughed, the sound was smooth enough to transfix a room. But it never quite reached his eyes.

Hopefully, all that might change.

Because he was also her future husband.

Possibly. Maybe.

Her mother refused to accept anything less.

And Maddie wanted a husband. Someone to share her life with, but she hadn't found anyone else to sweep her off her feet and kiss her to set her heart ablaze—not that such a thing could be managed in the dead of winter. No, if only she could manage to convince him of the fact before the end of this engagement party. But really, how hard could it be? She had already drawn up a rather ingenious husband-chasing plan. And there really was just one ingredient for success in such matters.

Dedication.

And Maddie had lots and lots of dedication. Other than that, there were only three steps to catch a husband that she had identified through reading numerous books. And perhaps this time, *The Handbook on Seduction and Matters of the Heart* might actually come in handy. But one could never know. It was equal parts advice and nonsense, but at least it gave her something to do.

But she'd borrowed it from Charlene just in case... Maddie was, after all, the only one of her group of four friends who hadn't caught the wedding fever yet.

This afternoon, the plan looked almost sensible: catch his eye (accidentally, achieved with a frog and a ruined jacket), stir his interest, steal his heart. Three tidy steps the handbook promised—though it had never met a duke who didn't smile.

"What's brewing in that head of yours?" Ashley, hostess, and one of Maddie's best friends and the bride-to-be for the master of this castle, the Earl of Linsey—Thomas to friends—piped up as she joined her in her little cocoon of heat. Fire crackled, adding a peaceful harmony to the scene.

"Step two of my plan." Maddie reached for another lemon cake. They were her favorite. Bright and fluffy, a delicious combination of sweet and tart flavors.

"If you are really going to proceed with this mad plan," Ashley plucked the lemony goodness from her fingers, "and it truly is mad, stop stuffing your face with these cakes and throw them at him instead. It's what he deserves for even being here— uninvited."

"The duke's not looking this way."

"Exactly."

Maddie glared at her friend but didn't snatch the cake back. It had only been her fifth cake.

"Well, at least the duke does not suspect your husband-chasing plan after yesterday's display. And yet, I daresay, my hope is that you'll chase him away and not into matrimony." She pursed her lips. "I suppose things could have been worse."

Maddie arched a brow. "How could things have been worse?"

"You could have jumped into his arms."

Maddie's face heated. "I would never do such a thing!" Although… the idea did hold some appeal. It might speed things up considerably.

"Just as well," Ashley said, motioning to a group of ladies surrounding the duke. "You're not the only one clamoring for his attention."

"There's no need for me to clamor. I already caught his attention."

"Right." Ashley inclined her head and didn't even try to hide her disapproval.

"Do not judge. Any attention is good attention."

"Remind me what books you've been reading of late?" Ashley narrowed her eyes.

Maddie clamped her mouth shut. It was the book, of course. They'd all consulted the advice of *The Handbook on Seduction and Matters of the Heart*.

In any event, Maddie still had some pride.

"Romance books," she said vaguely.

Ashley grinned but didn't press. Instead, she asked, "Have you heard from your family?"

Maddie scoffed. "Mother ordered me to stop reaching for my potions and the stars."

"That woman is really something."

Maddie smiled, but it didn't reach her eyes. Of course, her mother didn't understand her interest in potions—or anything else, for that matter. The subject was dismissed as a childish fancy, a dangerous quirk better hidden if she ever hoped to marry. She'd been told to be agreeable. To smile sweetly. To accept the first suitable offer that came her way.

Settle. Be grateful. Do not frighten anyone with too much enthusiasm for herbs or science or passion.

But the thought of it—of being chosen like a cow at auction, never seen, never wanted—had settled heavy in her chest.

She smoothed her gown. Once, she might have agreed. But not today.

Today, something inside her shifted. Not loudly, not all at once. More like a whisper beneath her skin. A rising hum of defiance.

No. She would not settle.

She didn't just plant her foot; she grounded herself. She burrowed in.

Let her mother worry about appearances. Maddie would worry about finding a man who looked at her as if he might burst from wanting her. A man who kissed as if he had gone mad. A man who saw her—and liked what he saw.

"Perhaps, after all, I'm not marrying the first gentleman who asks," she whispered to herself. "Not unless he makes me feel something."

"Don't look now," Ashley murmured beside her, "but the duke is looking your way."

Maddie straightened instinctively. She'd been trained by her mother to impress him. He was an ideal candidate. His pedigree was flawless, but his core was rotten.

Before she could turn, Ashley grabbed her hand. "Don't look. Be sophisticated. Not eager. Laugh."

Maddie hesitated—then let out a light, practiced laugh.

But inside?

Inside, she wasn't laughing. She was calculating. Debating. Choosing. Let the duke look. She was looking back—on her own terms. As soon as she knew what terms she wanted… You wait and see, Lord Paisley. *I'm not your fallback like your and my mother decided.*

So she smiled and gave a chuckle.

"Not like that. Are you a witch? Gentle laughter." Ashley shook her head.

Maddie yanked her hand from Ashley. "You are doing this on purpose, aren't you? Was the duke really looking this way?"

"No, but he is looking now. Though I'm uncertain that he ever sees a person as anything more than a sack of money or lack thereof."

Maddie didn't know whether she should laugh or cry at her friend's antics. "You are the very worst."

"Which is why you love me." Ashley winked. "I have another surprise for you. In my chamber."

"No more surprises, thank you very much."

"You'll love this one."

"What is it?"

"Is it a surprise if I tell you?"

"Why not surprise me right now?"

Ashley sighed. "Very well. I've brought dresses from London."

Maddie scrunched her brows. "And how is this a surprise?"

"Well, they are all for you."

Maddie blinked. "Me?"

Ashley nodded. "I had your seamstress design some new dresses for you. Something more suited for husband chasing."

Maddie looked down at her current evening dress. She thought the green matched the color of her eyes. Even if its sleeves puffed oddly and the lace scratched. "What's wrong with my dresses?"

"Well, for one, they cover up way too much, and I could never understand why your mother added so many frills. The dresses I brought are elegant and fit for a duke. And don't worry; I charged it to your mother's account."

Maddie laughed, and in her heart, she felt both sweet and sour at the same time, much like the lemon treats she loved so much. She didn't know what she had done to deserve such a loyal friend as Ashley, and she couldn't imagine stepping into this next adventure without her. Maddie hugged her friend tightly.

"Thank you."

She might be plain.

She might be awkward.

She might have more interest in her potions than in people.

But this season she was going against all the odds—and her family.

This season, she was determined to reach for one thing and one thing only…

The stars.

With a touch of potion.

Chapter Two

"MOORE. SEBASTIAN AUGUSTUS Moore, Third Marquess of Cambridge." Sebastian blew on his hands, bouncing from left foot to right. Movement kept his blood flowing. Or at least, kept his boots from freezing him to the ground. The terracotta floor tiles beneath him were just as bitter as the frost outside. His boots were soaked through, his toes aching.

"There ain't no reservation under this name," the gap-toothed innkeeper said from behind the worn walnut desk of *The Silver Thistle*, the last halfway-clean roof between here and nowhere.

Sebastian rubbed his arms and popped his collar, pretending the extra millimeter of wool might matter. His taupe cashmere scarf gave him a sliver of relief—until the door burst open behind him. Another gust of wind. And Paul. His poor coachman, soaked to the bone, shaking snow from his felt hat with trembling hands.

"Do you have any room at all?" Sebastian asked, laying five shillings on the counter. "My coachman needs a rest, too." He flicked a glance toward Paul and tugged his own wool coat tighter, though it made no difference.

The innkeeper pocketed the coins and checked the ledger. "No, milord. A hot soup is all we can offer ye tonight. 'Tis on the house."

A hollow kindness. For five shillings, the man could have served them something edible. Soup for two costs half a shilling. The rest was a tax for being titled.

Of course. The crest on the carriage—Sebastian had paid in advance for their contempt.

What they never saw—what none of them ever saw—was the price of those luxuries, not in coin, but in constant scrutiny. The smile required in every drawing room, plus the rehearsed charm. Even now, shivering in the vestibule of a backwater inn, he had to look vaguely dignified.

He might've laughed if his teeth weren't chattering.

Thomas would laugh. Thomas always did. Sebastian could hear it now: a dry chuckle and a too-casual, *"Did you really try to impress an innkeeper with your title?"*

That was the thing about titles.

But Sebastian did far too much because he ranked far too low and possessed far less money. It was the story of his life—paying to appear above the fray while fighting tooth and nail to stay in it. The old French adage his mother loved to repeat floated up like smoke: *Noblesse oblige.* Nobility obliges.

And it did. It obliged him to act grateful for a title that cost him his two-seater phaeton—sold to pay tuition. It obliged him to smile when he had nothing left but appearances. It obliged him to accept cold soup with grace.

That scarf soaked through and oddly stiff? Gifted last season. The boots? Repaired more than thrice. And still he stood, back straight, words polite.

He tugged at his cravat. Too stiff. He liked them starched—but it was suffocating like everything else in his mother's London townhouse, which was why he'd left right after the New Year to visit Thomas for his engagement festivities to Lady Ashley.

Mother—Lady Victoria Moore to those who cared about the whispers in the drawing rooms—had managed their home like she arranged his life—clean, polished, and impossible. There hadn't been enough left in his trust for the spring term. But she didn't worry.

"You will not be turned away," she'd said, "as long as your title maintains the respect of the realm."

Poor Mother. Still living in the golden echo of a fading world. She hadn't noticed that the Ton only stayed friendly so long as the money flowed. Nor that every debutante she paraded past him smiled at *his title*, not *his face*. Not one had fallen for *him*—because no one had ever truly seen him.

And wasn't that what he wanted? Someone who saw the man, not the marquess.

Back at Oxford, he'd have his tiny staff again—a housekeeper, a cook, a valet. Chatwick, the butler, ran the house with his wife and their twelve-year-old son, who'd taken to helping about.

A warm meal. An even warmer fire. Familiar faces.

He could almost taste the calm and joy of a fresh beer from Thomas's brewery while sitting near the fire and reading for his classes. Blissful times compared to… well… everything in Town.

The diluted broth at the inn was more salted water than soup, the kind Mrs. Chatwick would never serve, not even in a pinch. Still, after a few spoonfuls, Paul looked less like he might collapse on the inn floor.

"It's seven miles to Fort Balmore," Sebastian said at last. He couldn't wait to reach his best friend's castle in Elysian Fields. He'd nearly grown up there and missed it. "Think we can make it?"

"They don't expect you till tomorrow, milord," Paul replied, eyeing the snow lashing the windows. "You know the Earl of Lindsey doesn't like surprise visitors."

Sebastian did. Thomas Dunbridge—the Earl of Linsey—was his closest friend. He also hated surprises, but Sebastian wasn't worried. Not really.

They'd shared rooms at Eton. Spent summers in each other's homes. Every year after Christmas, Sebastian collected Thomas and they drove into the countryside and forgot who they were.

Just boys again. Before the titles mattered.

"All right," Sebastian said, straightening. "Let's surprise the earl, then."

 Chapter Three

MADDIE'S FINGERS DANCED over the keys of the pianoforte, the opening bars of Mozart's *Sonata in A Major* rippling through the quiet room. Her technique was questionable, but her love for the instrument wasn't. She always played alone—not because she was shy, but because she preferred to play as badly as she did without an audience.

The music filled the air, and for a moment, so did peace. Her left hand chased after her right in a clumsy duet—not a performance, but a conversation. One where no one interrupted or scolded her.

She closed her eyes and let herself get lost in it. Mozart didn't mind her mistakes. Mozart didn't ask about husband candidates Mother approved, or the sort of exciting man Maddie had hoped for instead.

When the final note faded, she took a deep breath and held it, trying to summon the courage the music gave her for just one more hour. It slipped through her fingers. Her mother would never stop pushing. And there was no harmony—not in her playing, not in her future, not in the face of choosing a husband like selecting fruit at market, lest she not land Paisley, whose mother was her mother's friend and… oh dear! He was perfect on paper and couldn't be more vexing in person. If she couldn't secure another proposal, Paisley would come for her and her dowry before her mother arrived. And if the viscountess found out that Ashley's engagement celebration turned into a hastened wedding, there would be no mercy, and Maddie would be all but thrust into his hands.

A cold chill ran down her back.

Her thoughts spun to the last few weeks. Every dance, every tea, every practiced smile. Sometimes, it felt like breathing through gowns laced too tight. She wanted to prove her mother wrong so desperately and to escape the scheme she and Paisley's mother had concocted for them—and yet...

She wanted to fall in love, too. And those two things never seemed to belong in the same sentence. She wanted something simple and impossible at once. Warmth that lasted.

There were ways to catch a duke.

None of them involved *affection*. But Maddie—for all her faults—wasn't ruthless enough to trap someone without feeling.

A cold marriage? *No, thank you.* She didn't need fireworks. But she needed warmth.

Otherwise, what would be the point?

The melody still hummed in the air. It quieted the storm inside her, just for now. Good that Charlene was nearby. She didn't know what she'd do without her. As for Ashley... Maddie shook her head. Her friend's engagement had been the sort of twist usually found in novels.

An enemy turned suitor. A proposal built on revenge. And somehow, love had crept in through the cracks.

Maddie had expected disaster when Ashley planned a vendetta against Thomas but somehow, they fell in love instead. What she got from watching her friend love so fiercely was proof that *anything* was possible.

Though Ashley had barely surfaced since the engagement was announced—odd, even for her. She'd even skipped breakfast claiming she couldn't eat in the morning. *So strange!* Still, Maddie had her own dilemma to manage.

Namely: how to catch the heart of a certain questionable, aloof, annoyingly attractive duke. If he had a heart, for which Maddie hadn't seen proof since they were children. And yet, she didn't know another candidate and her mother made it clear that she better be engaged by the end of winter or else…

The final chord fell into silence and her fingers grew too heavy to play.

Maddie sighed. She'd love to play another. But she really ought to find Ashley before she turned the castle upside down.

The last thing she wanted to be was a burden—

"An interesting take on the piece, Miss Madeleine."

Maddie spun, her eyes widening to full moons.

The duke stood a few feet away. Oh! He'd heard her play!

She swallowed hard. *Interesting take?* That was *the* piece. Mozart! What did he mean, *interesting*?

There was amusement in his eyes, if not a bit detached. Cold even. But she must just be imagining that. That faint glint of knowing that made her stomach flip—not in a good way but not in a bad way either.

Urgh. How confusing.

Her cheeks burned. First the frog and tea incident. Now this.

She was on a one-woman mission to destroy every remaining scrap of his hearing and throw in her dignity.

She straightened her spine. There was only one way out.

Play along.

"Thank you, Your Grace," she croaked, nodding. Then blurted, "I'm terrible at the pianoforte!"

His lips curved, just a little. Just enough to make her heart hiccup—not with excitement but that peculiar sort of embarrassment. Like he was superior to all and never let anyone forget it.

"This might come as a surprise, Miss Madeleine," he said, "but skill is not everything."

Is it not? Her brow pinched.

"You don't believe me?"

She bit her lip. "Without skill, many things cannot be accomplished."

He inclined his head. "Indeed. Some practices do require skill." He nodded to the pianoforte. "But sometimes, heart matters more than precision. And you, Miss Madeleine, play with heart."

A compliment from Paisley? What wonders!

"Did you hear the entire piece?" she asked, unable to help herself.

He nodded. "And the one before that. And the one before that."

"I didn't hear you enter."

"Of course not. I was already here."

Her heart plummeted. He'd *been* there? The entire time? How had she not noticed?

Ah, then she'd disturbed him?

Of course she had. She was *Maddie.*

What next? Stumble over his boots and land in his lap?

"My apologies, Your Grace," she said, already backing toward the doorway. "I shall disturb your peace no longer."

Then she fled.

Before she could ruin Mozart for him forever or the pianoforte for herself!

The music room exhaled behind her—banked coals, ticking clock, the faint sweet of lemon oil. She gathered what remained of her pride and slipped into the cooler corridor.

She turned the corner—straight into a wall of coat and chest.

"I'm terri—"

A single, alarming sneeze burst from a stranger. Heat. Damp. On her cheek.

Well, why not?

His hands found her arms—steady, apologetic—large and warm enough to fluster her in spite of everything.

"That will do," she said, voice even. "You sound unwell. To your chamber and a hot brick, sir. And a handkerchief."

His hands dropped and she started to bypass him with what little dignity remained, sleeve wiping at her cheek.

But when he looked up, she blinked.

He was… red. There was no kind word. Red nose, chapped lips, eyes glassy from illness. His skin was nearly translucent.

She wasn't shallow. Maddie prided herself on seeing character, not countenance. But this? This was not character. This was contagion!

She shuddered and stepped back. "Please take care not to sneeze on other people."

"I—"

She marched off without another word, scrubbing at her face harder. She didn't slow until she reached her room—only then did she let herself breathe again. Yet even then… those watery eyes haunted her. How his gaze made her heart flip! And looking at his eyes, they were surely the window to a brooding soul. This curiosity had to be stifled, she decided.

May she never cross paths with that man again.

SWISH!

Sebastian stood blinking in the hallway. What he saw—*no*, whom he saw—could only be a mirage brought on by frostbite. That young woman in pink? Far too lovely to be real. He gulped. Or… could she be real?

The girl in the light rose gown rushed past, skirts fluttering like petals. She vanished through the tall double doors toward the noisy chatter spilling from the Oak Room.

And just like that, she was gone.

He stared after her.

This wasn't wise. He should've stayed at the stables with Paul, his coachman. Since his father passed, Thomas had poured funds into his beloved horses. Two four-stall stables, two coach houses, grooms' quarters, and a small private brewery that produced everything from stout ales to something suspiciously like mulled cider. The point was the stables were warm. And Paul didn't expect conversation.

At least Paul could warm his toes. Sebastian had frostbite and a bruised ego on top of the chills.

But the pink girl—the lovely one—had scolded him. *Righteously.* And he couldn't stop replaying her voice in his head.

"Ha-ha-choo!" As if to prove the point, a fresh sneeze rattled his body.

He groaned. Even his sneezes sounded tragic.

His nose ached from over-wiping. His boots still squelched with dampness. The wind shrieked outside, snow brushing the windows. And somehow, even shielded by the walls of this grand castle, he was still cold, inside and outside.

The room echoed with his sniffles. He'd have laughed if his lungs weren't on strike. *Where did the beauty go?* He ought to apologize again for his sneezy outburst.

"Seb! You're early!"

"Thomas, your ability to tell time is uncanny."

He unrolled the scarf from his neck, the fringes frozen into miniature icicles that looked like sad lace.

The butler, McGulligan, took the soaked garment with a wince. "You're even wetter than the new kittens in the stables after they fell in a puddle, milord."

"Right, well." A soaked cat. What a lovely image.

"Milord, where shall we deposit the barrels of oysters and baskets of Billingsgate fish?" the man asked, voice painfully dignified for someone holding shellfish.

Sebastian blinked. "Oysters and what?"

"For the engagement festivities," the butler intoned, eyes narrowing in that uniquely Scottish acidity that said, *This is beneath my station, but I will persevere.*

"Bring them to the back," Thomas said breezily. "There's ice enough for the oyster platters."

Sebastian trailed behind him toward the grand staircase. The whole household buzzed, the air full of floral soap and simmering sauces.

It all reeked of celebration. And not the relaxing kind.

He frowned at the row of ancestral portraits. Every earl of Thomas's ancestry glared down at him as if to say, *Try not to sneeze on anything valuable.*

"You'll want to change and come down to dinner," Thomas said.

"Who's *we?*"

"Everyone," Thomas said, grinning. "The Expecting Party."

Sebastian missed a tread, then caught it.

"Ashley is with child," Thomas added, pride bright as a torch.

Sebastian found the banister and his voice. "Well. That explains the oysters."

Good for him. Warmth for a friend, and a small, sharp tug beneath Sebastian's ribs—find your own place, man.

Sebastian followed in a daze, water squishing from his boots with every step. The last time he and Thomas had been here, they were drinking port and debating the ideal saddle. *Now Thomas was hosting... baby-themed buffets?*

Everything in the castle was the same. His room hadn't changed—same books, same drawer with his letterhead, same dent in the armchair where he read. But everything else? Different.

His best friend had grown up. And he was going to marry the love of his life, Ashley, and they were going to be a family.

Sebastian stood in the doorway, soaking and silent, while Thomas flung himself across the bed.

"So," Sebastian said slowly, peeling off his socks, "an Expecting Party is a thing now?"

"It is when Ashley says it is."

"Does anyone else know?"

"You're the first I've told." He couldn't stifle his smile. "But she probably told her friends, Charlene and Maddie. Sera and the prince haven't arrived yet."

Sebastian snorted. "How long has she—?"

Thomas coughed. "Let's not talk about timing."

"Could've warned me."

"Where's the fun in that?"

Sebastian scowled. "Some of us like *warning*. Preparation."

Thomas only grinned. "Don't be jealous."

Sebastian sat straighter. "I'm not jealous!"

Thomas smirked. "Right. Of course not. Speaking of triumphs—Lady Swift has been unbeatable lately. She's going to dominate the field next season."

Sebastian blinked. "Your mare? What does your horse have to do with your unborn child?"

"She's of excellent breeding. Bold spirit. Lightning-fast gait." He paused for effect. "Just like you."

Sebastian gave him a long, unimpressed look. "Did you just compare me to a horse? And a female on top of that?"

"If the hoof fits."

"Please stop."

Sebastian rubbed at his temple. He needed a nap. A nap, hot tea with honey, and six blankets.

"A-a-choo!" Another sneeze, sharp and wet. He fumbled for his soggy handkerchief and dabbed at his nose, which had now developed that raw, flaking texture of early-stage misery.

"That sounds awful," Thomas said. "I'll send someone with tea and to light the fire."

"I don't need—" Sebastian sniffled again. "Fine."

Thomas headed for the door, pausing just long enough to deliver one last dagger. "Ashley's friends are already here. Rotheworth is here somewhere as well."

Sebastian's stomach dropped. Pink dress. Scathing scowl.

"I'm begging you," he muttered. "Don't let me say anything stupid."

Thomas grinned. "You? Say something stupid? Never. Just remember—girls talk."

And with that, he was gone.

Leaving Sebastian, damp and feverish, with the knowledge that the most beautiful girl he'd ever sneezed on was likely somewhere downstairs.

$$\mathcal{C}\!\!\sim\!\!\mathcal{D}$$

Chapter Four

"**I** CANNOT WEAR this. Absolutely not." Maddie stared at herself in the mirror, her breath catching on sight. Or more precisely, on her bosom. Two pale swells were scandalously perched atop the low-cut bodice, defying gravity and good sense. She hadn't shown this much skin in her entire life. Now Ashley had commissioned a few scandalous dresses designed to seduce.

Her mother would faint when she saw the bill. Possibly twice.

It's all to catch your duke.

Ah yes. Her duke. Paisley. The one her mother might have pursued herself had she not been wed to her father for three decades. And that was saying much. Paisley's mother, after all, was the viscountess's friend.

She rolled her shoulders back, squaring them like a soldier facing battle. The bodice would certainly catch his attention. Any man's, for that matter. But keep it?

She had her doubts.

Still… the gown *was* rather pretty.

Soft pink. Gentle and romantic. Not at all what she usually wore—and precisely why it felt so foreign. So dangerous.

"Men are visual creatures," Ashley said from behind, smoothing the hem with the ease of a general preparing her soldier for the front lines. "The duke won't know what hit him. That color does more for you than all your mother's gray and pale blue gowns combined. I've told you that for years."

Maddie lifted her gaze. She hardly recognized herself.

Her hair, loosened from its usual prison of pins and practicality, tumbled into gentle curls. A touch of rouge, a soft sheen on her lips. It was her—and yet not. A different version. One no one else had ever met.

She looked down again. "I do admire your taste," she said, dry as bone, "but surely catching a duke requires more than cleavage."

Ashley tilted her head. "That's how you start. If you want his heart, use your mind. But first—" she plucked a small glass bottle from the vanity "—we get his focus."

The stopper popped. "Lilies and sweet orange. I chose it just for you."

Maddie eyed the vial warily. "It's not poison, is it?"

Ashley's expression faltered. Just for a moment. But it was enough. "No, that I'd choose for Paisley."

Maddie turned to face her. "What is it?"

Ashley set the bottle down. Her fingers lingered too long on the glass.

"You know how I feel about Paisley."

Maddie exhaled. "Yes, yes, he wounded Thomas's pride at Ascot."

Ashley's eyes snapped up. "He did more than that. He humiliated him. Stole from him. Tricked him. Publicly. Cruelly."

Maddie blinked.

"Don't get that look," Ashley said, her voice sharp now. "I know he's a duke. I know he's titled and important and he walks into a room like he owns the world. But don't forget—he's human scum."

"Harsh," Maddie whispered, but her heart fluttered. *True.*

"No title will change that," Ashley continued. "And I don't want you, of all people, falling for a man just because he's powerful and polished. You're better than that."

Maddie felt heat rise to her cheeks—not from the gown, or the rouge, or the indignity of her exposed bosom. But from the weight of Ashley's words.

"You deserve a man who sees you," Ashley said, softer now. "Not just your dress. Or your title. Or your potential to birth heirs."

Maddie swallowed hard. The idea of Paisley's heirs made her cringe. She glanced at the mirror again. The woman in the reflection looked… capable.

Capable of seducing a duke.

Capable of falling for one, too.

And possibly, terribly, capable of choosing wrong.

Perhaps she could redirect her capability to a better man? Not just another title, another candidate, but a better man with a heart and soul? Perhaps she could just stand up to her mother this once.

Maddie sniffed. "It smells lovely."

"Dab your wrists. Neckline, too."

"What exactly will this *do*?"

"Men are ruled by more than their eyes. Scent matters. And speaking of senses…" Ashley's gaze flicked upward. "You'll want to touch him."

Maddie blinked. "Touch him?"

"Dancing, ideally. Or if fate's kind, a near fall into his arms will suffice."

Maddie narrowed her eyes. "And how do you know all this?"

Ashley's lips curved. "You're not the only one who reads."

She gestured toward Maddie's little apothecary collection on the shelf. "And how do *you* know so much about tonics and tinctures?"

"It's just for personal benefit." Maddie dismissed the topic swiftly. No one needed to know every detail of what ailed her—especially not during the warmer months. She breathed freely only in winter, when the flowers were gone and the world quieted. This was her season.

"You're always full of surprises," Ashley said softly.

Maddie smiled.

They'd known each other for years, though lately, Ashley had been swept away in the glow of love and impending marriage. Even now, standing beside her, Ashley practically shimmered with love and contentment.

She could hardly believe she had once worried Ashley was rushing into a disaster. But no. She'd chosen *right*.

Her mother's words flashed across her mind.

How could I have given birth to such an odd daughter? You have nothing to recommend you, Madeleine, except your dowry. Be glad our family has a fortune. Otherwise, who would even look at you?

Maddie glanced at her reflection.

No. She was more than a dowry. She had knowledge, wit, and friends.

She squared her shoulders. *I can do this.*

"I'm not just going to fall into his arms like one of those swooning geese," Maddie muttered, tugging at her bodice. "He'll have to *earn* my kiss."

"Ah, so we've moved from bashful to bold," Ashley said, crossing her arms. "That should be more than enough to win that man. His heart is another matter since I'm not convinced he's in possession of one. I just hope love can transform him."

"I don't know yet," Maddie said primly. "But I *must* find out."

Ashley arched a brow.

"I just… I'll *feel* it. In my bones. There'll be a shiver. A spark." Maddie swept her hands across her body, dramatically tracing the air. Somehow the duke didn't come to mind, though.

Ashley smirked. "And you're certain Paisley, the dreadfully scheming gambler *Paisley* can manage that spark? I still have my doubts."

"Of course." Maddie hesitated. "He's a duke. He's likely been very well educated."

And probably kissed a hundred girls.

The thought made her stomach drop. How would she *know* what a perfect kiss felt like unless she tried it?

And if she tried it, well, that was a different sort of ruin entirely.

A knock rapped on the door.

"May I come in, or shall I brace myself for a scandalous display of chemises and corsets?" Charlene's familiar voice called from behind the door.

"Char!" Maddie called, laughing.

"About time," Ashley said with a grin. "Took you long enough."

"Oh, hush. Rotheworth and I had a moment." Charlene swept into the room, curls bouncing like the heroine of a romantic novel. "I came straight in search of you when I heard the gowns had arrived. Oh, you look *ravishing*," she declared, halting mid-step to beam at Maddie. "I'm almost of a mind to swoon."

Ashley pulled Charlene closer. "She will steal everyone's gaze tonight."

Maddie scoffed. "For your sakes, I hope not. How many bachelors are here tonight? One? Two?"

Her friends laughed.

"You are both glowing," Charlene said before inspecting Maddie's gown. "But this is *sorcery*."

Maddie groaned.

"Our friend is finally dressing like someone with sense," Ashley said smugly.

"And she's griping about it," Maddie added.

Charlene surveyed her with a critical eye. "You must wear it. The world deserves to see your bosom."

"Char!" Maddie exclaimed. "You know my mother will faint if she finds out."

"She probably will," Charlene chirped. "But that's her problem."

"Where's Rotheworth?" Maddie asked about Charlene's

husband, the Duke of Rotheworth.

"Oh, he went to go inspect the horses, naturally."

"Again?"

"Of course." Ashley giggled like only a woman in love would indulging her husband's affection for his equestrian friends.

"Are you ready to head down?" Ashley asked, giving her a reassuring smile.

Maddie inhaled. "I'm ready." And as soon as she spoke the words, she knew she hadn't meant them. Being ready was terrifying.

Ashley beamed. "Then let us surprise everyone with your beauty."

"Wait," Maddie said, gripping Ashley's arm. "I'm not ready."

"Why?" Charlene asked. "What's the matter?"

Maddie let out a breath. "You'll think I'm foolish, but… What if everyone *laughs* at me?"

Ashley blinked. "Why would they?"

Maddie hesitated.

"If they do," Ashley said, voice firm, "it's only because they're intimidated. And that, Maddie, is their problem. Not yours."

Maddie laughed weakly. Jealous? Of *her*?

She glanced at her reflection again.

She'd dared to defy her mother. That had been difficult. Surely she could handle a little embarrassment. A little fear.

Embrace discomfort.

Yes, this counted.

This most definitely counted!

And Maddie was about to find out what happened when a girl like her dared to be seen. Even to a small group of people. Most of whom she already knew. The question was who did she want to see her?

SEBASTIAN TUGGED HIS greatcoat tighter around his shoulders as a chilly winter wind hit him from all sides. He wanted to be in bed but as Thomas's best friend, he felt a responsibility to greet the other guests. The good ones at least. Excluding, of course, Paisley.

His nose burned from the cold, but he had to escape the suffocating stuffiness of the castle, which reeked of perfume, smoke, and far too many logs burning on too many hearths. And whatever water the ladies were dabbing themselves with. His boots crunched on the frozen stones as he approached the barn. A faint nicker greeted him, followed by the comforting scent of hay and horseflesh as he stepped inside.

He inhaled deeply, ignoring the tickle in his throat.

Much better.

The air here was warmer, but not cloyingly so. Sebastian strolled past the stalls until he spotted the Duke of Rotheworth beside the sleek chestnut form of Lady Swift.

Right. The very horse Thomas had compared him to.

"She bites, you know," Sebastian said, his voice just rough enough to betray his lingering cold.

Rotheworth glanced over his shoulder, one brow rising. "She has excellent taste, then. You look like you should be tucked in a bed, Cambridge."

"Why, thank you," Sebastian replied dryly. "Just what every man wants to hear."

"I meant it in the most affectionate sense," Rotheworth said, turning back to Lady Swift. He patted her neck. "She's in fine form."

So he kept hearing. "I heard she won the Brighton run."

"Cleaned the field," Rotheworth said with a nod. "Even outpaced Paisley's stallion. Won me quite a bit of money."

Sebastian scoffed—then coughed. He leaned against a post and rubbed his nose with his handkerchief. "I hope he's still licking his wounds."

Rotheworth chuckled but didn't comment for a moment.

"You don't care for the duke?"

"Absolutely not." Sebastian didn't elaborate. Paisley had nearly forced Thomas into a marriage of convenience. Fortunately, Ashley had had other ideas. "I heard you're engaged. Congratulations."

Rotheworth turned, a smile playing on his lips. "We're married. Eloped."

Sebastian blinked. That had not made it into any letter. "Well then. Congratulations on your union."

"Thank you."

"Does anyone else know?" Please let the answer be yes. Ashley's pregnancy was more secret than he wanted to keep.

"I believe the whole of England knows," Rotheworth said dryly. "Except you."

What a relief. Still, something tight lodged in his chest, and he wasn't entirely sure it was the cold.

Married. Rotheworth. Thomas. Expecting.

It felt as if the entire world had taken a step forward while he stood still, pages missing from his story.

"I seem to be surrounded by people who catch wedding fevers," he muttered.

"Better than catching colds and real fevers," Rotheworth replied. "You sound like a man who's never considered it."

Sebastian shrugged. "I have. But I've yet to meet the right woman."

"Ah. She must be calm, gentle, and fond of silence, I take it?"

"No harridans, certainly." He glanced at Lady Swift. "Not the sort to gallop into storms or throw teacups."

"I can't claim to know many ladies who fit that bill. They sound fictional."

"And yet I live in hope."

Rotheworth chuckled, patting Lady Swift once more. "What you need, Cambridge, is a holiday from your expectations."

Sebastian arched a brow. "Doctor Rotheworth, prescribing rebellion?"

"Worked wonders for me. Too high expectations make for

too high disappointment."

"I'd rather risk disappointment than settle."

Rotheworth huffed a laugh. "You won't heed it. I can see that."

"Expect nothing, and you'll get exactly that."

"Some people find that comforting."

Sebastian shook his head. "I'm not one of them."

"Suit yourself. What works for one doesn't always work for another."

"I still don't envy you," Sebastian muttered. Though perhaps he did. Just a little.

"You sound like a man convincing himself," Rotheworth said, giving him a knowing look.

Sebastian said nothing. Something had shifted in him—some quiet storm building since Thomas's courtship, the engagement, the announcement. A restless discontent he couldn't name.

Rotheworth clapped him on the shoulder. "Relax. Enjoy the countryside. Focus on your health, not your heart."

Sebastian rolled his eyes, but Rotheworth was already walking off. Lady Swift tossed her head as if amused by the whole exchange.

"I hope you bite him later," he told her.

The mare blinked, entirely unbothered.

He should head back to his room. Rest. Drink something scalding and restorative. But still, he lingered, breathing in the quiet snuffling of the horses.

Too peaceful.

With a huff, he pushed away from the post and wandered farther down the line of stalls, pausing beside an old dapple-gray gelding. Half-asleep, the horse twitched one ear in acknowledgment. Sebastian scratched him behind it, then leaned against the stall.

Everyone's glowing, he thought. *Everyone's changing.*

He didn't want to change. Didn't want to glow.

But he did want something.

Someone.

To love, perhaps.

Yes.

He exhaled a long breath, one that fogged the air in front of him. The warmth of the stables clung to his coat, a lingering comfort he already missed. The scent of hay and hops still threaded through his senses, grounding him in something simpler, something real.

But he turned toward the castle anyway.

Up there, dinner awaited along with the carefully folded expectations of good breeding and even better behavior. He stuffed his hands in his coat pockets and trudged up the path. Maybe it was time to loosen his grip on some of those expectations. Maybe not everything had to be done the way it always had been. Maybe there was still time for him to change his heart? Or for someone to do that for him.

The thought unsettled him. But oddly, it didn't seem like dread. It felt... like hope.

So he entered the castle, almost ready to change and face the formal dinner.

He was halfway up the grand staircase when a blur of motion collided with his shoulder.

"Oof—!"

"I'm so sorry—!"

He blinked.

No. It couldn't be.

It was her. The woman he'd sneezed on—repeatedly, and to his eternal shame.

She gasped. "You!"

"Yes, me."

"You sneezed on me."

"And you fled like I'd grown pustules before I could apologize."

"I had just been sneezed on. Several times. Your blasts nearly unpinned my hair!"

He tried not to laugh. "Exaggeration." *But very nice hair indeed.*

"You were a menace."

He bowed slightly. "A recovering menace. The pleasure is all mine."

She pushed a lock of hair behind her ear, cheeks flushed from exertion or mortification—or both. "I didn't see you there."

"You didn't see a man halfway up a staircase?"

"I was in a hurry."

"To trample someone?"

"I didn't trample you." She lifted her chin, and all he could see was her perfect neckline.

Someone as sweet as you has permission to trample me, he thought, but pinched his lips flat so he wouldn't accidentally say it. New man, new expectations, less calloused behavior perhaps.

"My shoulder says otherwise."

She huffed, then narrowed her gaze. "You look dreadful."

"Charming," he muttered. "Do you insult all strangers, or only the ones you collide with?"

A twitch tugged at her lips. "Only the ones with handkerchiefs permanently affixed to their noses."

He lowered the linen in his hand. "As you might have noticed, I'm recovering from a cold."

"You should try to recover harder."

Her gaze swept over him again, slower this time. "You do look marginally more human."

"Why, thank you," he said dryly. "A compliment. I shall treasure it."

"I wouldn't," she replied, eyes dancing. "You're still clutching that wretched handkerchief like a weapon."

He stuffed it into his pocket. "I promise not to sneeze on you again. Unless provoked."

"Then I'll try not to provoke." She turned, ready to dash.

He couldn't stop himself. "Try not to knock down any more invalids."

"Try not to sneeze on any more innocent bystanders," she called back.

And then she vanished—up the stairs, a hurricane in a breathtaking gown.

Sebastian stood frozen on the step, blinking after her.

Well.

He really had to stop meeting people like this.

But at least he wasn't cold anymore. But was she truly just an innocent bystander now?

Chapter Five

S EBASTIAN REALLY DID not want to be here for this. A formal dinner, of all things, when what he truly needed was a quiet bed, a hot brick, and the right to wallow in peace. Soup in a plain cup. Tea with honey. Blankets. Silence. That was what a sick man required. Not polished silver, cravats starched within an inch of suffocation, and forced smiles across a sea of strangers.

But here he was.

Because Thomas was his best friend, and when your best friend summoned you to dinner with his fiancée and her friends, you showed up—even if you felt like death in evening wear.

He could feel the air stir with trouble. With eventfulness. With peace-disruptive, emotion-provoking nonsense.

He sighed and rubbed the bridge of his nose. He wasn't made for this sort of evening. But he was here now, so he'd do what was asked of him. That was something, wasn't it?

"Miss Madeleine Hunt." Thomas pointed toward a familiar young woman as they took a sip of whiskey.

The name rang a bell, but it was the sight of her that hit harder.

Miss Madeleine. Of course. He remembered her from the Royal Ascot. But this time, she didn't wear a big hat and her hair... not just that... there was something about her... Heat crept to his chest and he took a swig of the amber liquid. The burn was a welcome sting in Sebastian's throat, but he didn't care for the thin liquor. He preferred something velvety and rich altogether.

Speaking of velvety… she was just striking.

He hadn't noticed it before—perhaps because she'd been too busy shooting him glares like twin pistols—but now that he saw her from a distance, without the full brunt of her disapproval, she was… arresting.

If she weren't so clearly unimpressed by his existence, she might've even looked inviting.

His eyes stuck to her, a siren with a bosom that had Sebastian staring like a green boy.

Wham!

His friend elbowed him. "Ouch! What was that for?"

"This is Ashley's friend. Stop ogling her bosom," Thomas growled in a low voice.

Sebastian winced. Right. He was a guest, not a ruffian.

"If she didn't want me to look, why did she put it before me then?"

Whack!

Linsey stepped on his foot with the precision of someone who'd been waiting for that moment all evening.

Excellent. Now he was cold, congested, and quite possibly going to be challenged to a duel.

He muttered something unintelligible and lifted his glass again, reminding himself this was not the time for mischief. He'd promised Thomas he'd behave. He could manage that—for an hour. Maybe.

"Stop it!"

"I mean it. They are thick as thieves. You know, girls are more dangerous with their tongues than most men with a sword."

"She doesn't look dangerous," Sebastian muttered as he cocked his head. Even though his neck was stiff and his sinuses irritated, he wasn't too sick to appreciate the beautiful young woman across the room.

"Can you sit with her and behave like a gentleman?" Thomas asked, setting his glass down. "This is a celebratory dinner after all."

But Sebastian moved. He was nothing if not dutiful. With practiced ease—and an uncomfortable awareness of just how tight his trousers suddenly felt—he approached her.

She hadn't said a word to him, and honestly, that might've been a mercy. He deserved her silence after the sneezing incident. And the ogling.

But she was looking right at him now. Eyes sharp, lips soft, dress sinful.

With a bow—perhaps a touch too graceful—he pulled out the chair for her, fingers brushing the velvet fabric as he guided it into place.

He accepted his wine, though he would've traded it for a pint of ale and the blessed relief of distance. But he peeked at her lips again.

And regretted it immediately.

They were glistening. Crimson. Wicked.

"Do you like Chablis, Miss Madeleine?"

"Not particularly, my lord." She took a sip, her lips wet with the sheen from the wine.

Sebastian had never wanted to be wine before.

He cleared his throat and adjusted the napkin over his lap. "Please. Call me Sebastian. And shall we call a truce?"

"You mean because our first and second meetings were less than stellar?"

He exhaled. "Yes."

"Very well." She studied him. "Chablis. Is it one of your favorites?" she asked, and her tongue caught a drop of wine.

Sebastian forgot how to breathe.

He'd seen plenty of women drink wine. None had ever made it look like foreplay.

"Chablis is made from Chardonnay grapes in northern Burgundy. A waste of the grape, if you ask me."

He blinked. She wasn't just lovely. She was clever. And opinionated.

"You are a connoisseur, then?"

"Hardly." She set the glass precisely beside the water goblet.

"The Kimmeridgian limestone gives it its pale color and green apple acidity, with a hint of..." She licked her lips again. "Salinity."

Sebastian took a large gulp and nearly choked. "Too steely for me."

"That depends on the barrel. If it's aged in oak, it has a fresher finish." She blinked at him with slow, devastating lashes.

He was going to have a fresher finish if this went on. Right here. At dinner. All the more reason to go to his chambers, curl up under a blanket, and avoid polite society.

But something about Miss Madeleine made him want to be not so polite. Not rude, of course. Kind. Loving. Gentle. Slow at first, but then harder... *argh!*

Her collarbones glowed like porcelain beneath lace, and the pearl resting there looked criminally lucky. He wanted to kiss that spot. Wanted to press his mouth there and hear her gasp.

Now he needed stronger wine. Or cold water. Or the castle moat.

"I hear you are a bosom friend of Lady Ashley?" he asked, hoping the word "bosom" would not trigger his entire body into betrayal.

She lifted a brow. "Indeed. We've known each other a long time."

"So she tells you all her secrets?"

"I beg your pardon?"

"Girls talk," he said, feigning innocence. "I wonder if you know Lady Ashley's secrets... or her plans for the du—"

Clink!

Thomas tapped a silver spoon against his goblet, and the

room hushed. Footmen glided in with trays of champagne. The table held its breath.

Sebastian turned to Ashley, who sat composed and elegant, a sly smile just playing at her lips.

"My dear friends," Thomas began, his voice ringing clear. "It brings me great joy to make an announcement this evening."

He paused. "I am proud to say that Lady Ashley and I—" his voice softened as he turned to her, "—have set a date for the wedding. In seven days."

Sebastian had known they'd be in a rush with a baby on the way, but it still hit him like a shove.

Young. In love. Everything ahead of them.

It was oddly beautiful. And it stung a bit.

The table burst into applause. All but one person.

Miss Madeleine was frozen. Her hands clapped, yes—but her face…

Her expression cracked right down the middle. Surprise, certainly. But also something softer. Sadder.

As if she'd suddenly realized she was still waiting for her turn.

Sebastian leaned closer, his voice low. "Are you feeling quite all right?"

What he really wanted was to brush a hand down her spine, to draw her into his side until she could breathe again.

To tell her, your turn is coming.

But she didn't look at him.

She just smiled—a little too tightly—and nodded.

And it made him strangely ache.

Because she was the sort of woman who would always applaud for others, even when her own heart seemed to be breaking.

A WEDDING SO soon?

Charlene leaned in close, her breath warm against Maddie's ear.

"It's all so sudden, isn't it? She didn't even tell us," she murmured, voice low with mischief. "But then, I suppose Ashley needs to be a bride before her belly begins to show."

Maddie blinked. *Belly. Show.*

"You mean…?"

Charlene winked, pleased with herself.

"A baby."

Ashley with child. Joy startled through her—bright, a little blinding—and then the breath caught as the room went on cheering. Of course Thomas would know first. He should. Still, the old hedge-maze vows pricked—flowers in their hair, promises made side by side.

Maddie kept applauding. I am happy for you, she told her friend in silence, even as something tender ached open inside. Please let there be a turn for me as well.

One more misstep and the marriage proposals would vanish. As her mother warned. Replaced by an arranged match. To someone horrid, that was certain.

And now this.

A baby. Conceived before a wedding.

If her mother learned of it… she'd claimed Maddie to be ruined by association.

Love, choice, *hope* would be off the table. Permanently.

She darted a glance toward the duke. She had hoped to be seated beside him to perhaps better understand the man beneath the title but secretly dreaded speaking to him again. This evening could have been an opportunity. Instead, she was seated beside the unfortunate gentleman with the handkerchief.

He wasn't sneezing now. That helped. A little.

But that wasn't the point. Besides, who was he to call it if he'd been the slimy offender?

The point was, her dearest friend had just announced a rushed wedding—in public, sort of—for reasons unknown.

"Miss Madeleine?" Lord Cambridge's voice rasped through the haze. "Are you quite well?"

She turned slowly. "Did you know about this? You're like a brother to Thomas."

He looked at her, puzzled. "Only found out earlier. Why?"

"*Why?*" Maddie whispered. "They've announced their engagement, and this was meant to be an engagement celebration but it's being turned into a wedding!" Her eyes darted to Ashley—still poised, still smiling. "They're mad. Both of them!"

Her friend could at least have warned her! Well, Ashley knew about her mother, so perhaps she had tried to spare them. Or perhaps, it was a last-minute decision. She could hardly sit there and judge, she supposed.

The marquess, wisely, said nothing.

She slid her chair a fraction away from his. He noticed and arched a brow. The man seemed to notice everything.

"You might sneeze on me again," Maddie muttered.

"It was an accident," he muttered back. "I don't go about assaulting ladies with illness."

"You'll forgive me if I remain wary."

"I *have* apologized, Miss Madeleine. Will you not accept?"

"We shall see." *How vexing!*

She turned from him, trying not to let her trembling fingers show. She had come here hoping to follow in her friends' footsteps—to hopefully find love. Plus, she didn't want to give her mother any more reason to rule over all her decisions. And now she might be in a scandal that wasn't even hers. If someone like Paisley were to find out about the baby before Ashley's wedding... oh, she couldn't even think it.

"If I may ask, why do you keep looking at Paisley?"

Her head snapped toward him. "I am not."

"You did. Twice."

A pause.

"Why can't I?"

His eyes widened. "My apologies. You may. But if I may ask,

do you... like him?"

"I do *not*." Not yet. But she could. If he made an offer. If he rescued her from the life her mother had planned. Hah. Though, there did live a little doubt in her heart.

"Little liar."

She sucked in a sharp breath. Did he truly just call her that? "What cruel twist of fate seated me next to you?"

"If you must know," she hissed, "the Duke of Paisley is the perfect male specimen."

He scoffed. "Perfect? *Paisley?*"

"He is calm, composed, and yes, handsome." Not honorable if her friend, Ashley, was questioned about Paisley's character though. And suddenly Maddie realized that it was important to her what her friends thought of her potential suitors. *If only he could already be a friend...*

"He's *not that* handsome." The marquess combed a hand through his hair, which was denser, darker, and altogether rather invitingly a little messy.

"More handsome than you." Why on earth had she just said such a thing? Honestly! Well, at the moment, anyone would be more handsome than the stuffy, red-nosed marquess. *But not as wonderfully disheveled?*

His eye twitched. "I beg your pardon?"

Still, it *was* rude to point out his reddish nose if he was ill. "Nothing."

"Is it because he's a duke?" He folded the napkin in his lap into halves, then quarters, then eighths, and then twisted it into a bullet that Maddie could have sworn was meant for Paisley.

She gave him a tight smile. "Do you think me that shallow?" *Yes.* A little bit. However! If it were to be him, she did hope to still find love.

He said nothing.

Truthfully, she had followed her mother's wishes and aimed high. But not just for the title. For safety. For freedom.

"All ladies want a duke or an earl," he muttered. "Wealth.

Status."

"Well," she replied sweetly, "*you* just admitted he's wealthy. That makes him a catch in society's terms, does it not?"

His jaw clenched.

"You have me there," he said flatly. "If you think money can buy love, passion, and a happy family, help yourself to him." He looked down as if she'd vexed him.

Maddie took a sip of wine and tried not to look smug. Still, something inside her twisted. A strange sort of pressure. Why did he unsettle her like this? Why, when he spoke, did her heart beat the way it did when her mother caught her sneaking a novel under her bedcovers?

All around them, cheers and congratulations echoed. Ashley glowed. Thomas beamed.

And Maddie—Maddie sat frozen.

She didn't know if she felt betrayed by the surprise or left behind. Then again, that was also not her friend's fault or burden. But now was not the moment to dwell on the fact. She forced a polite smile to her lips and sat straighter. She meant to look back at Ashley, but her gaze darted instead toward the head of the table.

Toward Paisley.

No. No, don't look.

She forced her eyes sideways.

And met Cambridge's stare.

Heat rushed to her face. Of course, he'd noticed.

He arched one brow.

She arched one in return.

And so, it began. Again.

The brow waggling war.

Until a throat cleared near them, and Maddie snatched up her glass of wine and averted her gaze. If she had to survive an entire dinner beside this insufferable man, she would need more than a glass. A barrel, perhaps.

The man was impossible.

He was also too clever by half. And worse still, he saw too much. Of her. She pressed her palm to her forehead and drew in a slow breath.

She would *not* fall ill.

Not now, when her life was at stake and she needed to find the right husband as quickly as possible. Not just anyone would do.

But still… if she fainted… maybe the marquess would catch her?

Now that was an idea worth exploring.

Chapter Six

L ATER THAT EVENING, in his chambers, Sebastian sniffled. *Argh!* He blew his nose fully, then again into the handkerchief embroidered with Thomas's crimson initials.

A knock sounded at his door.

"I'm busy." All he needed was to suffer in peace.

Another knock. Then the latch turned.

"Anyone here?" a soft voice came, causing unbidden shivers to run down his spine.

"No," he barked, voice thick, from behind another damp square of linen. He might be the one blowing phlegm all over Thomas's name, but he'd rather not do it over anyone else. That did not stop the girl from entering, however.

Very well.

"Set it down there, please. The linens here and that there."

Wait. That voice was familiar.

Maddie?

Sebastian's head jerked up. Of course it would be her.

"Thank you," she added with a nod to the two footmen, who carried in a steaming pot of water and a pile of pristine white linens. "You may go," she told the elder footman, with a graceful flick of her wrist. "I shall ensure the Marquess of Cambridge is properly cared for and will return to my chambers shortly. You may leave the door open."

With a bow, the footmen retreated.

"I didn't ask for a nursemaid, Miss Madeleine," Sebastian muttered, feigning irritation. But, truth be told, she was a sight for sore eyes—and his were among the sorest.

She paid him no mind, carrying a stool from the far wall and setting it beside the small table bearing the steaming pot. "Sit here and hurry before the steam fades."

Then she untied a narrow leather case and unrolled it with a practiced flick, revealing a neat row of fabric loops, each holding a small glass vial.

Sebastian squinted. Was she here to treat him or seduce him with tinctures?

No, that was the fever and the building headache speaking. The door was open as per her specific instructions. She didn't invite scandal.

She selected a vial, uncorked it, and dropped a few beads of liquid into the water.

"Are you trying to poison me?" he asked, dryly. He couldn't help himself. Needling her had become oddly satisfying.

"Come here," she said, sending him an exasperated look.

For some unfathomable reason, he obeyed.

Sebastian leaned forward and Maddie's hand gently settled at the base of his skull, guiding him over the steam.

Then she draped one of the white linens over his head.

He bristled at first, outlined beneath the cloth by the hand of a beautiful woman. But the steam struck him full in the face, and with the first inhale of that sharp, minty vapor, his resistance began to dissolve.

"What is in this?" he asked from beneath the linen.

He heard her rifling through the case again.

"*Mentha piperita*—peppermint. *Melissa officinalis*—lemon balm. *Camphora officinarum*—camphor." A pause. "From a tree. A needle one. I know that for a fact."

Her Latin was flawless. Not just a pretty face, then. Not just a high-and-mighty heiress with a dowry and a mission.

He should not have wanted to run his fingers through her hair. And yet he did. Almost desperately.

"And where did you get this delightful poison?"

"Alfie," she said.

"Who in the world is Alfie?"

"My apothecary. Alfie Collins at 87 Harley Street in London."

"Of course."

"He made me this traveling kit," she added, almost defensively. "For… reasons."

"What sort of reasons?"

"Never mind."

Now that piqued his curiosity, but it was hard to press while being steamed like a Christmas pudding. The water began to cool. He cracked one eye open and caught sight of the shimmering surface, flecked with oils. Then the coughing started.

He yanked off the towel and doubled over, hacking a bit.

And there she was, already pressing a clean cloth into his hand instead of withdrawing.

If the cough had permitted it, Sebastian would have paused to acknowledge that every other lady he'd ever met would have first avoided him in his state, second not helped with a clean cloth, and third not be as gorgeous delivering minty oils for a steam bath.

He blew his nose again, trying to angle his body discreetly so she wouldn't see the results.

"Any better?" she asked, folding another linen with military precision.

"You knew exactly what I needed, didn't you?" he mumbled, a little foggy now. The lemon balm was kicking in, or maybe it was her voice, but the headache was eased with all that came out. "That helped, thank you." He tried to smile, but his skin felt tight, dry. Between the fire in the hearth and the steam, the air in his room was practically tropical rain.

Maddie opened another small jar—wider, paler—and dipped

her finger into a cream. Without a word, she rubbed her palms together, warming the mixture. Then she placed both hands on his cheeks.

Sebastian went utterly still.

She stroked the salve into his skin—soft, slow, rhythmic. It was a healer's touch. Except it absolutely wasn't. It was sensual. And entirely inappropriate. And very nearly his undoing.

He placed the handkerchief on his lap. Urgently.

"What is that?" he rasped.

"Chamomile with beeswax," she said lightly. "Good for inflammation. Soothing on the skin."

She rubbed the last of it into her knuckles, then reached up and brushed her thumb over his mouth, spreading a bit of balm along the seam of his lips.

"There," she murmured. "That should help your dry lips and skin. I reckon you stood in cold wind to end up so ill?"

He only managed a faint nod. His entire body ignited. With a fever, yes, but also something far more dangerous.

His heart thudded like a drum. His head spun—but not from congestion.

She was too close. Too composed. Too… touchable.

What was he supposed to say?

His throat worked uselessly, and then—

"Why are you so nice to me?" he asked, like an idiot.

The question hit her like a slap. She drew back. Slowly. Her hands fell to her lap, her expression shuttered.

She stood.

With calm, measured movements, she rolled her kit back into its leather sheath and tied it closed with one tight knot after another.

The warmth in her eyes was gone. Replaced by something colder. Controlled. Familiar.

"Set the pot by the hearth," she said, brisk again. "The steam will help while you sleep."

And with that, she was gone.

⟫⟫⟫⟨⟨⟨⟨

MADDIE SLOUCHED AGAINST the door the moment she stepped out, clutching her chest.

Oh dear.

The man was positively…

Ugly.

No—no, no!

He was sick. There was a difference. Maddie had never been a shallow person. It didn't matter whether someone was tall or short, wide or thin, rich or poor—she prided herself on seeing to the heart of a person.

But this man…

At least he hadn't sneezed on her again.

She touched her throat, then her temple. No fever. Good. As long as she didn't fall ill herself. Because then she'd have to dig into her vials and teach that man a lesson.

She thought of one particular blend—just a drop here, a splash there—and he'd itch for days.

She smirked.

Fortunately, she was not a vindictive person.

She harrumphed.

I certainly can be.

Which was precisely why she'd left. There was something about him that she couldn't place.

Never mind the fever-flushed face. The man was impossible—distant one moment, almost tender the next. And for some reason, he couldn't be close enough for her to be satisfied with… how odd. Perhaps she was falling ill after all?

Must be the cold.

Men did have a way of reverting to infants when unwell. That would explain the gentleness. Which would mean his usual disposition was rather… rude.

Still.

She pressed her ear to the door.

Silly. And yet she strained to listen.

Fine. She also felt guilty for leaving so abruptly. When he'd leaned into her touch… Lord.

For a moment—a very fleeting moment—she'd forgotten everything else. And in that same fleeting moment… she'd wanted to lean in, too.

Urgh!

"Maddie?"

Maddie whirled around to find Ashley watching her with lifted brows. "Are you all right?"

"Yes. Perfectly fine."

Ashley's gaze dropped to the small silver etui in Maddie's hand. "You usually only carry that when the gardens are in bloom… or when there are cats about. Why now?"

Maddie's throat tightened for a moment at the thought of sweet, purring fluffballs and the havoc they could wreak. "No reason," she said lightly, tucking the case into her reticule.

Ashley nodded toward the door. "Have you checked on Cambridge?"

Maddie gave a tight nod. "He'll survive. He just needs rest."

"You do not mind if I have a look?" Ashley started forward. "This is Thomas's best friend."

Maddie frowned. "Shouldn't you know him well? You are engaged to…"

Ashley shrugged. "Never spoken to him alone. I am curious."

"We just had dinner with him."

"I was not paying him any attention."

Of course she hadn't been.

"Why must you disturb a sick man now of all times?"

"Why else? I want to see what sort of man my future husband chooses as his closest friend."

"Can it not wait until morning?"

"Certainly not." With that, Ashley turned the knob and slipped inside.

Maddie bit her lip.

Oh, for pity's sake.

With a sigh, she followed.

They entered just in time to see the marquess hunched at the edge of the bed—shirtless, flushed, and gloriously disheveled.

Maddie froze.

His bare back was a map of taut muscle, each sleek line shifting under skin that gleamed faintly in the firelight. Heat had flushed his broad shoulders, lending them a sculpted, almost bronzed look, and a thin sheen of perspiration caught the glow like polished marble. His dark hair—thick and unruly—clung in damp waves at his temples, the disarray making him look more like a conquering hero returned from battle than an invalid.

He was… breathtaking.

Not in the feline way that would close her lungs, but in the heroic way that could make her knees forget their purpose entirely if he ever chose to kiss her.

He shifted, bracing his forearms on his thighs, and the movement set his chest in motion—defined planes and ridges revealed in the flicker of the fire, as if carved by some daring sculptor who knew exactly how to tempt a woman's eye.

Then he looked up.

The fever in his gaze was more than heat and illness—it was awareness, startling and sharp, catching her breath in her throat. For the barest heartbeat, it felt as though the rest of the room dissolved and there was only this—the quiet pull between them, humming low and hot in the space they shared.

He made a rough sound, half-cough, half-groan, and yet he didn't look away. Neither did she.

Her pulse stumbled. Her common sense whispered retreat, but her body—traitorous thing—leaned almost imperceptibly forward, drawn toward the heat of him.

He looked magnificent. No—dangerously magnificent. And Maddie, with her soft heart and unreliable knees, had no business being this close to him.

"Perhaps we should call for a doctor," Maddie murmured, her voice softer now, caught somewhere between concern and... something she didn't want to name. "He doesn't look well. He sounds worse."

"I'm fine," he croaked.

They both stared. It was the exact same thing he'd said earlier.

Only now, he looked one sneeze away from death—or seduction.

"You certainly don't look fine," Ashley said bluntly.

Maddie's earlier annoyance dissolved into something warmer. Something dangerously close to tender.

He looked so pitiful. Crumpled. Pale. Shaking.

But also... beautiful. A sick Adonis with a bruised sort of dignity.

What on earth had happened between the soup course and now?

"No need for a doctor," he muttered.

"You can still say that?" Maddie asked. "In the state you're in?"

He waved a limp hand above his head and collapsed back into the pillows, chest still bare, eyes glazed with fever—and something else as they flicked to her.

For a single heartbeat, it felt like she was the only thing anchoring him to this world.

Then his lashes dipped.

"Lady Ashley?"

Ashley cleared her throat. "I came to see how you were. Your... departure after the announcement at dinner earlier was rather sudden."

Maddie pinched her friend's arm. "Let's go. He's clearly in no condition to receive guests."

"Did you need something, Lady Ashley?" he asked, eyes half-lidded.

"No, she did not," Maddie said firmly, trying not to sound

breathless as she tugged her friend toward the door. "Sorry to disturb you. You need rest."

He grunted something unintelligible as she hauled Ashley from the room and gently pulled the door shut behind them.

But not before Maddie cast one last glance back.

His head had rolled to the side, mouth parted slightly, one hand sprawled over the linens, the other across his ribs.

Nothing like the infuriating, sharp-tongued sparring partner she'd argued with at dinner. He looked… vulnerable. Disarmed. Raw.

He looked like a man who needed someone.

And that shouldn't have made her heart ache.

Breakable.

She frowned.

If he knew she'd thought him pitiful, he'd be furious.

Not that it mattered. She was fairly certain his opinion of her wasn't particularly glowing either.

With one last look, Maddie slipped from the room.

They stepped into the corridor, the door clicking softly shut behind them.

"Thomas wants him at the wedding," Ashley said, casting a glance back. "But he looks like he's going to have a funeral at the chapel instead."

Maddie sniffed. "He does not. He has a cold."

"A theatrical one."

"I've been sicker than that and still attended my pianoforte lesson."

Ashley arched a brow. "You also boiled herbs like a hedge witch and drank things that smelled of shoe polish."

"Yes, and I recovered within the week."

Ashley looped her arm through Maddie's. "Which is why you should help him. For Thomas."

Maddie hesitated.

Then lifted her chin. "I will," she said.

But not for Thomas.

Chapter Seven

THE SUN HAD just risen over Elysian Fields, casting a soft, pinkish-orange glow over the freshly fallen snow. Sebastian groaned as he pulled his scarf over his riding gear, already regretting every decision that had led to this exact moment. His boots were polished, his coat pressed, and his bones aching. He knew Thomas wouldn't let him skip the morning's activities—not without reading disapproval into his absence. And if there was one thing Sebastian despised more than social obligation, it was being misunderstood.

Especially now, when he didn't even understand himself.

Sick as a dog, his misery felt prophetic. His head was heavy, his mouth dry from sleeping with it open, and his nose—well, better not to speak of it.

The cook's black tea had done little to soothe the raw sting in the back of his throat. Black tea, no matter how elegantly poured, couldn't hold a candle to the minty, lemon-laced magic Miss Madeleine had left for him the day before.

He hadn't tasted anything so gentle in years. Or been looked after quite like that, either.

He made a mental note to ask her what she'd put in it, the very next time he saw her.

Which he hoped would be soon. Imminent. Preferably now.

Sebastian didn't have a hat fit for the snow, but Thomas's staff had seen to his boots and coat. The beeswax on the leather gave off a faint scent of honey. He didn't feel good, but at least he'd smell good. Small mercies.

He stepped into the foyer and pulled on his gloves—then stopped short.

A delicate hand, gloved in dove gray, reached for the brass door handle. Soft, slender fingers curled with quiet purpose, so at odds with the sturdy metal.

Then she turned.

Miss Madeleine.

"What a lovely day," she said brightly, as if snowflakes weren't actively trying to murder his lungs. "Perfect for gathering pine tips. Honeyed tea is best when brewed fresh."

He stared. Was she truly venturing out into the ice for tea? For him?

She stepped into the snow, her boots leaving neat little impressions behind. Her hunter green pelisse swayed with each step, trimmed with rabbit fur at the collar. Wind tugged a curl loose from her bonnet, and she didn't fix it. That wild, unbothered curl undid him completely.

"Come on, Lord Cambridge," she called back, glancing over her shoulder with a smile that didn't just warm him. It dared him to follow. "Isn't the fresh snow wonderful?"

Sebastian exhaled. His breath steamed in the air like a dragon's sigh.

Wonderful? No. Misery, yes. But then again, if she was the reward...

He tightened his scarf and followed.

Never too sick to follow such a pretty lady.

She blinked into the sunlight like a girl from a painting—half innocence, half temptation—and he wanted, quite suddenly, to be the man who made her smile that way every morning.

She held a silver traveling flask cupped between her palms, the kind hunters used to carry hot cider. Steam trailed from the spout. The scent of cloves and cinnamon curled through the air like an invitation.

"I didn't bring any for you," she said, clearly unrepentant.

"Cruel," he murmured. "But fair." He stepped beside her and leaned down slightly. "Will you share this one?"

She looked down at the flask, her cheeks turning pinker than the sunrise. Then—still watching him—she unscrewed the cap and held it out, the steam rising like a secret between them.

Interesting.

"The cold doesn't bother you, Miss Madeleine?"

She inhaled deeply and his eyes fell to the buttons of her pelisse, stretching the delicate but lush bosom he now knew was tucked away in there. He'd fallen asleep to the memory of her cleavage in her dress at dinner last night and the things he'd like... where was his handkerchief?

Sebastian blew his nose and pulled the door shut behind them with one hand.

"You like the cold, don't you? Well, I didn't expect Tom to pair us up at dinner, I thought it was a fortuitous arrangement only." Fortunate actually, but he didn't dare voice his hope.

"Thomas—Tom? You mean, the Earl of Linsey?"

"Yes, Tom and I have known each other for a long time."

She crinkled her nose adorably, seemingly considering her response. "Well, I do prefer winter over summer."

"I daresay you're the only one."

"Nonsense," she murmured, then paused. "Do you know much about the Duke of Paisley?"

"I do not know much beyond his reputation from Oxford." *It was after their studies that he showed how truly vicious he is.* But Sebastian didn't want to worry her. She'd already obsessed over the duke last night. Sebastian didn't like it. Not one bit. Not that he had any interest in challenging Paisley for Miss Madeleine, but he suspected she possessed a bit more depth than merely angling for a duke.

Call it a hunch.

She seemed displeased with his answer, too. Had he gone too far to ask her to call him by his first name? She'd seen him in a state that only Thomas had, sick and sniffling as he wallowed in self-pity for having caught a chill.

"A-a-choo!" *Not again.*

"If you sneeze on me, I'll pour this hot water right down your cravat before we even put any pine needles in it."

Sebastian froze mid-sniff, leveling her with a dark look as he fished out his handkerchief. "You wouldn't dare."

Her smile widened, all sugar and mischief. "Try me." She tilted the cup just enough to make a point, the fragrant steam curling between them.

He eyed the cup warily, then her, and arched a brow. "Would you at least clean it off after burning me?"

She tapped her finger thoughtfully against the rim of the cup, her grin turning wicked. "I suppose that depends."

"On?"

"Physics."

"You reference science, Miss Madeleine?" he tested the words. She couldn't possibly think what he was... then why did she have this knowing grin?

"Yes, see, this liquid would cool and turn rather sticky. It's sweetened wine with clove, anise, and cinnamon. So there'd hardly be any injuries and yet the stains may never come out of your bright white cravat and would never match your bright white smile again."

Sebastian's mouth grew dry. He wanted to speak but no words came out.

Bright smile.

Sticky sweetness.

No, no, rein yourself in.

"So it depends on physics," Sebastian croaked like a green boy and he hated himself for it.

"And on how cooperative you are." Her voice dripped with

mock innocence, though her sparkling eyes gave her away entirely.

Sebastian sighed, smothering a laugh as he dabbed at his nose. "You're a menace, Maddie."

"And yet, you keep coming back for more," she countered, taking a small, triumphant sip of her wine.

His lips twitched despite himself. Her charm was insufferable. Sebastian had to defend.

"Back to Paisley. What was his reputation like back then?" She seemed more interested in the duke than the snowy path they set upon. In one hand, she still held the flask of steaming mulled wine that Sebastian was now imagining she'd pour over him and clean off. Dabbing him with the chemise he'd pulled off her. Then kissing his torso to make sure he was clean. And he'd most certainly return the gesture.

Sticky goodness.

No, be a gentleman! These are not Thomas's wild horses and you're not some stallion in the stables, he told himself.

But she held the flask so delicately, her fingers curved around the warmth, and he couldn't help but envy the flask for the comfort it received. Foolish though it was, he found himself wishing she'd clasp him with the same gentle reverence, her touch soft and steady.

Sebastian held out his arm and she took it.

She felt nice. Her arm fit perfectly into the crook of his arm and he flexed his muscles.

Not handsome, she'd said.

He inwardly snorted. Was he not quite a catch himself? "His reputation, much like everything else about him, Miss Madeleine, is impeccable. On the outside."

"So, you'd agree that he is perfect?" She sounded smug.

A lump formed in his throat. He hated discussing the qualities of the esteemed duke with this beautiful girl. For reasons he'd never understand, he much preferred to redirect the conversation.

"If externally perfect is what you desire, Miss Madeleine, like an empty urn." He shrugged. "Then you can do worse than Paisley."

"Desire? Why do you say it that way?"

He arched a brow. "What way?"

"So suggestive."

Argh! If she knew.

Sebastian stopped. They'd arrived at a gazebo far enough from the castle to have a private conversation. From here, the castle looked like a toy house in the distance. Beautiful old oaks lined the path and even though they could be seen from the windows of the parlor, Sebastian knew that all the guests were otherwise engaged.

But still, he couldn't help himself.

"Tell me, Maddie, what do you desire?"

She blushed and plonked down on the wooden bench in the gazebo, her back to the castle, her gaze cast down. She set the flask aside, seemingly forgotten.

And something inside of him stirred because he finally had her full attention.

And those beautiful green eyes looked at him in a way that made his stomach lurch.

"Will you stop saying it that way?"

"I'll stop if you answer the question.

She turned to him, blinking bashfully.

Sebastian grinned, and sat the other way, facing the castle, but he was close to her.

Very close.

She emanated just the kind of warmth that he didn't even know he'd longed for.

Ice crystals hung from tree branches like delicate jewels. The air was crisp, and Sebastian still saw his breath like a thin cloud as he spoke.

She pursed her lips thoughtfully for a moment, and said, "I want to prove my mother wrong. Beyond that, I wouldn't know."

"And to prove your mother wrong you must wed a duke?"

She cast him a glance. "Perhaps a duke. The perfect man for certain."

"But is Paisley what you want?" He itched to ask her about her mother—*Why do you want to prove her wrong? What happened?*—but sensed she wouldn't be open to discuss that topic.

She thought about this for a moment and then locked her eyes with his. "What I want, what I should want, and what I desire are not exactly congruent."

So, the duke wasn't what she wanted.

Good.

"I can imagine what you ought to desire to be duchess?"

Her eyes drooped away from his gaze. Sebastian brought a finger to her chin and nudged her gaze back to his.

She bit down on her lip.

"I can also imagine, Madeleine, that your desires transcend proving your mother wrong."

"H-how would you know what I desire, Sebastian?" It was the first time she used his given name. And just like that, his heart sank with the realization of why it bothered him so that she asked about the duke.

He wished she'd ask about him.

But he was no duke. She couldn't use him to prove her mother wrong.

Unless…

"Perhaps I could help you."

"Maddie, for my friends."

"I am your friend now?" His stomach leapt with joy, but it was also a shortcoming, for he wanted more than mere friendship with this beauty.

She bit her lip and gave a sweet frown. "You'd help me?"

"Always." His cold gone and the fog lifted from his head, he only had one thought on his mind. "Have you ever thought about your first kiss?"

She jerked back, her eyes wide.

"Excuse me?"

"To know what you truly desire, and whether it's worth proving your mother wrong, perhaps your first kiss shall reveal more of your desires than you imagine."

She arched a brow and swallowed visibly.

"Thus," Sebastian pressed on, "it's not merely the rank of a man or his ability to make you a duchess that should factor in the triumph over your mother." Sebastian tried to look away and looked back at the estate. They were truly alone. And he was absolutely incapable of resisting the urge to look deeply at her eyes. "Take me, for instance. All I could offer a woman would be the title of marchioness. But there are other factors, such as a proper kiss, that I am sure to add to the weighing scale in my favor as opposed to anyone else in the race."

What are you doing? Stop. Before there is no return.

Maddie's mouth fell open and there was the faintest gasp.

It was lovely.

The sort of angelic shock of a virgin that Sebastian would love to hear more often.

In even more secluded places.

She blinked up at him, and in her eyes he glimpsed the intrigue, the hesitation, and all the questions left unasked.

"Maddie?"

"I never thought about being kissed before." Sebastian stilled. She sounded too bloody intrigued. "Say, can a woman initiate a kiss?"

"I-Initiate." He tasted the words as realization washed over him. "Not good. A woman should never initiate a kiss."

"Never?"

Sebastian cleared his throat and amended, "Not if she's a lady. An unattached woman should never initiate a kiss."

"I see," she said, and a dark curl fell from her coiffure and hung over her cheek from under the ermine hat. Sebastian hesitated at first but then he reached for the delicate strand of hair and tucked it behind her ear.

"However, I hope your first kiss will be perfection."

"Why?"

"Then you'll know what you desire, Maddie."

And perhaps it will be me.

⤐⤐⤐✕⤏⤏⤏

WHEN MADDIE ROSE that morning, the last thing she imagined doing was walking arm-in-arm with the still stuffy-nosed Marquess of Cambridge.

And not just in the literal sense.

The man not only sniffled like a dying hedgehog, but he also had an infuriating knack for sticking his nose where it most certainly did not belong—into her thoughts, her principles, and worse, her desires.

He'd spoken of kissing. Desires. Her mother. In the daylight, it all felt inappropriate—unspeakably so. But it had also left a mark.

Now, walking beside him, her arm tucked neatly into his, Maddie could not stop thinking about that particular remark.

I can also imagine that your desires transcend proving your mother wrong.

Did they?

Maddie wasn't so sure. She certainly didn't want to dwell on the topic of her mother. Most of that was a subject she kept tightly shuttered, even from her closest friends.

And yet she had told him.

She'd told him she wanted to prove her mother wrong. That she was meant for more than the first gentleman who offered for her. She was worthy of more, wasn't she? Her gaze lifted to him briefly, only to be struck by the clean, heady scent of him. Not cologne. Something warmer. Soap, maybe. Or leather and starch and skin. Masculine.

It filled her head more swiftly than it ought.

And now that the feverish sheen had left his skin, she could appreciate his handsomeness more fully. And his build. His coat hugged him just so, the cut of his shoulders clear. The strong forearms beneath his sleeves. The easy strength in how he moved.

This man was all *man*.

And kissing Sebastian would be infinitely more interesting than kissing Paisley. As of late, when Maddie tried to picture the duke, her imagination faltered. The vision blurred. Because another man's mouth came to mind. One far more expressive. One far more maddening.

Maddie blinked hard. She had to stop this.

She didn't even know if a kiss could reveal so much. Could it? She imagined it perfectly, yes. Soft at first, curious. And then…

No. No, no. Madness.

She shook her head, frustrated at herself.

How had he gotten into her head so thoroughly?

She needed a distraction.

Maddie's arms slipped from his and she walked past him, straight to a thick, untouched patch of snow. She crouched, scooped a proper handful, and began patting it into a compact ball.

Perfect. Cold. Solid. Satisfying.

She may not have answers, but this, at least, she could control.

"What are you doing?" He directed a skeptical look at the snow. "Your fingers will freeze."

Maddie grinned at him before throwing the ball of snow at him, which exploded dead center on his chest. She loved the snow and had yet to meet an opponent who could beat her at snowball fights.

He cast her an astonished look. "Are you mad?"

"Who is the mad one here?" she quipped back. "Raising topics such as desire and kissing. I suddenly have a *desire* to pummel you with snow." She made another snowball. This one hit him square on the shoulder.

"Madeleine!"

She laughed at his use of her full name. "Have you never been in a snow fight?"

"I can't say that I have in years."

"I suppose you are no good at having fun."

Sebastian narrowed his gaze in a way that made her skin prickle—half mischief, half warning.

He bent, scooping snow with long fingers.

Maddie's eyes widened. "Oh no you don't!"

Too late.

He tossed it, fast and without ceremony, and she only just side-stepped in time. Her boots sank half a foot into a soft drift, snow clinging to her skirts, but she didn't care. She dropped to scoop her own handful, cold biting her gloves, and lobbed it toward him with a triumphant whoop.

It smacked the side of his head with a glorious thwack.

She punched the air. "Yes! Headshot!"

He turned slowly, snow in his hair, a smear of slush dripping down one brow.

"How is this possible?" he asked, dumbfounded. "How are you so good at this?"

"I've had some practice," she said sweetly.

"You are enjoying this far too much, I think."

"It's quite rejuvenating, I daresay. Exceptionally good for the mood."

He snorted and shook his fingers, sending snow flurries flying. "Now you're just mocking me."

She gave him her most innocent look—one he clearly didn't buy.

"My fingers are bloody freezing."

"Can't take the cold?" she teased. "Then surrender and I shall show mercy."

"I never surrender."

"Neither do I."

That was apparently the wrong thing to say. He lunged, and

she squealed as snow exploded at her feet.

Another snowball, this one striking her leg. The chill bit through her skirts, but the ripple of thrill was entirely unwelcome.

Or rather, far too welcome.

She bent and scooped a fresh handful, her breath catching as he grinned—grinned!—and ran in a wide arc to dodge. Too slow. Her snowball hit him square in the shoulder.

He clutched the spot, dramatically staggering backward as though mortally wounded. "I shall never recover."

"You'll live."

"But I may never live to truly love."

"Such a loss," she called, laughing as she danced backward. She hadn't laughed like this in ages—not the well-mannered chuckles of polite company, but a bubbling, unrestrained, childish joy that left her breathless.

Then splat.

A snowball caught her square in the stomach.

Her laughter stopped with a gasp. The cold seeped straight through the wool and petticoats to her skin. She stumbled a step back and clutched her belly. "Oof."

Sebastian's face went from smug to horrified in half a second.

"Oh no. I didn't… Are you…"

"I'm fine," she said between shaky breaths. Then she started laughing again, harder this time, her knees folding until she dropped to a crouch, hugging herself.

His shoulders relaxed. "You scared me."

"You hit me in the spleen," she managed, giggling.

He crouched beside her, snow dusting his hair and lashes. He looked absurd. And adorable. And far too close.

"I surrender," he whispered. "Truly this time."

Their faces were only inches apart now. Maddie's laughter quieted. Her breath fogged between them, visible in the space they didn't cross.

She swallowed.

This close, she could see the faint stubble along his jaw, the line of his lips, the way his brown eyes weren't so unreadable anymore.

They were warm. And trained entirely on her.

Her heart gave a hard thump.

He tilted his head slightly. "You look cold."

"I'm not," she lied. "But the flask is by now."

He reached up and gently flicked a bit of snow from her temple. The brief touch stole the warmth from her breath.

"I should get back inside," she murmured, not moving. "Perhaps I'll get some pine or tea later."

"Yes." But he didn't move either.

"So soon?"

He hunched down, breathing heavily. "I haven't recovered from my cold yet." As if to prove his words, he sneezed.

Indeed, Sebastian made a good friend. But one thing was for certain; he was a distraction. One Maddie couldn't afford, unless she wanted to give the wrong impression to the duke. One she even might want to give.

What should she do?

Chapter Eight

"LOOK AT THIS beauty," Paisley called out, holding a dripping hare by the ears. Sebastian winced in disgust. He'd taken the only seat in the brewery that was not a hay barrel, a three-legged stool that he was sure had been there since Thomas's grandfather's time. However, he'd much rather be in a snow fight than in the presence of this blackguard.

"Get that out, Paisley," Thomas called. "You're dripping on my floor."

"It's filthy already." Paisley had only come to show his hunting loot; why else would he have entered the brewery if he deemed it for staff only?

"That's hay. You are spilling blood on it." Sebastian rolled his eyes, and Thomas shook his head in disgust. Why did he always have to insert himself in their lives? Title certainly shielded the undeserving sometimes.

The brewery, at least, was one of Sebastian's favorite places.

So many memories with his friend.

Thomas's great-grandfather had built it when he was the Earl of Linsey. Sebastian remembered when he and Thomas sneaked in and took a few sips of liquor from a cabinet his grandfather kept hidden from them. Or so he thought. He couldn't even remember what liquor it had been. Cognac probably. It had been their first time trying spirits and they got so drunk that they lay flat on their backs in the drawing room later, laughing at the chandelier's crystals sparkling in the light of the fireplace.

That was before Thomas's father had renovated the castle and introduced gas lighting in every room. A big investment, and an admirable step toward modernity.

Thomas plopped onto a hay barrel and rubbed his thighs. "He's tirelessly efficient and skilled at any task he sets his mind to. He's gotten four hares, two foxes, and a deer today."

"Just perfect, isn't he?" Sebastian mumbled, picturing the servants skinning the poor animals that the duke had killed. Thomas caught his understatement and suppressed a grin.

"You are just jealous that you missed the hunting trip, Cambridge," the duke said. A stable boy appeared and caught the rabbit carcass in a chipped porcelain bowl and carried it off. "We won't be dining on anything you've caught tonight, hm?"

"At least we won't be stuffing the heads of innocent animals as wall decoration either, Paisley."

"Ah, well, you know I like to have some trophies to remind me of the fun we're having."

He poured himself a glass of whiskey and drank it without regard to the quality of the carefully aged liquor. Sebastian noticed that Thomas put on a placid face, ignoring that his guest completely failed to savor the expensive drink he'd so generously put out for Sebastian, not Paisley.

"Killing isn't a sport; it's not fun."

"You speak like someone who can't stomach the fowl, Cambridge. Sluggish appetite, eh?"

"I'm just saying that killing for sport is not—" but Thomas shook his head and Sebastian swallowed his words. They'd had this exchange time and again back at Oxford. It was no use arguing with the man. The duke hunted and engaged in every other sport that the men might admire, most garish as far as Sebastian was concerned. Also, Paisley was one to seek women out as a sport, burning his coin at the most expensive establishments in town. None were activities that Sebastian could ever favor.

"Now that you are walking down the aisle with a pretty blonde, maybe it's my turn to find a trophy of my own," Paisley said to Thomas.

"Lady Ashley is not a trophy. Watch your words," Thomas barked. Was he defensive of his betrothed? How odd.

"I never thought you liked her," Paisley muttered.

"You know nothing," Thomas snarled.

"Why are you harping on the past?" Sebastian jumped in. "Like follows introduction follows love."

"Always the romantic, Cambridge. You are too soft-hearted." Paisley poured himself a second glass.

Sebastian wrapped both hands around his dimpled mug with a nickel plaque of Thomas's crest. There were only three of these left, one for Thomas, one for Sebastian, and one locked away in the spirits cabinet for his late grandfather. Thomas's father never had a sense of the brewer's art.

"He wants to marry for love, like I am," Thomas said dismissively. "Some of us have more than a title to give."

"He's read too many books; they made him soft." Paisley hmphed.

"As far as I can remember, I outran you as a boy, Tom. I raced you on horseback and you were but a speck of dust behind me, Paisley. And I'm younger than you both." Sebastian crossed his arms and stared at his friend.

"All I'm saying, Cambridge, is that you have to guard your heart. Those girls may look harmless, but they steal your heart and crush your bones."

"Nonsense, Paisley. Not every girl wants to marry out of spite," Sebastian spoke to the duke but Thomas ought to know the reproach had been directed at him.

"Well, gentlemen, short of compromising a beauty, there is no sure way the woman of your heart's desire will have you, is there?" Thomas said.

"I don't want a woman to feel coerced into a union. If she wants me, she has to make it known," Sebastian spoke before he filtered his words. He really sounded like a weakling. Plus, it would take years to find such a woman. Decades. Centuries. Unless…

"You want perfection, Cambridge—always have," Paisley said, sloshing his drink as he leaned back. "But if you ask me, imperfections are far more accommodating. Give a little praise, and they'll give you everything. No chasing required."

The words sounded hollow.

Across from him, Tom gave a low chuckle and raised his glass. "There's truth to that. The ones who don't expect much rarely ask for anything in return."

Revulsion curled in Sebastian's stomach. He might be tired, still shaken from the lingering ache of his cold, but he wasn't so far gone as to stomach this line of thought.

"That's not something to be proud of," he said quietly, but neither man seemed to hear. Or perhaps they just didn't care.

They could keep their games. Sebastian had never found pleasure in the "easy". There was no appeal in taking something not freely offered. It was the depth of a woman's mind that intrigued him. Her fire. Her defiance.

Like the way Maddie Hunt had stood toe-to-toe with him in the snow, grinning as if she could topple him with a single look.

She probably could.

He lifted his glass and set it back down untouched.

"I don't want perfection," he said, this time loud enough to cut through the laughter. His tone was calm, but there was no mistaking the conviction in it. "I want someone who sees the world with clarity. Who wants something real. And who won't hand herself over for a compliment."

The room quieted, slightly.

Paisley gave a lazy shrug. "To each his own."

Sebastian leaned back in his chair, gaze fixed on the fire.

Let them think him stuffy or slow or overly principled. He

didn't mind. He knew what he wanted.

And somehow, despite all his rules and resistance… he had a sinking feeling she wore snow-dusted gloves and smelled faintly of peppermint and lemon balm.

My daughter,

I've been summoned to Lady Ashley's wedding and can only speculate why it has been arranged nearly four months earlier than anticipated. Not that the short notice concerned me as much as your new friendship with a certain marquess. When did you decide that a duke was too high to reach?

Do write and explain yourself.

Mother

Viscountess Tisdale

Maddie folded the letter slowly, smoothing its crisp edges with more care than necessary. At least the paper was neat if not her nerves. She placed it beside the untouched cup of chocolate on Ashley's vanity and took a calming breath.

The wedding was now just a few days away. Not four months, as originally planned. Mere days. And here she was, standing in Ashley's chambers, staring at the wedding dress her friend held up with delight.

"I had it commissioned when I thought we had more time," Ashley said with a soft laugh. "Now look—it's nearly too fine for a rushed wedding."

The pale-blue gown shimmered as it caught the light, the silk delicate as snowflakes and cool as Ashley's glacier-blue eyes.

"It's perfect," Charlene said, reaching out to stroke the hem. "Like something out of a dream."

Maddie nodded, though a strange tightness clutched at her chest. She should be overjoyed for her friend—truly she was—but still… a part of her ached. "You didn't tell us," she said, her voice low, nearly drowned out by the fire's gentle crackling.

Ashley blinked and lowered the dress as she paled. "Tell you what?"

"That you were with child."

Ashley's expression faltered, and the gown slumped in her arms. "I'm sorry. I was afraid to."

"Afraid?" Maddie asked. "Why?"

Charlene cut in gently. "You know what she means."

"No," Maddie said. "I don't understand. Unless I'm missing some facts. Why would you be afraid to tell us? I mean, I came with you to the Royal Ascot with a stomach potion in my satchel, prepared to take down a peer of the realm for what he did to you."

Ashley laughed, then quickly sobered. She looked down at the gown. "I know you wish to marry for love, and with all the things with your mother… I felt a little guilty."

"To be happy?" Maddie asked, aghast.

Charlene snorted. "No, I hope not!" she teased.

"Well…" Ashley laughed when Maddie sent her a glare. "I was also afraid you'd be afraid your mother found out, and you wouldn't be allowed to come. And I can't tell Char and Sera without telling you."

"Very well, I accept that," Maddie said. She'd suspected the reason, too. "But throughout your adventures, I have kept my own, you know."

Her friends nodded.

"And strictly speaking," Charlene said. "You told us before Sera now. Just when is she arriving, by the by?"

"Oh, should be in a day or so. I haven't heard anything to the contrary," Ashley said. "So, am I forgiven?"

"Always," Charlene said.

Maddie nodded. "I can defy my mother, you know. I've done it plenty. I might worry and be startled, but I do come around. So don't ever hold back on my account." She sighed. "You both have love, and I… urgh! I haven't even been kissed!"

Ashley's lips parted, but no sound came.

"I mean it," Maddie added at their shocked faces. "Not once. Not even a tiny stolen peck. I've read everything in this book," she retrieved *The Handbook on Seduction and Matters of the Heart* from her reticule and flung it on the bed, "even your notes, and according to it, if you recall, a lady must never initiate a kiss. So then tell me, how am I to show a man he has permission?"

Charlene laughed. "That book is utter nonsense."

"I know," Ashley said. "But it works. I remember it said something about how a lady must always maintain mystery. 'Only in the stillness of her virtue will a gentleman approach.' What does that even mean?"

Maddie let out a short laugh. "Exactly. I don't know how to be mysterious and still somehow make it clear I want him to kiss me."

Charlene grinned and nudged her shoulder. "It's not about being mysterious. It's about… openness. You let your guard down, linger a little longer, give him reason to hope. No man wants to get slapped for leaning in."

Ashley grinned. "You have more power than you think, Maddie. You don't need to speak it. It's all in the eyes. In the way you look at him."

"Or in the way you smile at his terrible jokes," Charlene added.

Ashley wrinkled her nose. "Or when you nurse him through a miserable cold and dab chamomile salve on his cheeks."

Maddie groaned. "How did you find out?"

"I knew when I saw him and smelled it. You'd been in his chambers before I arrived, hadn't you? You weren't there by chance; you had just come out."

The three of them burst into laughter, and some of the tightness in Maddie's chest eased.

Ashley set the dress aside and took Maddie's hand. "You're not alone, Maddie. You never have been. And for what it's worth… I have always been in awe of you."

"And I you," Maddie whispered. "Always."

Ashley blinked down at her stomach and grimaced. "Do you happen to have one of your elixirs? For nausea? Because I feel I might faint before I even make it to the vows."

Maddie laughed and opened her satchel. "Peppermint, lemon balm, and just a touch of ginger. Sit down, dear bride. I have a solution for every ailment."

And somehow, she hoped this would hold true for matters of the heart, too.

Chapter Nine

S EBASTIAN LEANED BACK against the cool stone wall in the hall beneath Thomas's grandfather's portrait, arms folded, jaw tight. If the man were alive, he wouldn't allow the kind like Paisley to cause problems. Therefore, Sebastian decided he had to find a way to protect his friend from any trouble that may arise before his wedding. He was getting married soon, and if Sebastian was a good friend, he'd make sure there were no hitches.

He didn't understand how Paisley could speak of women as if they were prizes to be seized. As if affection could be won with a few compliments and handed over like spoils. Sebastian didn't want spoils. He wanted a woman who would look at him and see him. Who wanted him because of who he was—not what he had. Not a conquest, but a connection. A meeting of equals, not a victory lap.

And for some reason, his mind wandered straight to Miss Madeleine Hunt.

Maddie.

The name slid into his thoughts like a whisper he didn't want to forget. He wasn't sure when it had happened—perhaps somewhere between her commanding him over a pot of steaming mint and brushing salve over his face—but she'd unsettled something in him.

Would she ever let him kiss her?

Their first kiss should be special, and he'd do anything to make it unforgettable if such an honor fell on him... *Confound it!* Why was he thinking about her first kiss? His body reacted instantly to the thought.

He hadn't meant to think of her that way. Well, not at first. Especially not while he was sneezing and dripping like an invalid. But she'd sat so close. Touched him so gently. Her fingers had grazed his lips with an innocence that touched him deeply.

What man wouldn't react?

And then she'd looked at him. Not through or around him. At *him*.

She didn't simper and feign false charm. No angle to work. Just those steady eyes that made him feel like a man worth considering for life. And in the gazebo in the snow, when her gaze had flicked—just briefly—to his mouth, something inside him had locked into place. As if his entire body understood something he hadn't dared name.

He'd kissed women before. Far too many, if he were honest. But none of them had made him want the way Maddie did. Not just to taste, or touch, or win—to deserve her. He dragged a hand through his hair and exhaled slowly. His chest felt too tight. His thoughts too loud.

She was everything he hadn't expected. Polished, yes. But not cold. Proper, but not unfeeling. Curious. Quick-witted. Surprisingly kind. And even when he irritated her—especially then—she looked at him like he wasn't just the Marquess of Cambridge, but a man capable of more than he'd ever let himself believe.

Would she kiss him back? Just another perspective of the same question: Will she let me kiss her?

If she did, he wouldn't rush it. He'd kiss her slowly. Thoroughly. As if a kiss were a promise and he truly meant every word of it. Sebastian pushed away from the wall and adjusted the towel slung over his shoulder. Maddie deserved more than idle fantasies. If there ever came a moment when she wanted him—

truly wanted him—he intended to be ready. Not because she was beautiful, though she was. But he looked back at the painting of Thomas's ancestor and thought to himself that with Maddie, he'd like to pose for a portrait. To stand for a legacy for their... he gulped... children.

Am I falling into affection?

Because when she looked at him, he felt like a better man. And he'd be damned if he let that feeling slip away.

A tall shadow flicked by and Sebastian lost his train of thought.

Male with a thick coat.

Sebastian pressed his back to the cold stone wall, holding still as footsteps approached.

A faint sound broke the silence.

Meow!

He frowned. Not the sharp, warning cry of an adult cat. This was higher, whinier. A kitten.

The shadow stretched before the corner. Sebastian shifted slightly to catch a glimpse of the intruder.

It wasn't a servant.

Paisley.

The duke walked into the corridor, a wicker basket swinging from one hand. From the basket came the mournful cries of a mother cat, white as the snow outside, with five tiny kittens wriggling beneath her. Sebastian's jaw clenched. The kittens from the stables... They were barely old enough to leave the hayloft, much less be dragged through the drafty castle.

Paisley crouched, his seemingly expensive coat brushing the flagstones, and plucked up the smallest kitten. The runt. The little claws caught on the lace handkerchief Paisley had inexplicably produced from his pocket.

Sebastian's gut twisted. That kitten needed its mother more than any of the others. Whatever this was, it wasn't kindness.

Cradling the squirming ball of fur, Paisley tucked it inside the handkerchief and straightened, moving quickly toward the main hall.

Sebastian followed.

He knew the layout of the castle far better than the duke did. While Paisley took the long route, Sebastian slipped through a side door, cutting into the same hallway ahead of him. He ducked behind a carved screen just as Paisley joined a waiting companion—one of the footmen who served as his shadow and a maid from upstairs.

"You got it, milord?" the man asked in a low voice.

"Better than I hoped," Paisley replied, glancing down at the small bundle in his arms. "Perfect for the plan."

The maid leaned closer, curiosity in her tone. "You sure it's old enough?"

"It'll do," Paisley said flatly. "I don't care about the animal. The point isn't to keep it alive for long. Once Miss Madeleine is near this cat, her dowry is as good as mine."

Whatever did that mean? Even for Paisley, this was a stretch… he'd have to marry her first. Sebastian wrinkled his face at the thought. *Not while I'm alive.*

Staying out of sight, Sebastian's hands curled into fists. He knew the kind of man Paisley was but hurting a kitten was a low even for him.

The duke's voice was calm. They also carried a touch of cruelty. He spoke as though this kitten were nothing more than a prop, a disposable tool for whatever evil scheme he had in mind for the day.

Sebastian's throat tightened as the maid—he recognized her from the upper floors—peeked into the bundle. Her eyes widened. "Your Grace, she's hardly weaned. She won't survive long without her mother."

Paisley's mouth curved in a smile that did nothing to soften him. "Then she'll have to manage. I paid you both, so do the job."

The maid looked down at the kitten again, stroking its tiny head. "If the mother won't take it back, there's no saving the poor thing."

Sebastian didn't wait to hear more. Whatever Paisley had planned, he was not leaving that defenseless creature in his hands. Not tonight. Not ever.

The duke might think no one had seen him.

He was wrong.

MADDIE SAT CURLED in the soft embrace of the drawing-room armchair, a book on herbal remedies propped in her lap. She traced a finger under a passage about nettle leaf's virtues in easing inflammation, and murmured aloud, "If only nettle could cure all my troubles."

The quiet was pleasant—until the maid appeared with a feather duster and a determined expression.

At first, Maddie only noticed the occasional floating mote in the air. Then came the sniffle. Another. Her eyes began to prickle. She gave the maid a polite smile and bent over her book again. No sense making a fuss about a little dust.

Through the corner of her eye, Maddie saw a bulge under the maid's apron. Did it move?

The air seemed to thicken, almost… musky. Her breaths felt shallow. That odd, too-tight ribbon about her chest pulled tighter. She shifted, trying not to draw attention to herself.

And in that uncomfortable stillness, her mind slipped—unhelpfully—toward a certain marquess. She remembered the way Sebastian's voice dipped when he spoke to her, how his gaze seemed to hold her in place even when she wanted to look away. It was absurd to think of him now, with her eyes watering and her throat prickling, yet the thought came anyway, uninvited and warm. As if some part of her had begun seeking him out, even in the quiet.

She blinked hard and fixed her gaze on the page, willing her cheeks to cool. Thinking of him was not part of her plan.

The door opened again. As if beckoned by her thoughts, Sebastian strolled in with his easy, unhurried gait—until he caught sight of the maid. His expression sharpened.

"Maddie!" he said, then he glanced at the maid and corrected himself. "Miss Madeleine, how do you do?" but without waiting for an answer, he stepped toward the maid. "You," he said, the single word carrying far more weight than his casual tone.

The woman froze, duster in hand. "My lord?"

"Where did you take it?"

Maddie's head came up. *It?* Her frown deepened. Was he in the habit of interrogating staff so bluntly? Had she perhaps been mistaken and he was no less arrogant than Paisley?

"The kitten," Sebastian said. "From the stables. Where is it?"

The maid's fingers tightened on the duster as if she were trying to cover up the bulge beneath her apron. "I—"

Before she could continue, another figure emerged from the hall—Paisley, looking far too pleased with himself. "What's all this?"

Sebastian didn't even glance his way. "Where," he repeated to the maid, "did you take the kitten? It wasn't even weaned."

"Is this how you treat the staff, Cambridge?" Paisley ignored the maid and shot Maddie a grave look. Almost theatrical.

The maid's hands trembled now, her lips pressing together.

And in that moment, Maddie understood Sebastian wasn't cowing her. He was protecting something small and defenseless. Kittens.

Her chest constricted again, sharper this time. "Wait," she managed, breathless. "Cats? Here?"

Sebastian's head snapped toward her. "Maddie?"

Her throat tickled, her nose twitched, and the next moment she was sneezing so hard she nearly dropped her book.

She fumbled for her handkerchief. "It's nothing," she wheezed, though it was decidedly something. Her lungs felt as though they were filling with wet wool.

Sebastian crossed the room in two long strides, his coat

brushing her knee as he crouched. "You're pallid," he said low, scanning her face and the faint rash beginning along her neck. He turned on the maid and Paisley. "Out. Now."

Paisley came with a smug face from behind Sebastian, his expression carved into a vicious smile just like he had when he was a boy.

"You accept the friendship of a man who's hunting a maid down for kittens from the stables? How low can you fall, Miss Madeleine?"

"Out, Paisley," Sebastian said, his voice a whipcrack.

But Paisley only tilted his head, his tone dripping with mockery. "What will your mother think if mine tells her you've decided to befriend a man who'd rather return a runt of the litter to its feline mother than find his place in society?"

Without waiting for a reply, he turned on his heel and strolled away tsking, every inch the satisfied predator.

Maddie's pulse thudded in her ears. "A kitten?" she croaked, her voice barely above a whisper.

Sebastian nodded once. "Yes. He took it from the stables. But why?"

Her chest burned; each breath felt heavier than the last. "Because he's known my reaction to cats since I was a child. Our mothers are friends..." She pressed a hand to her middle, the room tilting.

And in that dizzying moment, she wasn't sure what unsettled her more—whether she was about to collapse into Sebastian's arms... or whether that was precisely what Paisley had hoped she'd do in his.

The instant the door shut, Sebastian turned back to her. "How bad?"

"I'm—" She caught herself on a cough. "—quite... pink, I imagine."

"That's one word for it." He slipped a cool handkerchief from his pocket and pressed it gently into her palm. "Do you have something for this? In your remedy etui?"

"In... my chamber. Third drawer left side. Under the lavender satchels."

"Right." He straightened as if ready to fetch it himself, then hesitated. "Do you need me to carry you?"

She narrowed her eyes over the handkerchief. "I may be spotted and wheezing, Sebastian, but I still possess the use of my legs."

"You were swaying."

"I was startled."

"You're still gripping on to the arm of that chair like it owes you money."

Her lips twitched despite the prickling heat on her skin. "You are enjoying this far too much."

"Not true," he said, sliding a hand beneath her elbow. "I'm only enjoying about half of it—you are holding me. The rest is abject concern that you might collapse before we make it to the stairs."

She let him draw her up, pretending she didn't need the steadying pressure of his arm. "Rogue."

"Protector of kittens and damsels in distress," he corrected, curling her fingers into the crook of his elbow. "Come on, Maddie. Let's get you breathing again."

And though her skin burned, and her chest ached, she let herself lean into him just a fraction more than necessary.

❖

SEBASTIAN SLOWED HIS stride as they reached her chamber door, every muscle taut with the effort of not drawing her closer still. She'd held on to his arm the entire way, her fingers light but constant, the contact igniting something warm and treacherous under his ribs.

He hated the faint rasp in her breath, the unnatural flush on her cheeks. Hated her discomfort.

And yet... he loved that she hadn't let go.

"I should apologize," she murmured, pausing just inside the doorway. "Bothering you while you're unwell—"

"Bothering me?" His voice came out low, rougher than intended. "Maddie, you've seen me sneeze on half the household. I think we're well past politeness."

Her lips curved, the ghost of a smile tugging at them, and for a moment he forgot entirely about the faint ache in his own chest. Her illness mattered more than his. She mattered more than—than anything. He would carry her up every stair in the castle if it meant she could breathe easily again.

He stayed in the threshold, bracing a shoulder against the doorframe. He should leave her to rest, fetch a maid, maintain the fragile propriety they'd both been raised to protect. But the thought of turning away now, of not seeing her steady again, tightened something deep in him.

"Ring for a maid," she said softly, as if reading his thoughts. "For propriety's sake."

He didn't move. "I'll wait."

"Sebastian—"

"I'll wait here," he amended, though his gaze remained fixed on her in a way that was anything but gentlemanly. Not across the threshold, no, but close enough to see the faint rise and fall of her breath, the way the pulse fluttered in her throat. Close enough to imagine crossing those few feet and catching her face in his hands.

If anything happened to her... The notion alone was enough to put a heavy, unfamiliar weight in his chest. He could picture it too clearly—her crumpling in the corridor, Paisley standing by with his smug detachment. That man would run at the first sign of trouble, finger outstretched to assign blame. Sebastian would never—could never—understand what drove a man like Paisley to be so unfeelingly cold and sheer evil.

"Eucalyptus oil," she muttered as she dripped something from a vial onto a handkerchief.

She sank onto the edge of the bed, turning her face away to press the handkerchief to her nose. He watched her, the fierce urge to protect her warring with the dangerous truth he'd been keeping at bay: somewhere between her lovely smile and her odd concoctions, she had slipped past his guard entirely.

He'd thought he could keep this in hand. But standing here, watching the soft curve of her shoulders rise with each careful breath, knowing how close he'd come to losing her—even to something as small as this—he felt the last of his resistance snap.

I think I might be falling in love.

Think?

In fact, I know so.

She glanced up and caught him watching her. Neither of them looked away.

If he stepped forward, if he touched her now, there'd be no mistaking it for gentlemanly concern. But he stayed where he was, holding himself in check by sheer will. His heart had already surrendered; the rest of him was only waiting for the right moment to follow.

Chapter Ten

B Y THE TIME the sun set, Maddie lay propped against her pillows, the glow of the fire casting a soft orange light across her chamber. Her skin still prickled faintly from the earlier rash, but the worst of the tightness in her chest had eased. Beside the hearth, her discarded gown hung over a chair, and a pot of cooling chamomile tea sat on the table.

It was Sebastian she had to thank for her being here at all. He'd all but carried her up the stairs, one strong arm at her back, the other braced for any falter in her step. And once inside her room, he hadn't crossed the threshold but stood in the open doorway—guarding her like some determined sentry—until Ashley arrived.

Ashley swept into the room just as Sebastian was standing guard in the doorway. "I came as soon as I heard—Maddie!" Her gaze darted over Maddie, still pale and propped against the pillows.

Sebastian stepped back, giving her room, but not without one last, steady look at Maddie. "She says she'll be all right," he murmured, almost as if to reassure himself.

"I will," Maddie said, though her voice was still breathless. "Thank you."

For a moment, his eyes searched hers—warm, intent, as

though he wanted to say more—but he only gave a short nod and took his leave.

The instant the door closed, Ashley turned back to Maddie, eyes wide. "What happened? I nearly tripped over the maid sobbing in the corridor. She's convinced she nearly killed you! Did she?"

Maddie shook her head. "No, she didn't. It was… cats."

Ashley blinked. "Cats?"

"One tiny kitten," Maddie clarified, pushing herself up against the pillows. "Paisley brought them in from the stables."

"Why?"

"I don't know. But I think she hid a kitten under her apron and dusted the room so I'd breathe in cat hair. Paisley put her up to it."

The shock on Ashley's face turned to outrage. "He what? Everyone knows you can't be near cats!"

"I don't think he cares about my safety," Maddie murmured. *Consider him the last person I'd ever wed!*

Ashley's jaw set. "Oh, he knows. That was deliberate." She reached over, taking Maddie's hand. "You poor thing. No wonder you swooned."

Maddie managed a faint smile. "I didn't swoon."

"You nearly collapsed," Ashley countered, her eyes softening. "Thank goodness Sebastian was here. And in his condition, what a hero."

Maddie looked down at her lap, unwilling to admit just how grateful she'd been for his steady presence.

"Where are the cats now? Did he bring the little white ones? They are only two weeks old!"

"All I know is that Paisley brought them in from the stables. I didn't even see them at first, but the moment I started feeling that—" she gestured vaguely to her chest "—it all made sense."

Ashley's lips thinned. "What a bore with a title."

Maddie gave a small, wry smile. "Apparently."

"Oh, he's no good, Maddie. When will you realize that you

can do better?" Ashley said darkly. "You'd best steer clear of him entirely."

Maddie didn't disagree. Still, in the back of her mind, she couldn't shake the image of Sebastian—standing watch in her doorway, ready to chase away anyone who dared come near.

AFTER SEBASTIAN HAD seen the kitten safely returned to its mother—no small feat with Paisley lurking about—he found himself in need of a drink. Something strong. Anything but another cup of herbal tea.

Somewhere between fending off Paisley's petty cruelty, the ever-approaching wedding, and Maddie's breathless, pale-faced episode in the corridor, he'd clean forgotten about his own wretched cold.

If he could forget the weight in his chest in favor of watching over her... perhaps he was recovering after all. Or perhaps she'd simply made him forget everything else.

"Are you going to make one?" The old butler who'd served Thomas's grandfather and now Thomas—who'd known Sebastian since he was a lad—had that extant twinkle in his light blue eyes. The butler was a dear man and the fuss over the hasty wedding wore him out.

"I was going to the kitchen to whip up a batch, yes." Sebastian winked with one eye and the butler had understood. "Will you let the earl know?"

"Certainly, milord," the butler said with a smirk. The title always sounded respectful, except when it came from him. Eh, Sebastian shrugged, the old man had known him for so long. There wasn't a tale of his boyhood that didn't have one version or another of McGulligan, the butler, carrying him and Thomas back to bed—usually bringing them back from the brewery. When the milkmaids joined the stableboy to taste a new concoction that Thomas had invented, the nights got a bit wild.

Sebastian tiptoed quietly through the silent halls of the castle, making his way to the kitchen. He didn't want anyone to know he was sneaking down to cook himself a nightcap; he'd only share it later with Thomas. He'd leave a cup in the cabinet behind the cheese for McGulligan. He knew where to find it.

Once he arrived and greeted the cook on her way out, he went to work, gathering the usual kitchen utensils he needed.

"Whipping up a flip, milord?" she said with a smile. She, too, had known Sebastian since he was a boy. "Shall I set aside some strong coffee in the mornin'?" she teased. When he was fourteen, there'd been this one time when the egg-flip hadn't agreed with him… oh well, that was a long time ago.

"I'm three-and-twenty, Mrs. Thatcher."

"All grown up, milord, I know." Her tone was wistful. This wasn't his castle, and Sebastian didn't need to be the head of household here. The staff were his friends, to the extent propriety allowed—and a little beyond.

He grabbed a pewter tankard for the beer, and a long-handled egg-spoon to stir in the eggs, sugar, and nutmeg. He carefully cracked the eggs into a bowl and added a spoonful of sugar and a pinch of nutmeg, then beat them together until they were light and frothy.

Next, he poured a quart of ale into a large iron pot and then added the egg mixture to the ale as it heated up over the open flame of the fire. Using a long-handled iron poker, he stirred the mixture vigorously, careful not to let it boil. As it warmed, the egg-flip thickened and became smooth and creamy. By the time he was finished, the staff had dispersed to other parts of the house. The servants turned in early at Fort Balmore.

Sebastian enjoyed the silence in the kitchen. Only the metal of the poker rubbing against the pot disturbed the light crackling of the fire as the sweet aroma of nutmeg and sugar filled the air with an enticing scent.

"Smells malty." A voice came from behind Sebastian just

when he poured the frothy treat into three cups. "Who's this for?" Maddie sneaked up on him.

Sebastian's surprised gaze flew to Maddie. In the kitchen. "This is not a place for a lady."

"Says who?"

Well, what could he say to that? "Can I help you with something?" Sebastian asked as he took a fourth cup from the shelf and poured a ladleful into it.

"I've come for some hot milk. It helps me to sleep," she said, her eyes surveying the used utensils in the copper pan. The cook would have them washed in the morning.

"Why didn't you tell me that cats make you sick?" Sebastian spoke to Maddie in that newfound tone, full of promise. What, he didn't know yet. Friendship? Maybe more.

"I love animals. They don't make me sick."

"But you cannot be around them?"

She shook her head. "That's why I carry a small apothecary with me when I travel."

"The vials and essential oils you showed me?"

"Yes, they help me breathe when everything—" she showed a clenching motion around her chest and throat, "—when something is in the air and I cannot breathe, there's usually a smell that opens up my chest again."

Sebastian felt terrible for her. After only a few days with a head cold and stuffy nose, he'd been miserable enough.

"When does it happen?"

"In the spring and summer, all the time. Around animals, especially the sweetest and fluffiest ones." She wrung her fingers. "Sometimes at the library and always in the attic."

Poor dear. Something in the air made her ill. "That's why you like the winter?"

"Oh yes." She inhaled deeply, and her mein brightened. She was beautiful and Sebastian's heart leapt. The more he got to know her, the closer he wanted her. The more he wanted to know. "When the rainy period starts in late October, I blossom."

Suddenly, she bit her lip and blushed. "I mean, not blossom, but... ahem..."

"I know what you mean," Sebastian said with a smile. So she was thinking along the same lines as him? Interesting. "Continue."

"Well, when the rain comes, the cold, and even the snow, I can finally breathe. The kind of breaths that let all the life into my chest." She inhaled and her breasts rose. Sebastian tried very hard not to stare. He probably failed miserably.

"Why didn't you tell me earlier today?"

"You were so upset and when you were feverish, I tried... but most people don't like the winter and think me odd."

"But it's your favorite season."

"Yes." She looked around.

"Pardon me, where were my manners? Please join me, Maddie." Sebastian said as he pulled a stool over for her to sit and handed her the cup. "This works better than milk and honey."

"Why is mine only half-full?" Maddie stretched her neck to compare the cups. She was adorable.

"Because you are a lady." Sebastian blew on the cozy drink in his cup. It had formed the thin layer of skin on top, just the way he liked it.

Maddie cradled the cup in both hands and inhaled deeply. She closed her eyes for a moment, and Sebastian felt his stomach do that thing again. It would have been unsettling if Maddie hadn't had such a satisfied smile. In the orange glow of the kitchen fire, the little curls hanging from the side of her head were almost golden. He wished to wrap one around his finger... *stop it!*

"What is this?" she asked.

"An egg-flip." Sebastian took a sip. Hmm, perfect. He'd have to bring the cup for Thomas upstairs soon lest he come and search for him.

"Is it like a rum-posset?" she asked.

"How do you know such a thing, Miss Madeleine?"

She shrugged and Sebastian's eyes fell to her deeply cut

gown. He was starting to feel warm, and it couldn't have been from just a sip of his drink. His fever was gone now, but a different heat lingered whenever Maddie was near.

"Well, we make it with beer here. It's not rum." He took another sip but he couldn't stop staring at her cleavage.

"What else goes into the flipping egg?"

Sebastian broke into a laugh. "It's an egg-flip, not a flipping egg." He licked his lips. "You are—" He stopped himself just in time before he told her just how sweet she was. "I extracted the juice from the rind of a lemon by rubbing it with sugar and a piece of cinnamon, nutmeg, and voilà. I boiled it gently in the beer and then poured it on the eggs."

"And how did you make it so creamy?" she asked as she took her first sip.

"A lot of stirring," Sebastian answered but his voice trailed off when he watched Maddie's lips lay on the rim of the thick cup. Her perfectly manicured fingers wrapped around the rustic cup, a thumb looped through the handle, she held the drink in her mouth for a while. A long moment that erased all other thoughts from Sebastian's mind.

When she raised her gaze again and set the cup on her lap, Sebastian's mouth was dry.

THE WARMTH OF the egg-flip lingered on her tongue, sweet and rich and utterly unexpected. Maddie held the cup in both hands, letting the heat seep into her fingers. Her lips still tingled where the creamy drink had touched them, and as she glanced over the rim of the mug at Sebastian, she caught the way he looked at her.

Not politely. Not casually.

But like a man who had forgotten, for just one moment, what he was supposed to do next.

It did strange things to her insides.

She lowered the cup carefully to her lap and fought the impulse to reach for her face—because she could feel it, couldn't she? A touch of foam on her upper lip. Surely that was why he was staring.

He was trying not to laugh. Or perhaps—no, not laugh. Linger.

"Do I have something on my…" She gestured vaguely toward her mouth.

His gaze dropped, just for a heartbeat, before he set his cup down.

"Hold still," he said softly.

His voice felt like a thread of silk drawn over bare skin, impossible to ignore. Maddie stilled. Not because she had to, but because something in his tone had rooted her to the spot. The fire popped behind them, but all she could hear was the sound of his breath reaching for hers.

He hesitated. Just for a heartbeat. A flicker of uncertainty—or restraint?—crossed his face. His hand hovered in the air, and she caught the barest tremble in his fingers. From the cold?

For one wild second, she thought he might cup her cheek instead. And she wanted him to. Her skin ached for it. Her whole body leaned ever so slightly forward, a pull she wasn't even aware of until her balance shifted on the stool.

Then, he brushed the pad of his thumb just beneath her nose.

Not a sweep. Not even a press. Just a whisper of contact, warm and slow. A single pass beneath her nose, deliberate enough to banish the foam, but tender enough to cause her heart to flutter.

The touch ignited something low in her belly. A trembling. A tug. The kind of sensation she imagined poets wrote sonnets about and never quite captured.

She forgot to breathe.

She felt it all the way through her.

His fingers lingered a fraction too long, as if he were memorizing the curve of her lip. And in the firelight, with shadows dancing across his features, he didn't look like a marquess or a scholar or a guest in someone else's home.

He looked like a man on the precipice of desire, and terribly afraid to fall.

Her gaze lifted to his. And in that look—unspoken, un-rushed—something passed between them. Something ancient and new all at once.

A question.

An answer.

A beginning.

"There." His voice was lower now. "Gone."

And yet, he didn't move away immediately. Not even when she met his eyes.

She should look away. That would be the polite thing. The wise thing. But she didn't want to. His face was so close—closer than it ought to be, and she was perfectly aware of it. She could count every thick, dark lash framing those eyes. She could smell the faintest trace of spice and nutmeg from the drink, and something else. Something deeply him.

It wasn't the fire making her warm anymore.

"I suppose I ought to thank you," she said, her voice barely above a whisper.

Sebastian smiled—but slowly, like he didn't want to give it all at once.

"Any time, Maddie."

The way he said her name—it curled around her like velvet.

She reached again for her drink, needing to do something with her hands before they betrayed her. Her fingers trembled slightly as she lifted the cup to her lips and took another sip, hoping he wouldn't notice.

He did.

But instead of teasing her, Sebastian leaned back slightly on the stool, one elbow resting carelessly on his knee, the corner of his mouth curving into that smile she was beginning to recognize as rare. Private.

Just for her.

"You know," he said after a moment, voice low, "you're the only one who hasn't asked me for the recipe and then immediately tried to improve upon it."

Maddie blinked, surprised. "That's because I know better than to improve something already perfect."

The words had slipped out, warm with sincerity before she could temper them. But the quiet that followed made it clear what he'd heard… and what she'd just implied.

His expression barely shifted, yet something in his gaze deepened, heat gathering like embers in a grate. He looked at her as if she'd just revealed a secret he very much wanted to keep for himself. And now that he'd seen it, he wasn't about to look away.

Her pulse tripped. She dropped her gaze first, studying the swirl of froth in her cup as if it were suddenly fascinating. She wasn't ready. Not entirely.

But she was perilously close.

The fire beside them popped, sending a warm rush of air over her cheek. Neither of them spoke, but the silence had weight—not awkward, not empty. It felt like something was settling between them, unseen yet undeniable.

She lifted the cup and let the creamy warmth slide over her tongue, the faint spice of nutmeg lingering. A sigh escaped before she could catch it. "This is very good," she murmured, softer than she'd intended. "Far better than milk and honey."

He didn't answer at once. When he did, his tone lowered, threaded with something deliberate.

"I like the winter now, too," he said.

Her head came up, startled by the intimacy in such a simple statement.

His eyes caught hers, steady and unhurried, and in them she saw the same thing she felt: an awareness neither had named, but both acknowledged. It was the kind of moment that made a woman feel… chosen.

And Maddie, her heart trembling like a leaf on a still branch, felt the most dangerous thing of all…

She was choosing him back.

She didn't speak it aloud. She didn't need to. In the glow of the hearth, with the scent of nutmeg in the air and the warmth of the cup cradled between her palms, she met Sebastian's gaze and knew—

Something had shifted.

And she would never be quite the same.

Chapter Eleven

L ATER THAT NIGHT, Maddie lay curled beneath the counterpane, her room lit only by the faint orange glow from the hearth, the fire reduced to embers now, whispering softly to the silence. She'd taken down her hair. Her skin still felt warm from the heat of the kitchen, but it wasn't just the fire or the drink that clung to her now.

It was him.

Sebastian.

She remembered the first time he'd let her feel his forehead for fever. The way he hadn't flinched, even when her fingers brushed his hair.

Or how he'd once fallen asleep mid-sentence, mouth slightly parted, lashes resting on his cheeks like shadows. That had been the night she stayed an extra half hour, just watching him breathe. And the day he made her laugh when she was meant to scold him for not drinking his tincture. Every moment had chipped away at her resolve until she didn't know where admiration ended and infatuation began.

Her hands were restless beneath the covers, one curled around the other. Her thoughts wouldn't stop tumbling. Every time she closed her eyes, she saw his. That amused tilt in his smile. The warmth in his voice when he said, "Please join me,

Maddie."

He'd called her Maddie again.

And somehow it had sounded more intimate than... a kiss?

She sat up, pushing the counterpane aside, and reached for the small wooden box she kept tucked inside her nightstand. Her fingers brushed over the worn leather as she lifted the lid.

Her etui.

Inside, nestled in velvet-lined compartments, sat her small brown vials—glass glinting like amber in the firelight. She touched each gently, familiar with the feel and weight of every one. The eucalyptus bottle rolled beneath her fingers. Almost empty. She uncorked it, inhaled—sharp, cool, comforting.

But somehow, her support, her medicines, her oils and ointments didn't hold the same comfort as his smile. His attention.

His touch.

The chamomile was nearly gone too. That soft, honey-sweet scent lingered on the air, reminding her of warm clothes and quiet evenings and the comfort of a hand held just a little longer than necessary.

Except that it struck her: Sebastian hadn't needed her oils today.

He was almost entirely well.

Which meant...

No more excuses.

No reason for her to knock on his door with a prepared tincture or a satchel of remedies. No reason to linger in his room under the guise of care. No reason to touch his hand or hear the deep rumble of his thanks or... No reason to see him alone.

She was not the sort of woman men pursued.

She wasn't the kind they ruined or even risked for. And yet, when he looked at her like that, like she was the only thing in the world holding his gaze together, it felt... possible. That was the trouble with longing. It turned sense into fog and temptation into poetry. She had always lived carefully. Quietly. She had been told her heart was too soft, her mind too fanciful. But Sebastian... he made her feel like softness could be strength. Like her wildest thoughts might not be foolish at all.

She gripped the sides of the box, the leather cold beneath her palms.

It's not proper.

Of course it wasn't. She should never have spent so much time by his bedside. She should not have gone to the kitchen, alone, late at night. She should not have laughed with him. Let him touch her. Let him look at her like that.

But she hadn't been able to help it.

She'd forgotten propriety.

She'd forgotten everything when he looked at her. The castle, the staff, the very air around them—it had disappeared. The world had narrowed to the glow of the fire, the scent of nutmeg, the sound of his voice.

And his eyes. So brilliant. So alive. So focused on her.

She snapped her lips together, suddenly aware of the cool air on her mouth.

Oh no.

She had longed to kiss him.

She still did.

I don't even know how to kiss!

The thought struck her like a bolt of lightning. She hadn't meant to think it so plainly, so openly, but it was the truth. It had settled low in her belly and bloomed like something shamefully beautiful. She wanted to know what his lips would feel like. She wanted to tilt her face up, stand on tiptoe if she had to, and just feel him.

She imagined his palm cupping her cheek, steady and sure. How he might tilt her chin up and whisper something. Something that would undo her. Would it be slow? Gentle? Or would he kiss her like he couldn't bear to wait another second? And if he did... would she melt? Would she forget the whole of the world the way she had by the fire? Her lips parted at the thought. She curled deeper beneath the covers, torn between shame and a strange, dizzy kind of happiness. His mouth, his hands, the sound he might make if…

Maddie shut the etui.

She couldn't think about this. It wasn't right.

And yet…

No matter how tightly she pressed the lid, no matter how she tried to calm her heart, the thought lingered. The memory of his smile. The smell of warm beer and spice. The gentle press of his thumb to her upper lip.

She'd never felt so seen. So wanted. So… deliciously undone.

And the worst part—the most dangerous, wonderful part—was that she didn't want to forget.

Lying back against her pillows, she clutched the etui to her chest and whispered into the night.

"I'm falling in love with you."

The words hung in the quiet like a secret meant only for shadows.

And Maddie, her heart aching with the truth of it, closed her eyes—and dreamed of egg-flip, firelight, and the way Sebastian looked at her like she was something worth breaking all the rules for.

⇢⟫⟫⟩✺⟨⟨⟪⟪⟵

THE FIRE HAD dwindled to a low glow, its soft flicker casting long shadows across the stone walls of his chamber. Stillness had settled around him like a second skin. But inside, he was anything but still.

He was all chaos and storms.

Sebastian leaned back in the large, high-backed chair before the hearth, his boots kicked off and discarded somewhere near the bed. His shirt was open at the collar, sleeves rolled to his elbows, yet still he felt too warm. Stifled. Like he'd walked straight into the heat of the kitchen again. Or maybe it was memory that made him sweat now.

Maddie with froth above her lip.

The feeling of her skin beneath his finger as he swiped it away.

And the way she had looked at him…

Like he mattered in a way that no one had ever made him feel before.

Maddie.

He let her name tumble silently through his mind, the sound of it… almost magical. Too intimate, perhaps, and yet—he had called her that. Softly. Almost daringly.

Maddie.

He exhaled and tilted his head back against the chair, eyes drifting shut. He could still see her in the kitchen. The way the firelight danced in her hair, the way she held that cup with both hands. And then she'd looked at him, just over the rim. Lips parted. Foam on her mouth.

That had undone him.

That picture had landed somewhere near his ribs and refused to let go.

A muscle jumped in his throat. He swallowed hard. It had been nothing—on the surface. A simple touch. But warmth had transferred to his finger and still it burned.

He shifted in the chair, dragging a hand down his face.

It should not have meant anything. It should not have happened. But it had. And now… now his blood wouldn't quiet. His thoughts wouldn't still.

He pushed up from the chair, pacing.

He wanted her.

Not just the curve of her mouth or the scent of her skin or the feel of her fingers. He wanted her. Her voice, her mind, her spirit. The way she'd argued over the smallest things. The way she'd tried to hide her smile when he teased her. The way she just… existed.

He stopped at the edge of the bed, gripping the post as if it might balance him.

It didn't.

Not where it mattered.

His mind betrayed him, conjuring her again. Not the prim Miss Maddie with her vials and her lectures, but the one with firelight in her eyes. The one who leaned in close and smelled like crushed herbs and soft linen. The one who looked as if she didn't yet know what it was to be kissed but was thinking about it.

Sebastian pressed his palm flat to his chest. His heart was still there, still pounding. That was something, at least.

He dropped onto the mattress, elbows to knees, and pressed his hands to the back of his neck.

What the devil had happened tonight?

She'd crept under his skin, that's what. Not with intention—he didn't believe that for a moment—but simply by being.

He wanted to touch her again. Properly. Deliberately.

He imagined it: her breath catching, the slight tremble of her fingers, the softness of her mouth beneath his.

Would she sigh? Would she make a small sound of surprise before melting into him? Or would she press close, greedy and unknowing, and make him forget every bloody rule he was supposed to remember?

He groaned and dropped back onto the bed, one arm flung over his eyes.

It was not proper.

It was not wise.

And yet—

And yet…

And yet.

He would break rules for her. Had already broken a few.

He had not meant to want her. Not like this. Not in ways that kept him awake and aching. Not in ways that filled his nights with heat and his days with distraction.

But tonight had undone him.

Because it hadn't just been desire. It hadn't just been hunger.

It had been comfort. Companionship.

The sense of being seen.

She had looked at him as if he wasn't a burden or a patient or an obligation. She had looked at him like a man.

Like her man.

The realization came suddenly and sharp, as if it had been waiting just beneath the surface.

He sat up slowly.

The firelight reached the edge of the bed, golden and flickering. He stared at it. Then reached for the blanket, fingers closing into the folds.

He could still feel her here in his room, his chair, his breath.

Sebastian pressed his fingers to his lips. As though that could transfer the sensation of hers over.

A kiss by association.

A beginning.

A promise.

And he wanted to see it through.

He wanted to unpin her hair and watch it fall. He wanted to see her cheeks flushed not from embarrassment but from pleasure. He wanted to taste her sighs and count her freckles and make her forget every lesson in propriety she had ever been taught.

His breath shuddered out of him.

If he kissed her, he would not stop at just one. He would kiss her until she forgot her own name and whispered his instead. He would kiss her until the fire died and came back to life. He would kiss her until there was nothing left but the two of them and the ache they'd carried alone for far too long.

But she wasn't here.

And maybe that was the only thing saving them both.

Sebastian leaned back on the pillows, staring up at the beams overhead.

She would return to her chamber. She would bury herself in blankets and the memories she was probably trying to forget.

But he wouldn't forget.

Not tonight.

Not ever.

He closed his eyes, letting her image fill the darkness. The way she had looked up at him. The shape of her mouth. The hesitant desire in her gaze, barely disguised.

She wanted him too.

He was certain of it now. And that certainty was the most dangerous thing of all.

He lifted one hand to the air above him, watching the firelight catch on his fingers. Then slowly, he closed it—

As if holding on to something precious.

As if she were already his.

And in a whisper meant only for the shadows, he said, "I'm already yours." A secret promise sent into the dark. And Sebastian, heart thudding and body far too warm, let himself dream of herbs and firelight.

And the girl who made him want to break all the rules.

Chapter Twelve

EARLY THE NEXT morning, with a fresh layer of snow blanketing the world outside, Sebastian stood by the window of his chamber, a steaming cup of tea in hand and a blanket draped loosely around his shoulders. Though his nose remained a little stuffy and a dull ache lingered behind his brow, the worst of his illness had passed and with it, the dreary weight that had kept him trapped not only in bed but in his own thoughts.

Today felt… lighter.

The fire crackled softly in the hearth, the scent of burning oak curling into the room alongside the sharper eucalyptus from Miss Maddie's salve. She'd left it for him two mornings ago, along with her own blend of tea and an oil she claimed would help him breathe better. He didn't know if the remedies were to credit for his improvement, or if it was simply the memory of her voice, her hand brushing his as she passed him the steaming cup, the faint flush on her cheeks when their eyes met.

She had come without hesitation, walking into his chambers with tinctures, essential oils, and fresh herbal teas each day as if it posed no inconvenience. As if nursing him back to health was something she wanted to do.

No one has ever taken care of me like that.

Not personally, at least. Sure he'd been sick as a boy, but mother had always sent his governess or the servants for help.

Maddie... ahem... Miss Madeleine was different. Special. Precious.

Sebastian sipped the tea. The taste was odd—earthy with something floral, not unpleasant but not quite to his usual preference. He'd finished every drop.

Outside, the estate grounds shimmered in the pale morning light, the snow transformed into a sea of silver. The frost on the glass windowpane sparkled like a thousand tiny stars, each one shaped delicately, intricately, uniquely. He ran a finger down the edge of the window, watching the fog recede slightly beneath his touch, and thought—strangely—of the way Maddie had smiled when he'd offered her a taste of his egg-flip the other night in the kitchen.

That's what her eyes looked like, he realized, staring at the frostwork. Bright. Alive. Not pitying, not shocked. Just... amused. Warm.

He hadn't been able to stop thinking about her since.

He'd never been a man prone to illness. Or to helplessness. But this cold had gripped him hard, rendering him a shell of himself for days. The fever had taken his appetite, the aches had stolen his sleep, and worst of all had been the sensation of futility. And yet... she'd stitched him back together with the golden threads of her heart.

Or so it felt at least.

But it was daring to presume that she'd felt the same.

Sebastian revisited their encounters. There was that time when Maddie had walked in, wrapped in her practical wool cloak, her hands full of unlikely treasures, and without making a fuss, had sat beside him. Not once had she looked at him as if he were a burden. Not once had she treated him with exaggerated gentleness. She'd simply existed in the space with him, quietly making things better. Propriety didn't matter. Humanity did.

That's how wonderful she was.

Now, as he took another sip and let the heat work its way into his chest, Sebastian exhaled slowly and let his gaze drift over the horizon. The morning had that peculiar stillness only snow could bring. Even the crows had quieted. The castle grounds lay silent, white-dusted and untouched.

He should go out.

The thought struck him with unexpected urgency. For the first time in days, the idea of dressing and stepping outside did not seem a chore. His body still ached, yes, but something inside him had shifted. He no longer felt dull and feverish.

Sebastian set the cup down and moved to the wardrobe. He dressed slowly, carefully. His muscles protested when he bent to pull on his boots, but he didn't mind. When he finally straightened, wool coat buttoned, gloves in hand, he caught sight of himself in the mirror.

His reflection startled him.

There were dark circles beneath his eyes, the stubble on his jaw darker than usual, and he still looked paler than he'd like—but there was something else, too. Something steadier in his eyes. Something determined.

Outside the corridor, the castle remained hushed. Most of the staff were still below stairs, preparing for the day. He took the stairs down two at a time, ignoring the way his chest tightened slightly at the exertion. The door to the east wing opened with a creak, and he stepped out into the cold.

The wind hit him first, sharp and clean, biting through his coat with its icy fingers and pulling at his breath. But instead of retreating, Sebastian inhaled deeply, the pine-sweet scent of the woods mingling with smoke and earth. His lungs stung with it. Alive.

He made his way down the familiar path leading to the stables, each step crunching in the snow. The boots left a trail behind him, the only footprints in an otherwise pristine landscape.

And then he saw her.

Maddie.

She was crouched at the far end of the gardens, wrapped in that same dark-green cloak, her hair tucked beneath a knitted cap. She was tending to something at the base of a stone wall, her gloved fingers brushing frost off the stems of a hibernating plant. There was nothing particularly extraordinary about her posture or movement, and yet Sebastian stopped as though struck.

She hadn't noticed him. That was what did it. That she moved so freely, so confidently, when she believed herself unseen. That she was out here at all, when she could have been warm in the kitchens.

He approached quietly, but not to startle her, only to delay the moment when she would look up. He didn't know what his face would reveal. He didn't trust himself not to reveal every-thing.

"Maddie," he said finally, his voice lower than intended, roughened by disuse.

She looked up at once, a smile already forming. "Sebastian!"

And just like that, the world seemed warmer.

"You shouldn't be out here. You're barely recovered."

He shook his head, stepping closer. "I needed air."

Her gaze scanned his face, pausing just a moment too long on his mouth. She was worried. He saw it in the way her brows pinched slightly. In the way her gloved hands fidgeted with the folds of her cloak.

"I'm quite recovered. Truly." He hesitated, then added, "Thanks to you."

She didn't answer immediately, just stood and dusted snow off her knees. When she looked at him again, her cheeks were pink, and not from the cold, he suspected.

"It was nothing," she murmured.

"No." He stepped closer, feeling something solid and sure beneath the words. "It was everything."

The snow crunched softly between them. The space was small now. Not quite close enough to touch. But enough that the warmth of her breath mingled with his in the frigid air.

Maddie glanced away, her lashes brushing her cheek. "I only brought what anyone would have. You'd have done the same."

"Not everyone would have come." His voice was quiet now, steady. "And not everyone would have known what to bring."

She didn't answer.

Sebastian reached out, gently lifting one of her hands. Through the glove, he felt the shape of her fingers. Small. Strong. Real.

"I missed you," he said.

Her eyes snapped up to meet his. Wide. Shining.

"I didn't go anywhere," she whispered.

"You did," he said, his thumb brushing the top of her glove. "You didn't stay after you brought me tea. And the castle—my chambers—felt empty without you."

And that's when he realized it.

My heart is empty without you.

Something shifted in her expression. The kind of vulnerability one tried to hide but failed to—just as he had failed to ignore the ache of her absence.

"I only stayed away because I thought—" She shook her head. "Because I thought you needed rest."

"I needed you," he said simply.

The words hung in the air between them, misting in the cold.

She didn't smile, not yet. But her hand tightened in his, just a fraction.

And Sebastian knew, with more clarity than he'd known anything in a long time, that this was what he'd been waiting for—not just the lifting of a fever, or the clearing of his head. But this. The feeling of being seen. Of being cared for. Of wanting something enough to reach for it.

"I'm glad you're better," Maddie said softly.

"I am." His gaze didn't leave hers. "And I think… I'm only just beginning to feel like myself again." *But I will never be the same without you.*

A gust of wind rushed over them then, stealing her cap from her head. Her hair tumbled out in soft, dark waves, and she laughed—startled, shy, lovely.

Without thinking, Sebastian caught the cap mid-air and stepped forward to replace it. His hands brushed her hair, and she stilled.

When he met her gaze again, she wasn't smiling.

She was waiting.

He didn't kiss her. Not yet. But he leaned close enough that she would know he wanted to.

And close enough to know she wanted it, too.

THE SNOW CLUNG to every branch like silken ribbons, and Maddie, standing in the pretty rose garden with frost melting into the hem of her cloak, had never felt so aware of every inch of herself.

She wasn't cold.

She should have been. After all, the nippy wind danced past her ears and tugged at the strands of hair escaping from beneath her cap, but inside, she burned. She could feel the heat rising through her chest, warming her limbs, her fingertips, her throat. It had everything to do with the man standing just a few feet away, looking at her as if she were the reason spring returned each year.

Sebastian.

He'd recovered. Mostly. His eyes still held a faint shadow, and the red flush on his cheeks was certainly due to the morning chill, but his mouth curved with the ease of someone no longer fighting to breathe. He looked alive again. Gloriously, handsomely alive.

She should have said something. Anything. But her voice caught in her throat.

She wanted him to move closer. Just a little. One step. Two. That was all it would take for her to reach him. To feel his coat brush against her skirts. To know if his breath still held the scent of the tea she'd made with trembling fingers the night she had walked to the castle in the storm.

She stepped forward.

Just slightly. Barely a shift in the snow.

It was the boldest thing she'd ever done.

Her heel hadn't even left the ground, but she'd moved. Toward him. And heaven help her, she couldn't take it back. The air between them felt charged now, shimmering with possibility. Every inch of her skin tingled with awareness, as if her body already knew something her mind refused to admit.

She wasn't the kind of woman who reached first. She was the quiet one. The thoughtful one. The one men noticed after they'd flirted with everyone else. But Sebastian wasn't looking past her. He was looking at her.

And oh, how she wanted him to meet her halfway.

To close the space she couldn't quite bridge alone. To see her, truly see her, and choose her—not because she was proper or pleasant or conveniently nearby, but because something in him couldn't bear the distance.

Just two steps, she thought.

Two steps, and I'll know.

The distance between them seemed to shrink, and her heart surged with wild, silly hope. *Come closer.*

He didn't speak. Not right away. But his gaze flicked downward—to where her boot had moved. And then his eyes lifted again, slowly, to her mouth.

Her lips parted on instinct. She didn't know if she was about to speak, or if she was already imagining the feel of his mouth against hers.

The silence stretched between them. And still, he didn't look away.

The moment trembled.

Somewhere behind her, a window creaked open. Maddie stiffened.

The sound came from the castle, just behind the hedges, one of the ground-floor windows of the east wing. She didn't need to turn to know what it was: someone opening a shutter, slowly and carefully, as if they didn't want to be seen.

They were being watched.

Her stomach twisted, but she didn't move.

If they were watching, they could watch. Let them. I've been thinking of this for days.

But it felt like a lifetime culminating in a moment.

She let her gaze drop to Sebastian's mouth. If someone wants a show, she thought wildly, then let them see what it looks like when a woman loses her breath entirely.

He took a step forward. Then another.

And then he was in front of her.

His hand reached out, not urgently, but with the reverence of a man about to touch something precious. His glove was warm from his pocket, and when his fingers curled around hers, something inside Maddie gave way.

"Thank you," he said, his voice low and slightly hoarse. "For being so wonderful."

She swallowed. "As I said, it was just tea," she whispered. "And some medicine. Nothing."

He shook his head slowly, his eyes never leaving hers. "I didn't mean those things." Her breath hitched, but he spoke again, "I meant you."

Her fingers curled instinctively around his. The weight of those three words settled into her chest like a velvet cloak—heavy, warm, and far too beautiful to bear.

"You're wonderful, Maddie." His thumb brushed along the side of her hand. "And beautiful."

The word landed like a spark against dry parchment.

"And so very sweet."

Her knees very nearly gave out. The wind wrapped around

them, but she didn't feel it anymore. Not really. Not when her whole body was leaning toward his.

He stepped closer. His body almost touched hers. Just a breath away. Her gaze lifted to his eyes. They were so dark and so warm, crinkling slightly at the corners as he smiled, and dear heaven, that smile. The boyish tilt to it, the way it melted the last of her defenses. Her lungs forgot how to fill properly.

And then he leaned in.

Slowly. Intentionally. As if he wanted her to feel every moment before their lips met.

His breath mingled with hers, and she swayed toward him.

She didn't stop herself. Didn't try.

She wanted him to teach her. And she most of all wanted to know what he felt like. His lips. His touch.

Her heart beat so fast she was sure he must hear it. Every part of her ached for him to kiss her. She could already feel it—what it would be like. His mouth firm but tender, his hand lifting to cup her jaw, the press of him, finally, gloriously—

She trembled.

His nose brushed hers.

Closer.

Closer.

Please, she thought. Please kiss me.

And then followed footsteps. Crunching over the snow just behind the hedges.

Maddie froze.

They weren't passing by. They stopped. Then came the voice—sharp, loud, unmistakably scandalized.

"Madeleine!"

She flinched.

The voice rang across the garden like a bell cracked in frost.

Chapter Thirteen

"WHAT AM I interrupting here?" Paisley's voice rang out, sharp and smug, slicing through the quiet like a blade. He stood with his legs planted wide, arms crossed over his chest, and—Maddie's eyes narrowed—was that a rifle tucked in his belt?

Sebastian took a step back, distancing himself a bit. He turned slightly, gaze shifting away from her as if he needed the cold air to still the heat that had risen between them. He didn't look at her.

Why won't he look at me?

Her breath still came too fast. Her skin still tingled, her chest too full. The world had changed a moment ago, had tilted on its axis when he stepped toward her like a man who might kiss her. And she'd wanted it. Oh, how she'd wanted it!

But now he wouldn't even meet her eyes.

Because of Paisley?

Or her?

A thread pulled taut inside her chest, a strange combination of hurt and shame blooming where hope had just bloomed seconds before. Had she misunderstood everything? No—no, she couldn't have. He had leaned in. He had looked at her like she mattered. And yet, the space between them had never felt wider. As though Paisley's voice had shattered the spell between them and scattered the pieces too far to gather.

Was he ashamed? Embarrassed? Or just protecting her, now that there were witnesses?

Now that someone might think he cared.

Maddie's fingers curled at her sides, trying to hold on to something. The memory. The closeness. The possibility. Her cheeks burned… not from the cold. From being caught in the act of… what, exactly?

Of wanting.

Of hoping.

And suddenly, she hated that Paisley had seen it. Hated that Sebastian had let him see her vulnerability and responded with distance instead of defiance.

She swallowed down the ache. This wasn't the end. It couldn't be.

But for now… she stood alone in the garden, heart pounding for a kiss that hadn't happened, and a man who no longer looked at her like it might.

Paisley was grinning like a man who thought he'd walked in on something he could control. "It looked like—"

"Have you nothing to do?" Sebastian cut him off smoothly, the question polite in phrasing but steely in tone. "Nowhere to be?"

Paisley shrugged, not bothering to hide his delight, yet there seemed to be an underlying malice, if she were not mistaken. "Nothing more important than looking after good old Maddie here."

Maddie bristled. The moment was gone—stolen—and now Paisley was draping himself across it like a dog over a feast.

"Don't call me that."

"Oh, please," Paisley drawled, as though the matter were settled. "Our mothers have been closest friends since the cradle. It's practically tradition."

She held her ground, chin lifting. "I'm not your friend. There's no tradition. You're not my family."

He turned to Sebastian with a sly smile. "But our mothers

wish for us to be more than that, don't they? She'd make a lovely Duchess of Paisley, wouldn't she?"

The words landed with the subtlety of a cannon blast.

But Sebastian didn't flinch.

Maddie watched him, stunned. His jaw didn't tighten. His voice didn't sharpen. Instead, something quieter crossed his expression. A strength that needed no proving. He didn't dignify the bait, didn't rise to it—not because it didn't touch him, but because he wouldn't give Paisley the satisfaction of seeing it.

But it was there, plain to see if one took the time to look.

Maddie admired him more in that moment than any other.

And by it, she meant the envy. He was claiming her.

And oh, how she wanted him to succeed.

Sebastian turned to her with exquisite poise. "Well, it's cold," he said, gently. "You should go inside before you catch a chill, Paisley."

Paisley barked a laugh. "Like you? Hah! Didn't you just nearly faint with the flu?"

"A cold," Sebastian corrected, with all the elegant assurance of a man immune to insult. "A bit befallen, yes. But not weak and certainly stronger for having survived it."

He paused. The gleam in his eye was unmistakable.

"I wouldn't expect you to risk such a condition, Paisley. You never know. Some colds are known to linger… others to strike a man in his, ah, most delicate faculties."

Paisley blinked. "What?"

Sebastian shrugged, deadpan. "Oh yes. I've heard tell of fevers affecting the… continuation of one's line. Quite tragic, really."

He brought one gloved hand to his mouth as if to cough, but Maddie could see it. He was biting back a laugh.

She leaned in toward him, voice solemn. "I've been to the apothecary when men came in seeking cures for… you know."

Paisley's gaze darted between them.

"There weren't any," Maddie finished.

Sebastian let out a sound that might have been a snort—or a

suppressed explosion of mirth.

Paisley paled. Truly paled.

"Well," he said at last, voice wobbling with a flicker of panic, "as a duke, I do rank higher than you, Cambridge. I must take my leave. It's rather important I ensure… everything is in working order. For the sake of my… ahem… heirs."

And with that, he turned on his heel and fled.

They watched him disappear through the castle doors, and when the latch clicked behind him, silence followed before Sebastian exhaled.

And then, they laughed.

They broke into it together, sudden and helpless, laughter spilling into the cold morning like a warm wind. Sebastian's was rich and deep and beautiful. Maddie's own laughter bubbled up too fast, too full.

Her cheeks hurt. Her ribs ached.

"Oh," she gasped, trying to breathe, "did you see his face?"

Sebastian nodded, his eyes dancing. "When you said there were no cures, he turned positively green."

"He truly thought…" she started but couldn't finish for laughing.

Sebastian leaned forward slightly, shaking his head in disbelief. "I'm fairly certain he's galloping to the nearest doctor as we speak."

Maddie couldn't look away from him.

His eyes sparkled like black coffee kissed with sunlight, his cheeks pink from the cold, his smile warm and impossibly dear. His laugh wasn't aristocratic. It wasn't measured or poised. It was real. Joyful. Full-bodied. It was the sound of a man she was no longer resisting falling in love with.

And as the laughter faded into soft breaths between them, Sebastian reached out and—without thinking, perhaps—rested his hand on her shoulder.

It was light. Barely there. But warm. Steady. Intimate.

Maddie turned her face toward him, and the gesture undid

her. His fingers on her shoulder, his laughter lingering in the air, the way his mouth was still slightly parted. It was too much. And not enough.

Her heart swelled so suddenly she thought it might crack.

He was so lovely.

Did he even know? If not, she would tell him. Someday.

When she could breathe again.

⟫✦⟪

THE FIRE IN the brewery had burned low, casting a faint amber halo over the stone floor. Shadows clung to the barrels, stretched across the worktable like fingers. The scent of scorched grain and sweet malt lingered in the air, and Sebastian sat at the edge of it all, hunched over a tankard with the same brooding silence he'd worn since she left for her chambers. How long ago was it? Two hours? More?

He wasn't taste-testing anything. He wasn't brewing. He was drinking.

Drinking too much.

Not enough to dull everything, but just enough to take the edge off the ache that had started earlier that day, the ache that had Maddie's name carved into it like a secret confession.

The door creaked behind him, and he didn't look up.

"You're a long way from your bed," Thomas said, his voice low with casual mischief as he stepped inside, shaking snow from his boots. "Planning to drown the remaining fever in brandy, are we?"

Sebastian said nothing. Just tipped the tankard to his lips and swallowed.

Thomas didn't press. Not at first. He crossed the room slowly, the way a man does when he's walked in on something delicate.

"Let me guess," he said finally. "This isn't about the flu. Or the brandy. This is about a woman."

Sebastian snorted, but without heat. "You're insufferable."

"True," Thomas said lightly, dragging out a stool. "But I'm also right. The house is full of them since Ashley brought her friends here for our wedding. Girls, dresses, feathers, pearls. Soon they'll paint the halls pink and put lace on the saddles of my horses."

Silence.

Sebastian stared at the fire like it might offer absolution. It didn't.

"She almost kissed me," he said quietly.

"Who?" Thomas blinked. "Almost?"

Sebastian nodded. "I didn't let it happen."

A pause. Then, "Why not?"

Sebastian's grip tightened on the tankard. "Because Paisley was there. Watching. Smirking like the bastard he is. Maddie's mother seems to like him. She might, too. A little."

And the moment shattered.

Because of Paisley, yes, but not just him.

Sebastian had seen it in her eyes. That bare flicker of longing. Of trust. And it had near undone him. He could have kissed her. Saints, he'd wanted to. His whole body had leaned into it, had ached for it. One breath more and he'd have felt her lips against his. And maybe she'd have kissed him back. Maybe she would've let him pull her closer, bury his fingers in her hair, taste the softness of her mouth.

But what if she regretted it afterward? What if the spell broke and all she saw was another man who wanted something from her?

He knew what it meant. That it wasn't just about desire. Not with Maddie.

She wasn't a game. She wasn't a woman to ruin, or tempt, or steal a moment from. She was… everything he'd stopped believing he was worthy of.

And that terrified him more than Paisley ever could.

Because Paisley would offer for her. With her mother's blessing. With an estate and a title and a smile that never quite reached his eyes. Sebastian had no illusions about it—he was the more dangerous choice. The unknown one. The one with quirks.

And yet, Maddie had looked at him like she didn't care. Or maybe she did care and still wanted him anyway.

That was the part that undid him.

He didn't want to take her innocence. He didn't even want to steal her first kiss. He wanted to earn it. Every inch of it. The trust. The surrender. The way she might one day reach for him—not because she was caught in the moment, but because she knew him and chose him still.

But to have that… He'd have to become the kind of man she could choose. Not the kind who sat in the shadows of his family name, letting bitterness dictate his choices. Not the man who made women laugh at dinner and then left before morning. Not the man who ran from feeling anything real because it was easier to pretend nothing mattered.

He rubbed at his chest.

She mattered.

More than he'd expected. More than he might be able to handle.

Thomas frowned. "He saw you two? How much has he seen?"

"Enough."

Sebastian leaned forward, elbows braced on the table, the firelight catching the angle of his jaw. He looked like a man trying not to feel too much and failing.

"He wants her," he said. "Everyone knows it. He's even arrogant enough to say it out loud without letting her know first."

"And what do you want?"

Sebastian's throat worked. He didn't answer.

Thomas let the silence hang. When he finally spoke again, it was quieter.

"You're in deep."

Sebastian looked up sharply. "It's not just that she's beautiful. Or kind. Or clever. She makes me feel like—"

He broke off, then pushed back from the table, rising to pace across the room.

"She makes me forget everything I hate about myself. And everything I've spent my whole life running from."

Thomas watched him. "Your mother?"

Sebastian laughed, but it was hollow. "She'd adore Maddie. She's exactly what my mother's always hoped for. Polished, poised, unscandalized. Sweet. Good. Too good for me."

"So what's the problem?"

Sebastian turned, his eyes dark. "I never wanted to be the son she could be proud of."

"But now you want Maddie."

"Yes," he said hoarsely. "And she's the one woman I can't have without becoming exactly the man I never meant to be."

The words settled in the air between them, thick and unspoken.

Thomas stood and walked over slowly. "Sebastian."

"What?"

"You already are that man."

Sebastian stared at him.

Thomas shrugged. "The one who didn't kiss her. The one who walked away when everything in you screamed to stay. That's the man you didn't know you were."

Sebastian didn't answer. He didn't have to.

Thomas's expression softened. "Have you kissed her before?"

"No." The word came out like regret.

"Why not?"

"Because she's innocent," Sebastian said, the words raw. "Because she's precious. And I didn't want to start something I couldn't finish with the right intention."

Thomas raised a brow. "And what is your intention?"

Sebastian hesitated. His voice came out rough. "To keep her. If she'd have me."

Thomas's lips quirked. "You're worried you'd scare her?"

Sebastian nodded. "I don't want to rush her. Or touch her in a way that—God, she's not like the others."

Thomas grinned then, a slow, wicked smirk. "You do realize she's best friends with Ashley, right?"

Sebastian frowned. "Yes…"

"And you don't think she's had questions?"

The realization landed slowly.

Thomas clapped him on the shoulder. "Trust me. If she wanted answers, Ashley gave them."

Sebastian groaned. "You didn't."

"Oh, I did," Thomas said smugly. "Every question. In detail."

Sebastian rubbed his face with a groan. "I can't decide if I want to thank you or throw you into the snow."

Thomas laughed. "You're welcome. And I'll add this—Maddie may be innocent, but she's not breakable. If she looked at you the way I think she did—then you're already halfway to trouble."

Sebastian leaned against the edge of the table, the firelight soft against his features. For a long moment, he said nothing.

Then quietly, "I think I'm falling in love with her."

Thomas's voice dropped, the humor gone. "Then stop trying not to."

Chapter Fourteen

THE NEXT MORNING, Maddie hesitated in the corridor outside Ashley's dressing room, her fingers twisting in the edge of her sleeve. She was not here for anything in particular. Certainly not for advice. And if her cheeks were warm from walking too briskly through the corridors and not from thinking of Sebastian's eyes—or his mouth—well, that was entirely her business.

She knocked lightly.

"Come in!" came Ashley's familiar, sing-song voice.

Maddie opened the door to find her friend perched on the edge of a velvet-cushioned chair, swathed in a dressing robe of pink silk and half-lost in a cloud of soft hair ribbons. Her lady's maid bustled behind her, arranging perfumes and hair combs like a tiny military operation.

Ashley turned with a bright smile. "Well, don't you look suspiciously sweet this morning."

Maddie stepped in, tucking a curl behind her ear. "I brought you some of that rosehip balm you like. For your hands." She held it out.

Ashley accepted it with a raised brow. "That's thoughtful. And not at all a distraction tactic."

Maddie perched on the arm of the chair and gave an innocent smile.

Ashley narrowed her eyes. "What's happened?"

"Nothing."

Ashley waited.

"Almost nothing," Maddie amended. "Well… something. A little something."

Ashley leaned in with a grin. "Maddie…"

"It wasn't a kiss," Maddie blurted. "Not really."

Ashley clapped her hands once. "I knew it! I saw the way he looked at you yesterday. Like he wanted to tuck you into his coat and never let go."

Maddie groaned, hiding her face. "Ashley, I'm serious."

"Oh, I am, too." Ashley angled toward her, voice low and conspiratorial. "So? What happened?"

Maddie hesitated, then sighed. "We were in the kitchen. Late. He made this drink—egg-flip? I don't know. It was frothy. And warm. And…"

Ashley's eyes sparkled. "And?"

"And I had a bit of it on my lip, and he…" Maddie trailed off, cheeks burning. "He wiped it away. With his thumb."

Ashley gasped with delight. "Scandalous."

"It wasn't!" Maddie said quickly. "It was… sweet. But also… something else. I couldn't breathe properly for a full minute afterward."

Ashley bit her lip. "Did he lean in?"

Maddie nodded.

"And did you?"

"I wanted to," Maddie whispered. "So much. But then—Paisley showed up."

Ashley winced. "The human bucket of cold water."

Maddie burst into laughter, then sobered. "I haven't stopped thinking about it. About him."

Ashley tilted her head. "And you've never… kissed anyone? Not even a peck?"

Maddie shook her head.

Ashley softened. "Oh, darling."

"I don't want it to be just anyone," Maddie said quietly. "But with Sebastian… last night I hoped he would. And now I can't stop wondering what it would be like."

Ashley leaned forward, her voice warm and a touch wistful. "It's like… your whole world tilts a little. Like something new unfurls inside you. And if it's the right person," she smiled, "you feel it everywhere."

Maddie pressed a hand to her chest. "Even there?"

Ashley laughed. "Especially there."

The maid returned with a polished comb, and Ashley waved her off with a wink. "Give us a moment, Sarah."

When they were alone again, Ashley looked at her more seriously.

"If Sebastian is the one," she said gently, "you won't have to wonder much longer."

Maddie looked down, her thumb brushing the edge of her bodice. "I hope… next time he doesn't stop."

Ashley reached for her hand. "He won't."

And suddenly, the moment was too lovely, too full of possibilities, to bear.

Maddie looked out the window toward the snowy gardens, heart fluttering in her chest.

"Do you think he's thinking about me?"

Ashley smiled. "Oh, he's absolutely ruined."

Maddie twisted the ring on her finger until it nearly slipped off. Then, in one breathless rush, she asked, "Ashley… if one were to want a man to kiss her… how would one… give him permission?"

Ashley blinked. Then burst out laughing.

"Oh, Maddie," she said through a smile. "You're absolutely delicious."

Maddie flushed. "I'm being serious!"

"I know," Ashley said, her eyes softening with fondness. "That's what makes it so wonderful."

"I just… what if he's waiting for a signal? A sign?" Maddie

gestured helplessly. "What if he wants to but is too gentlemanly to presume and I've ruined it all by... *not* signaling?"

Ashley grinned. "All right. Let's say it did come to that. What would you do?"

Maddie's eyes widened. "That's what I'm asking you!"

Ashley leaned back, arms crossed. "Well, for one, you could look at his mouth."

"I do that already!"

"And?"

"He looks back at mine!"

"Perfect." Ashley clapped her hands once, delighted. "Then you're halfway there."

Maddie looked half-horrified, half-hopeful. "But what if he doesn't know that means yes?"

Ashley smirked. "Darling, if he's a grown man with eyes and blood in his veins, he knows."

Maddie let out a strangled sound and flopped dramatically onto the edge of the chaise. "This is mortifying."

Ashley just laughed again, leaning over her like a cat about to pounce.

"And if you want it to come to that," she said slowly, "you simply step closer."

Maddie peeked up at her. "Closer?"

"Closer. Into his space. Linger. Look at him like he's the only man in England. Like he's already kissed you, and you'd like him to do it again."

Maddie bit her lip. She might already be doing that. "What if I get it wrong?"

"You won't," Ashley said gently. "Because if you're thinking about him this much, I promise, he's thinking about you more."

Maddie sat upright, brows drawn in determined concentration. "All right. So I step closer. I linger. I look at his mouth. And I... tilt my face?"

Ashley's eyes sparkled. "You're really planning this."

"I'm trying not to blunder through it!" Maddie said, exasperated. "What if I tilt the wrong way? What if he leans in and I trip on something, and we bang noses and he reconsiders everything and—"

Ashley flung an arm around her and laughed into her shoulder. "Stop, stop. You'll be perfect. You're already perfect."

Maddie exhaled into a smile. "I just want it to be… special."

Maddie smoothed her hand across her skirts, suddenly too aware of every crease, every stray thread. Special. She'd said it like it was a simple thing. But it wasn't simple at all.

What she wanted, what she ached for, wasn't just a kiss. It was that look he'd given her in the snow. The almost-touch. The not-quite kiss that had felt more real than anything else in her life. She wanted a moment that meant something. That marked her. That she could hold onto in all the quiet years to come, when she doubted herself, or the world, or the way her heart still dared to hope.

She wanted to know what it felt like to be wanted. Not politely. Not passingly. But deeply. Intentionally.

And she wanted it from him.

He made her feel different. Like she wasn't just a quiet girl with neat hair and clean hands. With him, she felt wild. And visible. And very much alive.

She wasn't sure she'd ever felt like that before.

And if he kissed her—if he *chose* her—it would mean she hadn't imagined it. That she was more than just safe and sweet. That she could be the kind of woman a man like Sebastian would wait for.

That, to her, would be special.

Ashley looked at her for a long, quiet beat. "It already is."

"I NEED YOUR advice," Sebastian announced to his friend as he entered the study.

His friend looked up from his newspaper, bemused. "Good happenstance to you too. What's the matter?" He folded the pages and set them aside.

Sebastian slumped into the armchair opposite him. "Romantic agony," he said grimly. "Which you are experienced at, no?"

Thomas grinned, the kind of knowing smile reserved for a man who had weathered a few stealthy storms before marriage. "Well, of course. A wife does that to a man."

Sebastian stared at the flickering fire. "Miss Madeleine…" was not exactly his wife.

Thomas chuckled softly. "Ah. Miss Madeleine. I thought as much. You've been struck hard, haven't you?"

Sebastian's jaw tightened. "More than I expected. She's been tending me, fussing over… my ailments…."

Thomas leaned forward. "The lady, tending to you, all alone in your room?"

"How did you—"

"I know everything.

Confound it.

Sebastian sighed. "Yes. That moment… It changed everything. Well, perhaps it's more apt to say it shifted everything. All moments shift everything with her. She looks at me in a way that I… I don't know… mattered to her. And I wanted to kiss her. I nearly did. Still do."

Thomas smiled knowingly. "So, why haven't you?"

Well, that particular moment… "Paisley interrupted." Sebastian sighed. "Which was perhaps a mercy. But now I'm tangled in thoughts. How do I make her understand what I feel?"

Thomas raised an eyebrow. "Is it possible she already knows?"

Sebastian swallowed hard. "Perhaps. But I fear I might ruin it by moving too fast or saying the wrong thing." He wasn't exactly known for his charm with women. He wasn't known to charm at all. In fact, his interactions with them had been limited in the sense of flirtation. He'd always had other things on his mind.

Thomas stood, poured two glasses of brandy, and handed one to Sebastian. "Then move with care. But don't hesitate. If she's the one, she'll welcome your touch, your words. And if you're waiting for a sign, well—she gave you one."

Sebastian let the warmth of the drink soothe him. "Saints help me. I think I'm falling for her."

Thomas laughed softly. "Too late, my friend. Too late."

Sebastian smiled. True. "Then I suppose I must be brave enough to meet her halfway."

"Yes, well, she did a good job keeping you alive with poultices and whatnot."

Sebastian gave a half-smile. "She was. Is. And yet... last night..."

Thomas leaned forward, his interest piqued. "Go on."

"We were in the kitchens. Late. She couldn't sleep. Neither could I. There was egg-flip involved. And firelight."

Thomas raised a brow. "I can already see where this is going."

Did he? Still, he needed to get it off his chest. "She had a bit of foam on her lip. I wiped it away. With my thumb."

Thomas grinned. "Scandalous."

"It was meant to be innocent. It wasn't."

"And what happened then?"

"She looked at me like… like I was the only man in the world. And I couldn't breathe."

"Let me guess. You nearly kissed her again."

Thomas was quiet for a moment, then said, "But you didn't."

"Yes, and I don't know what that would have meant."

"It would have meant that you wanted to kiss her. Which, judging by the tortured look on your face, is no secret."

Sebastian groaned. "That's the problem. I do want to kiss her. But not just that. I want her. All of her. Her mind, her laughter, her maddening insistence on propriety while flouting it completely. And the way she looks at me. Like I'm worth something."

Thomas's gaze softened. "You are. Worth something. You're worth a great deal, my friend."

"I don't know how to do this." Sebastian stood and paced. "She deserves someone who knows how to court her. How to make her feel cherished."

He dragged a hand through his hair. He'd never been shown how to love someone properly. His mother had wielded affection like a tool, something to be granted when he behaved, withdrawn when he failed. Love, to her, had been about appearance. Poise. Status.

He couldn't remember the last time anyone had loved him without condition. Certainly not with softness. Certainly not with hope.

And yet, Maddie…

She'd looked at him like he could be better. Like he already was. And that terrified him. Because what if he failed her? What if she leaned in, gave him her heart, and he ruined it—because he didn't know how to hold something so precious without breaking it?

He wasn't practiced in courtship. He wasn't clever with compliments or dashing with flowers. But he felt everything. Deeply. Perhaps too much. And he wanted her. All of her. Not just for a season. Not just for the thrill of a kiss. Maybe that was enough. Maybe wanting her with that much meant he was already half the man she deserved.

"And you don't think you can?"

"I'm not sure she knows I want to."

"Women are not puzzles to be solved, Sebastian. They are novels. You read them, slowly. Carefully."

Sebastian stared into his glass. "She hasn't been kissed."

Thomas arched a brow. "And you have."

Sebastian gave a huff of laughter. "Point taken. But this feels like more than just a kiss. Like something sacred. Like I said, I don't want to ruin it."

Thomas clapped a hand on his shoulder. "Then don't. Plus, it seems that she wants you too, no?"

Sebastian thought of her eyes, wide and shining. The way her breath had caught when he touched her lip. How she'd leaned in, just slightly, before the interruption.

"I believe so, yes."

"Then that's your answer. The next time you're alone with her, don't waste it. You're not a fool. And she's not indifferent."

Sebastian took a long sip, letting the warmth of the drink settle something restless inside him.

Right. He shouldn't waste any opportunity.

He glanced out the window in thought. "I keep thinking about how she held that cup. How her fingers trembled when she lifted it again. She didn't say much after. But she didn't need to. It was all in her eyes."

Thomas leaned back against the desk. "Then what are you going to do about it?"

Sebastian turned, resolute. "I'm going to give her a reason to keep looking at me like that. I'm going to show her I see her too." If she hadn't read him like a book already. But then, even if she had, he'd make sure she kept reading. That she never stopped.

"Good man."

"Thomas. Thank you."

His friend raised his glass in salute. "Any time. Now go make her fall in love with you."

He chuckled.

Yes, and if he were lucky, she was halfway there. All he had to do now was prove he was worth the rest. Prove that she was the woman for him. And prove that if she chose him as her life partner, he would spend all his days loving her more than anyone else.

Chapter Fifteen

M ADDIE HADN'T MEANT to vanish the next day for luncheon. But after a morning surrounded by stolen glances and shared laughter, and none of it hers, she'd quietly excused herself and slipped away from all the loving couples. It was all rather silly, really. All her friends in love, so she ought to feel thrilled for them. Instead, she felt… displaced. Like a supporting character in someone else's grand romance.

And then there was Sebastian. Temptation on legs. Tall legs. Temptation that she didn't know how to approach. Which was why she had decided to take her luncheon in the conservatory, nestled on a small table beneath an overgrown tangle of ferns and flowering vines—in the hopes of clearing her head a bit. Think. Process.

However, she never imagined she'd be followed. By the very man that tempted her beyond all reason.

She stared at him.

He stared back with a grin.

She poked a fork at her cold cucumber sandwich and gave a long-suffering sigh.

Get a grip, Madeleine. How could I fall in love with a man with sneezed on me?

Well…

He did also save you from allergies.

And he has an impossibly good bone structure.

She glanced at the fern brushing against her elbow. "Is it right to fall in love so quickly, though? Is it love if it's quick?"

The fern offered no comment, though one leaf did sway suggestively. So yes? No?

Urgh!

She picked at her sandwich and looked over at the little fountain in the corner. Its steady trickle was far calmer than the mess in her head.

She didn't resent her friends. Of course not. She was thrilled for them. Deliriously, outrageously thrilled. Especially for Ashley and Thomas, who now couldn't seem to be in the same room without blushing or smiling like fools. It was… beautiful.

And nauseating.

But mostly beautiful.

Still. Everyone seemed to have paired off in tidy little duets. Everyone except her. Even Sebastian—who had no business being as charming or as witty or as entirely distracting as he was—had become something of a problem. But only because… She wanted to seduce him but couldn't. She couldn't just seduce a man. She had to think of the future or her mother…

Not that he'd done anything inappropriate.

Not yet.

Oh no. Worse.

He'd *smiled* at her.

He'd *listened* to her.

He'd *held her gaze* just a beat longer than necessary, and now she was ruined.

Entirely. Thoroughly. Hopelessly ruined. And not in the way of ruined, ruined. Just her heart.

What did she desire? Other than him shirtless in a pond?

Oh, heavens. Just the thought of such a sight… She fanned herself with her napkin. Even her thoughts had become unlady-like.

She used to be such a reasonable person. Measured. Steady. The sort of girl who color-coded her potions. Now she was debating her feelings with a fern and contemplating her moral downfall over a cucumber sandwich.

It was entirely Sebastian's fault.

Everything about him seemed designed to unravel her. His lazy smiles, the sharp cut of his jaw, the way his voice dipped low when he was amused, like he was sharing some private joke with her and only her.

Stop. Stop it.

Maddie pressed her palms to her cheeks, which were now burning.

What she desired most was clarity. That was sensible, wasn't it?

To understand her own mind.

To know whether this flutter in her belly meant something real—or was simply the result of one too many sleepless nights spent imagining how it might feel to be kissed by a man who looked at her like she wasn't a background character in his life, but the whole blooming story.

Not just in the hallway yesterday, or when he'd reached out and wiped the foam from her mouth, though her heart had nearly launched itself into the nearest flowerpot then, but this morning, at breakfast, when someone mentioned music and she'd laughed at something ridiculous. He hadn't even smiled back. He'd just watched her, like the laugh was a song only he could hear.

She hadn't eaten much after that.

Desire, it turned out, wasn't all smolder and lust and swooning against marble balustrades. It was sticky and inconvenient and lodged right behind her ribs like a pinch that refused to leave.

Worse, it made her uncertain. It made her reckless.

What if he kissed her? What if she let him?

What if she wanted him to?

Maddie stared at the fern again.

"I'm not being dramatic," she told it, mostly because no one else was around to disagree. "I'm simply trying to understand myself."

The fern rustled in a breeze that did not exist, which felt vaguely judgmental.

Maddie dropped her fork with a sigh and pressed her forehead to the table. "I'm going mad. Full, bonnet-on-backwards mad."

She stayed like that for a moment, breathing in the scent of moss and old wood polish, before lifting her head again.

A new plan. That's what she needed.

She would march right up to Sebastian and ask him something perfectly reasonable. Something like—

What does desire mean to you?

No. Too forward.

Do you believe in love at first sneeze?

Absolutely not. Not even she did.

"Ugh," she groaned, letting her forehead thunk back down.

Footsteps approached, and Maddie turned her head to the side, heart leaping as two legs entered her view.

Her gaze trailed up those legs.

And there he was.

Sebastian.

Grinning like a wolf who'd just located a stray lamb.

Her pulse decided to throw a party of its own. With violins. And wine. And some form of undignified dancing. Could one heart flutter so much?

"How did you find me?"

"I saw you weren't at luncheon."

"So you hunted me down," she accused, before she could stop herself.

Sebastian had the good grace to look mildly abashed. "Well. Yes. But in the least creepy way possible."

"There's a *scale?*"

"I believe so. Somewhere between sweeping all the hall and chambers and making a few enquiries."

He was still grinning, though it had softened into something more amused than roguish. His shirt collar was slightly crooked. His coat hung open. His hair, unruly at the best of times, looked like it had been at war with a stiff breeze and lost.

He looked… unfairly edible.

"Why did you come looking for me?" Maddie asked, smoothing her skirts for no reason whatsoever. "I mean—did someone send you?"

"Do I look like an errand boy?"

"Yes," she said instantly. "A tall, dangerous one with impeccable boots."

He gestured to a chair next to hers. "May I?"

"No. This is a private luncheon. I'm in the middle of consulting with the flora about my dramatic spinsterhood."

He glanced at the fern. "Does it have strong opinions?"

"It thinks I should ravish you and get it over with."

He paused.

She flushed.

"I was joking."

"Were you?"

"Yes."

"How disappointing."

"Sebastian."

He grinned and pulled out the chair anyway, settling in. "I thought you might appreciate the company."

"I was appreciating solitude."

He poured himself a cup of her tea.

"Highly sacred, very necessary solitude."

He added sugar.

"Which is now entirely ruined by your big, beautiful head."

Sebastian took a sip and sighed, utterly at peace. "Yes, but you're smiling again."

"I always smile."

"You didn't smile when I entered. You looked rather… head in the table."

Her face heated.

He reached across the table and nudged her untouched sandwich. "This yours?"

"I don't see anyone else here."

"May I?"

He wanted to eat her half-eaten sandwich? "I—"

He took a bite.

Maddie's breath hitched. How could such a thing be so sensual? "You are the worst sort of guest."

His grin widened. "I am the best."

They sat in silence for a moment—her pulse rioting, his foot brushing hers beneath the table. The light from the windows caught the edge of his cheekbone. She looked away too quickly.

Sebastian leaned in, voice gentling. "What's bothering you? Perhaps I can help?"

Help? Saints! He was the last man that could help her and the only man. "It's… a feminine thing."

He cocked his head. "I can still help."

She swallowed hard. His closeness. The smell. His eyes. It was all too much.

"It's nothing, truly. I was just… processing. That's what the plants are for, right?"

"They do seem terribly wise."

She eyed the fern. "More than some men."

Sebastian leaned back, smile still intact. "Then perhaps I ought to earn my keep and offer some wisdom of my own."

"Oh, really?"

"Yes. For instance…" His eyes seemed to blaze. "You are perfect as you are, so never try to strive to be perfect or for a moment to be perfect, a life, a future. Perfect is right now."

And just like that, her heart was no longer hosting a party. It was hosting a revolution.

A very inconvenient one.

With torches and declarations and possibly even fireworks.

All because of him.

Temptation on legs.

Tall legs.

And the one man who just might see the heroine in her before she saw it in herself.

SEBASTIAN TRIED NOT to stare at her mouth. He failed. It was the way she'd said it, so offhand, like it meant nothing. And yet somehow, it struck him like a lightning bolt to the chest. A perfectly ordinary, teasing response, delivered in that soft voice of hers, threaded with wit and something he hadn't quite learned how to name.

She was brilliant.

And entirely unguarded in this moment. Maddie, sitting there with crumbs on her skirt and a fern leaf tangled in her hair, all around her, really, was more captivating than any finely powdered debutante in a Mayfair ballroom. She wasn't performing, wasn't posturing. She was simply *being*.

He wanted to reach out and tuck that stray curl behind her ear. Not because it was in the way, but because it wasn't. Because it was wildly, wonderfully out of place—just like her.

He shifted in his seat, the warmth of the conservatory pressing around him. Her scent drifted over, sweet and something earthy. He doubted she even knew how distracting she was. Which only made it worse.

Or better.

Depending on how much longer he could resist touching her.

"I meant what I said," he murmured. He smiled. "About you not needing to change. Not for anyone. Not even for some idiot who can't stop staring at you."

Her eyes widened.

Did he just say that aloud?

Yes, he had.

Too late to take it back now.

"You said something rather intelligent the other day," Maddie said.

"I'm known to have the occasional moment of insight," Sebastian chuckled. "What was it that struck you as particularly noteworthy?"

"That I need to find out what I desire."

Sebastian's smile melted away. He swallowed hard, his Adam's apple bobbing under the tight cravat.

"And I have a question about that," she continued, batting her eyes like a young fawn. Almost teasing. No, most definitely teasing. He tried not to stare at her green irises and her bright pink cheeks, but she was absolutely too pretty not to be admired like a masterpiece portrait at the British Museum.

"Ask then."

"How does a kiss relate to what I desire?" Her eyes sparkled. "I mean, is there a connection?"

Saints, what this question did to him! The images it conjured. His whole body hardened and his mind trailed to forbidden pleasures. On second thought, why were they forbidden? He'd already peeled her out of her dress in his fantasies a thousand times to reveal all of her. *Everything.*

He played along. "A kiss can ignite a spark. It's such an intimate contact. When you kiss the right person, the effect is like feathers tickling you all over, your heart quickens, and your body wants more."

She bit her bottom lip. Such a sweet lip, he longed to taste it. But he mustn't overstep. Be too hasty. Rush. Plus, she was only just beginning to explore what she wanted. Sebastian shook his head as if to stop his thoughts from going in the only direction where they'd been recently.

She cocked her head. "And if you kiss the wrong person?"

"That's like kissing a dead trout."

"Disgusting! And how would… you know?"

"Many fish, never the feathers."

"Then what makes you so sure that the fireworks version is

possible?"

"I can feel it. I've seen it."

"How? Where?"

He thought about this for a moment. Then he dared. Sebastian gently took her hand, which had been resting on the side of the table. She hung on to his every word. "You've seen Ashley and Tom, right? Have you not spoken to Ashley?"

She blushed furiously and that was all the answer he needed.

Slowly but deliberately, he unfolded her finger that curled around his and placed her palm on his chest. "I know in my heart. All that's left now is to find it to confirm the right person."

Maddie's eyes changed to a darker hue, her pupils large. Her breath quickened and she looked more alert than he'd ever seen her. That intelligent sparkle in her gaze was a fire now that nearly intimidated Sebastian, had he not wanted to meet it with equal ardor.

"I want to know," she whispered.

Sebastian leaned forward but didn't close the distance. He had to be sure that she was asking him for what he hoped. A mistake would cause irreparable harm to the trust he'd built with her. He cleared his throat, trying to cool his blood in vain.

"If I show you, Maddie, and if there is more than the passion of a dead fish, it cannot be undone. It would mean something."

She gave a faint nod.

"Are you sure?"

Another nod. She gulped and pinched her lips together.

Sebastian caught her hand and placed it on his chest, testing her response.

He dipped his head and she blinked so deuced innocently.

She's so precious.

After this, she'd lose a bit of her innocence and Sebastian felt as if he were cradling an eggshell porcelain cup. A kiss would mean holding her up to the light to see the true design, what her heart desired. If there were fireworks, Sebastian knew deep down, he would never be whole again if he let her go.

She licked her lips as she'd done in the garden before. Bashfully blinking at him, she leaned forward. Sebastian lingered as close to her as he could without touching her. She smelled seductively like the dew on a waterlily, pure and fruity, enticing his senses with luminous allure. He pinched his eyes shut to steady himself, trying to slow his pounding heart but he had no time. Maddie pressed her mouth against his, puckering her lips. Sebastian froze. And then he could only gasp, slightly parting his lips. Maddie did the unthinkable and pressed further. He hadn't planned on moving so quickly but she didn't give him a choice. Ever so tenderly, he darted his tongue toward her mouth... she reciprocated.

Sebastian let go of her hand and wrapped his around her back, trailing slowly up and down. She leaned into him and moaned delicately.

And then she broke away and ran.

MADDIE GASPED FROM lack of breath as she came to a stop. What on earth happened? Why had she run?

Why? Why? Why?

She had wanted this. Wanted to kiss him. Wanted so much more. And then, she'd dashed off.

A perfect moment.

And she'd fled from it.

Maddie stood frozen, caught between the lies she told herself and the truth standing so very near. None of this was proper. And yet, propriety had always recently become to her a fickle sort of guide, draped in rules that offered answers without clarity. How, after all, was a lady to decide if she didn't understand? The usual criteria, parroted endlessly by her mother and aunt, had never soothed the restless questions beneath her surface.

They were the cause of her headaches, the very reason she

sought ointments and tonics for relief. But there was no salve for not knowing. Ignorance, it seemed, required something far more daunting to cure—knowledge.

And if there was anything to be learned from science, then knowledge came from experiments. She needed to experiment.

Kissing.

With a willing subject. A handsome one. With dark brown hair that she longed to run her fingers through. There was surely something in the handbook about not doing this. Back to the experiment... So, to gain knowledge, one must study, mustn't one? That was a virtue. Surely no one would fault her for thorough research.

Maddie winced. It was false logic but it was, oddly enough, what she wanted.

Perhaps desired?

Sebastian, she thought with a whispered thrill of defiance, was research. His confidence, his maddening ability to unsettle her, were the questions she needed answering.

She seized the thought, clutching it like a lifeline, and with it, the moment's stolen power. Slowly, cautiously, she leaned in.

Sebastian closed the space between them like he had all the time in the world, his gaze steady, unrelenting, but softened by something she couldn't name. Her breath faltered as his hand rose—not roughly, not quickly, but with a deliberate tenderness that left her rooted to the spot. His touch on her cheek was impossibly warm, his thumb brushing along her skin as if memorizing her.

"You're always running from me," he whispered, the depth of his voice sending an unruly shiver down her spine. "But not this time, Maddie."

She wanted to laugh, to scoff, to break the delicate tension curling around them like smoke. She knew how to deflect, to pull away when things got too real. But there was no deflecting from him, not now.

Why had she run again?

Why wasn't she fleeing right now?

Would she dash off the moment their lips touched again?

Sebastian dipped his head, and for just the briefest of moments, his lips hovered above hers, his breath a soft warmth against her skin. Maddie held perfectly still, the world narrowing to just this moment, just this man, just the light press of his hand against her back as he closed the final, impossibly small distance between them.

Then he kissed her, and everything she thought she knew evaporated.

She was beginning to understand… It wasn't merely an exchange, not merely the meeting of lips. The softness of his mouth covered hers with such aching care that her chest tightened, crushed beneath an entirely foreign wave of feeling. It started there, where their mouths touched, and shivered through her, weaving into places she didn't even know could respond as they did.

Sebastian didn't rush, didn't demand.

The kiss deepened, his lips coaxing hers gently, matching the rhythm of her hesitant responses and silently asking for more. When his other hand slipped to the nape of her neck, his fingers threading into her hair, something inside her gave way. She melted, all her arguments dissolving in the warmth of his touch, the surety of his mouth on hers. Her hands betrayed her uncertainty. They hovered for a breathless moment, trembling at her sides, before giving in, coming to rest lightly against his chest. His heart beat steadily beneath her palms, anchoring her even as her knees softened, threatening to leave her unmoored if he stopped.

This wasn't the kiss of a man trying to steal her senses or win a fleeting conquest. No, this was something so heartbreakingly deliberate, so full of restrained yearning, that her heart ached beneath its weight. It wasn't just their mouths finding each other—it was Sebastian's unspoken charm showing her what a real connection could feel like.

His lips parted slightly, and she followed, startled by the depth of her own response. He tasted like wine and something darker, something wholly his. Maddie leaned closer, her body pulled by an invisible thread as though she'd been made for this very moment, and only now realized it.

Her breath hitched, her heart stuttering as a sensation unfurled low in her belly, warm and electric. She didn't just feel it; she lived it. The world dissolved utterly, leaving only his touch, his steadiness, his impossible tenderness.

And then, finally breaking through the blissful haze enveloping her, came the understanding. This wasn't just a kiss. It was so much more. Sebastian was showing her something she had avoided her entire life. Not just pleasure but vulnerability, not just passion but intimacy.

Her fingers curled into his coat, a desperate motion to keep hold of him as if he might otherwise slip away. She matched him, first timidly, then with a confidence that bloomed as he met her halfway.

When he finally drew back, his forehead resting lightly against hers, Maddie found herself trembling. She didn't open her eyes right away, afraid the spell might break.

"You feel that?" he murmured, his voice rough, intimate, barely above a whisper.

She nodded, unable to trust her words, her lips still tingling from his kiss, her heart still soaring into uncharted skies.

"Feathers?"

"So much more," he whispered hoarsely.

His hand slid from her hair to cradle her cheek, tipping her face up so her wide, uncertain eyes met his. The way he looked at her was molten, unreadable, but full of something that left her chest tight and her throat dry.

Maddie wanted to speak, to find some breezy, clever remark that might make her feel like herself again, but none came. Because she wasn't that Maddie anymore. Somewhere between the first brush of his lips and the quiet intimacy that lingered now, something had shifted. It wasn't just a kiss. It wasn't just Sebastian. It was a truth she couldn't turn away from. And for the first time in as long as she could remember, she didn't wish to.

"You can tell?" Maddie asked, her voice barely above a whisper. Already, she felt the pull of him again, an ache low in her belly for the exact moment she had just lost. A foolish kind of longing, really, considering he was still so very near. What had become of her?

Sebastian's gaze flicked to her lips before finding her eyes again, steady and deliberate. "This is it." His thumb trailed along her cheek, his touch a contradiction of softness and certainty, before tilting her chin up. The gesture wasn't forceful but rather guiding, like she belonged in the exact place he wished her to be. "This only happens with the right person, Maddie. And I knew it would be you."

Her breath hitched, her lashes lowering for a moment to break the spell of his unrelenting stare. "But you… You said you'd never felt it," she managed, her voice faltering even as sparks of curiosity flickered to life. "And yet you claim you knew?"

He nodded, the edge of his mouth curving slightly—not in his usual faintly arrogant smirk, but in something softer, more earnest. Gone was the quirk of his brow or the playful challenge that typically danced in his gaze. His eyes now burned, dark and unshakably sincere.

"I knew," he said simply. "I know it's only you." The words weren't dressed up, weren't elaborated on, but they carried a quiet conviction that stole the air from her lungs.

Maddie blinked, her cheeks warming under his touch. That conviction, that certainty, it was entirely too much. Could anyone truly know such a thing? Yet the sincerity in his voice, the steady way he waited, as though her trust was not demanded but freely given, did something to her resolve.

And there it was. A terrifying, wondrous thing she hadn't allowed herself to consider until now. She'd trust him. Suddenly, entirely, she would trust him with what she couldn't yet name.

But the thought came, overwhelming and immovable.

My heart, the words whispered through her mind unbidden. They lingered there, echoing softly as he leaned so that his forehead brushed lightly against hers.

"Tell me you feel it too," he murmured, his voice rough and intimate, the kind meant for only one person to hear.

Her answer caught in her throat, her eyes searching his desperately, trying to make sense of what was happening inside her. Was it fireworks? Was it everything he claimed it could be? She didn't know what to say. But her chest tightened, her lips parted, and before she could find the words, she nodded. Just once. Enough.

Chapter Sixteen

H E'D FOLLOWED HER up the grand staircase, keeping his stride measured despite the way his body still thrummed with the lingering imprint of her warmth. He'd stopped at the landing to see her to her chambers, the door to the left that he now knew she slept behind. There had been so many things he'd wanted to say, a thousand foolish impulses to demand more of her time, more of herself.

But she was a lady.

A perfect, maddening lady who belonged on a pedestal he hadn't the right to touch, even if he wished to drag her down to meet him in the chaos roiling beneath his steady composure. He would not follow her into her chambers. He would not demand the taste of her lips again tonight.

No.

His jaw tightened as he turned away, his own door shutting firmly behind him as though that could be the end of it. Except it wasn't. It couldn't be.

Sebastian leaned against the door frame of his chamber, his hand resting on the sturdy wood as though it might somehow keep him upright. He dragged a breath into his chest, shallow and burning, but it did little to steady him. The faintest scent lingered in the air, something soft, floral, and wholly hers, and it undid him all over again.

The memory of Maddie's lips on his own was as fresh as though it had happened mere moments before. Her mouth had been impossibly soft, pliant under his, and yet teasingly bold in the way she'd responded. He closed his eyes, shoving a hand through his dark hair as if to shake the thought free, but it was of no use. He could still feel her. Her hesitant touch, the almost clumsy, daring way she'd boldened, trailing her tongue against his in a way that had nearly broken him apart.

Sebastian pressed his hand to his chest, his palm flat against the hammering beat of his heart. What had he done? Or rather, what had she done to him? He'd kissed many women before, plenty of them beautiful and perfectly willing as society demanded. But not one—not a single kiss in his twenty-five years of living—had touched him like this.

Because it wasn't just a kiss.

It was Maddie.

Miss Madeleine Hunt, his best friend's fiancée's closest friend, the woman who was meant to vex him with her endless complaints and penchant for tired remedies. The lady he should regard with the faint affection reserved for long-standing acquaintances and nothing more.

And yet...

She had undone him. Fully, entirely. Maddie's sweetness, her tenacity, the fragile vulnerability she tried so valiantly to guard had cracked his chest wide open. He'd been foolish to think he could remain indifferent, that she would remain nothing more than the vague requirement of society to "find a suitable match." Nothing about her was vague.

His brows pulled together as he stared at the darkened corridor. He should go to bed and leave the night and its confounding emotions safely in the hours past. Yet he couldn't move, couldn't stop turning over the scene in his mind. The truth of it settled heavily in his chest, a weight and a wonder all at once.

He was falling in love with her.

Too late.

He already had.

I love her.

Sebastian didn't bother denying it. He'd always been quick on his feet, sharp when it came to matters of logic and reason, and this was no different. He was a man who knew his own mind, and everything in it was pointed squarely at her. Maddie. Of all the women he might have imagined entwined in his life and future, she was an unexpected twist of fate. A lady who didn't fit the image his mother so persistently conjured but who now stood, unapologetically, at the heart of his desire.

I love Maddie.

The moment he was inside his chambers, he stripped off his jacket and cravat, the crisp fabric creasing as he tossed them aside. His boots followed, dumped carelessly near the foot of the bed, something completely out of character for his practiced routine. For a man who prided himself on control, he was utterly stripped of it.

Sebastian sat heavily on the edge of the bed, staring into the flickering firelight as though it could provide the answers he lacked. His shirt came next, the cool night air brushing over his skin, though it did nothing to temper the heat coursing through him. He lay back across the covers, one arm flung over his eyes, willing his body to relax.

But it refused, burning with an ache he hadn't expected.

He could still feel the tremble in her fingers as they slid along his jaw, still taste the uncertainty and hope mingled on her lips. That kiss hadn't been practiced. It hadn't been polished. It had been honest. Terrifyingly honest.

And now, with nothing but silence and firelight to distract him, a darker truth gnawed at the edge of his mind: What if he'd ruined it?

What if his hunger had overwhelmed the moment? What if she now sat in her room, unraveling it all, wondering if she'd misread him? If she'd been too bold?

God, the thought hollowed him.

Because he hadn't just wanted her—he'd wanted her to want him too. Not just his mouth, not just the way he made her laugh when he wasn't trying to—but him. The man who didn't know how to court. The man who never expected to feel this much. The man who wanted her enough to rewrite his future around her.

He pressed the heel of his hand against his chest, as if he might keep his heart from leaping straight out of his ribs.

He hadn't meant for it to go this far. But now that it had, there was no going back. No forgetting her taste. No pretending he could want anyone else.

He didn't need the fire crackling in the hearth, nor the blanket folded neatly at the foot of the bed. He felt as though he'd swallowed a sun, the warmth of her touch lighting him up from the inside out.

His breath came out in a low, frustrated huff. It was madness, and yet it felt like the only truth he'd known in years.

He was hot.

He was hard.

He was in love.

The last admission struck him harder than the rest, a vulnerable whisper coursing through him, stealing the breath from his lungs. And the source of it all was not some idealized duchess or carefully selected debutante.

No, it was Maddie. Maddie, who wore her heart on her sleeve even as her guard shot up against the world. Maddie, whose clever tongue had more than met his in words and in action. Maddie, who made him ache in more ways than he cared to name.

He wanted her.

Only her. Forever.

MADDIE SHUT THE door behind her, the soft click of the latch unnaturally loud in her quiet chambers. For a long, trembling moment, she just stood there, her hands pressed flat against the polished wood, as though pinning herself in place might somehow stop the world from spinning. But it did spin. Oh, it spun and swayed, and before she knew it, her knees had given out beneath her, her back sliding down the door until she sat in an ungraceful heap on the carpeted floor.

Her fingertips brushed over her lips, still tingling with the memory of his kiss, and her chest gave a faint, startled heave. Of all the things she had expected of this evening, of him, of herself, this… this was not among them.

"Oh, what a kiss," she whispered, the words tumbling out before she could stop them. Her laughter poured out next, bright and startled, bouncing off the walls of the small room. It was ridiculous, truly. If she had known kisses were such things as this, she might have set to practicing years ago.

Her gaze caught on the handbook resting on the nightstand, the leather-bound tome her aunt had thrust upon her with no small amount of solemnity. *A Young Lady's Guide to Matrimonial Understanding and Proper Behavior.* She snorted, that wild laugh threatening to erupt again. Oh, if only the author of that precious manual had felt this. Maddie doubted it very much.

"Perhaps it was written by a man," she mused aloud, shaking her head, her voice trembling with suppressed giggles. Surely no woman, having known what Sebastian had just shown her, could write such drivel with a straight face.

Her eyes drifted closed, her head tilting back against the door as her finger, slow and reverent, traced her lower lip. The sensation was still there, scorched into her skin. Could anything put words to what she had felt? To his warmth, the way he tilted her chin as though she belonged nowhere else, the unmistakable gasp that had escaped her, unbidden, when his tongue brushed hers. Surely, there were no words, no sentences, elegant enough to contain that.

And good.

Good that there were none.

Some things weren't meant for books. This was a moment carved out of time, stolen and too special to reduce to mere instruction or description.

I want to know more.

She pushed herself up gingerly, her legs still wobbling from the effort, and crossed the room to the washstand. The water in the basin was cool against her flushed skin, dampening her neck and the edges of her sleeves as she splashed it over her heated cheeks. It did little to chase away the rising warmth that lingered, curling low in her belly and quickening her pulse every time her thoughts wandered back to him.

Sebastian.

Her hands froze, gripping the edge of the basin, as if the name spoken only in her mind might somehow give her away. Maddie shook her head and moved toward the bed, shedding her gown with slightly fumbling fingers before slipping into her nightdress.

She slid beneath the linens and found no rest, only the kiss lingering like heat along her mouth. His touch haunted every shift of fabric.

You weren't ready for this, she told herself—and knew she wanted more. Sensible had been easy. This, not at all.

She wanted to be seen the way he had seen her. With eyes that didn't just look—but lingered. With hands that didn't just hold—but knew. She wanted to be chosen. Desired. Treasured.

Her fingers curled into the sheet.

Was it too much to wish for?

Because in the heat of that kiss, she had tasted a future that terrified her with how much she wanted it. A world that belonged not to good girls and rule-followers, but to women who stepped forward. Who asked. Who took.

And perhaps—perhaps she wanted to be that sort of woman.

Not just for any man. But for Sebastian.

He had kissed her like she was worth waiting for. Like he

didn't dare ask for more, but would give her everything if she only let him. And though the kiss had ended, the invitation had not.

She could still feel it… the humming beneath her skin. Waiting.

And what would she do with that?

She didn't know yet.

But she would know.

Soon.

She had told herself propriety was her guide, her shield, and perhaps it still was. But right now, with the memory of his kiss etched into her like her favorite song, propriety could wait until morning.

Chapter Seventeen

SEBASTIAN NEEDED AIR.

Not the sort one found, thick, in a London ballroom, nor the stifling scent of hearth fires or mixed perfumes at the castle. No, he needed the kind of air found in taverns: warm, sour with ale, and soaked with male laughter.

"I still don't understand," Thomas muttered, scowling over the frothy head of his tankard. "We have an entire bloody brewery. Why are we in this particular pub drinking this horse piss instead of our stout?"

"Because," Sebastian drawled, slouching comfortably into the battered booth, "I needed a moment outside the castle walls."

Rotheworth let out a low laugh and knocked his tankard against Sebastian's. "So you dragged us to this den of spilled pickles and regret. Women really, truly are something."

"It's charming," Sebastian said, eyeing the cracked plaster walls with a tilt of his head. "And it's exactly what the night calls for."

Thomas raised a brow. "You're rattled."

"Define rattled."

"Do I really need to put words to it? I just have to look at this place and have my answer."

Sebastian sipped his ale and said nothing. He was rattled.

Thoroughly.

Not because of Maddie. Very well, yes, partly because of Maddie. But also because he didn't quite know how to approach the matter. He had never courted a woman, and he was pretty sure he was doing everything wrong. In fact, could he be considered courting her at all?

That terrible, lovely woman who had kissed him like it meant something—and then gone to bed, leaving him a man unmoored. He could still taste her on his lips. Sweet. Curious. Bold. He wanted more.

Wanted everything.

"He's quiet," Rotheworth noted. "He's never quiet. This is unsettling."

"He's in love," Thomas muttered. "Or mad. Possibly both. Know I am."

Rotheworth nodded. "I can drink to that."

Sebastian gave a slow blink. "Can one be mad with love?" He didn't read much poetry, but he thought one could be. He just had to look at the men at this table. That is, after all, why he dragged them along.

"Only if you're an idiot," Thomas said.

He couldn't fight the claim. "Then I am a bloody imbecile."

Rotheworth leaned back and rubbed his jaw. "So what are you planning to do about Miss Madeleine? Her mother is rumored to be quite stubborn."

Yes, and she'd probably want a duke for her daughter, not a marquess. "What about her father?"

Rotheworth shrugged. "Haven't met the man, but what I've heard he seems to be sensible."

Sensible didn't mean much now, did it?

Thomas snorted. "You'll have to win his favor. After all, you can't just keep watching the woman like she's the last éclair on a dessert tray."

"I don't watch her."

"Right. You gaze. Dreamily."

"Rubbish." But he could feel a flush rush across his skin. Did he? Probably.

"Then what's that expression on your face right now?"

Sebastian slumped deeper. "How am I supposed to know? I can't see my face."

Rotheworth chuckled.

Sebastian swirled his tankard. "I feel I'm longing for a future I'm not sure I'm allowed to want."

Thomas grimaced. "God. That's nauseatingly poetic."

"You just feel this way?" Rotheworth asked. "Makes sense."

Sebastian looked over at the man. "It does?"

"Aye," Thomas echoed. "It does?"

Rotheworth shrugged. "I felt the same way about Charlene. Sometimes I still do. It's only natural when you meet a woman whom you believe deserves better than you."

Better than him… Did he believe that?

"If you thought you were no good for your wife, why did you marry her?"

"Too selfish to let her go."

Selfish… Sebastian didn't believe he was a selfish man, but thinking about Maddie… Yes, he could be selfish. He could most certainly be selfish. He wanted her. He didn't want anyone else to have her.

"That, I can understand."

"So, what do you suggest I do?" He hated even bloody asking.

Thomas smirked. "You ask me for romantic advice? Good God, man, are you trying to lose her?"

Rotheworth snorted into his tankard. "He has a point. He was more worried about his horses than his fiancée. If he had been to court his wife without the wager… Let's leave it at that."

Thomas raised his tankard in a mock toast. "It all still worked out in the end."

"From what I hear, barely," Rotheworth muttered.

"Barely is still working out. What about you?"

"I pursued the woman I love with my unrivalled charm."

Sebastian rubbed the back of his neck. "You're both useless."

"You don't need advice," Rotheworth said after a beat. "You need to decide what you want, although it seems you've already done that; now all you need to decide is how to ask her." He paused, his expression softening. "Then stop sulking in a piss-scented tavern. The lady seems taken with you, after all."

Sebastian let his head fall back against the seat, eyes fixed on the warped ceiling beams. Ask for it. The words rang oddly in his chest. He didn't ask for things. He inherited them. Managed them. But Maddie?

She was not something to be inherited. To be managed.

"I don't want to be another disappointment in her life."

Thomas shook his head. "In my experience, give your chosen woman more credit."

Chosen woman…

Sebastian liked that.

"You need to talk to her," Rotheworth said simply. "Not flirt. Not banter. A real conversation. Tell her what you want. Your dream for the future. See if hers aligns."

Sebastian lifted a brow. "What if I don't know what that is yet?" The future stretched long, did it not?

"Then you listen," Rotheworth said. "And figure it out together."

Thomas drained his drink. "There is a problem with that?"

"The problem is," Sebastian said with a sigh, "we're not officially attached. I can't just ask her questions about the future because we kissed, and I suddenly dream of things I never dreamed before."

"Why not?"

Sebastian gave them both a flat look. "Because she deserves… I don't know, but not a steamroller of a proposal from a man halfway to madness."

"You know there is a lodge on our property," Thomas said, leaning back with a smug tilt of his head. "I'm just saying. It's yours to use and use to woo if you want."

Sebastian blinked at him. "You want me to abduct her?"

Thomas rolled his eyes. "I'm suggesting you *invite* her. Like a gentleman."

Sebastian eyed his friend skeptically. "Invite her for *what* exactly?"

Rotheworth choked on a laugh. "He says it like it's a mortal sin."

"It *feels* like one," Sebastian muttered. "An invitation. To a lodge. Where we will be alone."

"Do whatever you want." Thomas blinked. "Or not want."

He scoffed.

But still… the lodge. It *was* secluded. Private. Far enough from the main house to be free of prying eyes and whispered speculations. If he asked Maddie there—invited her properly, respectfully, with whatever decorum was required—it might buy him the space to speak with her plainly. To ask the questions he'd kept swallowing every time she looked at him like she might feel something more.

It was a ridiculous idea.

It was a perfect idea.

"I'd have to arrange a proper escort," he said slowly, his mind already racing ahead. "Make it look respectable. Not some scandalous assignation."

Thomas snorted. "You're asking her to take a walk, not climb into your bed. Though if she decides to—"

Sebastian threw a crust of bread at him.

"Just being supportive," Thomas said cheerfully.

Rotheworth leaned forward, the tavern candlelight casting shadows beneath his eyes. "If you do this, Sebastian, don't make it a half-measure. Don't take her to the lodge just to fumble around the edges of what you want. Be clear. Ask her if she sees a future—with you. Not someday. Now."

Sebastian's throat worked. "What if she says no?" This was his biggest fear.

Thomas didn't flinch. "Then at least you'll know. And you'll have done something most men don't."

Sebastian tilted his head. "What's that?"

"Had the courage to tell a woman what she means to you before it was too late."

There was a long pause.

MADDIE WAS NOT inebriated. Not on beer, at least. She was, perhaps, *pleasantly marinated*—not in beer, but in thoughts of a certain marquess—which was exactly the sort of mood required for the conversation now taking place inside the Linsey family brewery. The rather lovely space—normally bustling with workers—was quiet for the afternoon, giving her the opportunity to catch up with her friends.

And quite timely, Sera arrived on the estate not even a quarter of an hour ago, which made the moment even more perfect. They'd practically dragged her from the courtyard straight to the brewery.

"Where is your prince?" Maddie asked. "I cannot believe he let you travel alone."

Sera snorted. "Did you *not* see my retinue? I am never alone and miss Alex.

"Will your prince not be joining us then?" Ashley asked, brows furrowing.

"Oh, he will. He has some business holding him up and I refused to wait a second longer! So, tell me everything that happened in my absence."

And they did, bursting into laughter at the various degrees of shock on Sera's face. When it came to Maddie's latest little adventure, her nerves all knotted in her stomach.

"So let me get this straight," Charlene said, kicking her boots up onto the bench across from Maddie. "He kissed you—*you* kissed *him*—and now you're hiding in a brewery with us. Wait, is this the reason why you ushered us all here so urgently?"

Maddie groaned. "I think I'm panicking." But not exactly *hiding* as her friend suggested.

Charlene patted her hand sympathetically. "Darling, I once panicked so hard I agreed to marry a duke. It happens."

Ashley snorted. "Are you calling love panic now?"

Sera chuckled. "I somehow completely understand. I'm just cross I couldn't arrive any sooner. Heh."

Charlene laughed. "I once panicked and broke a vase on a man's face."

The other three women blinked.

"He was *fine*," Charlene assured them with a smile that was almost sly. "Just a scratch."

Maddie lifted her head slowly. "Why are all of you so *much*?"

"Because you are surrounded by women of future legends," Ashley said, raising her tankard. "Now drink. Then tell us what happened."

Maddie took a generous sip of the honeyed ale and inhaled sharply. "It was… perfect. Not the kiss, well, *yes*, the kiss, but more the moment before. During. And after. Everything."

"And was the kiss?" Sera asked, intrigued.

Heat flushed her skin. "Well, of course."

Charlene leaned in. "Tongue?"

"Char!" Maddie squeaked.

Ashley smirked. "I take that as a yes."

"Does it even matter?"

"Of course it does," Sera said. "The one is chaste, the other is not."

"A kiss from a man by its very nature isn't chaste."

Sera shrugged. "That might very well be true."

"Well, ours was *nice*," Maddie muttered. "Too nice. Now I don't know what to do."

"You do what any self-respecting woman would do after kissing a man she's clearly halfway in love with," Ashley said. "You panic, drink ale, and demand answers from your friends."

Maddie feared *halfway* in love was an understatement.

"I don't recall you ever doing it!"

"We all manage our panic differently."

Charlene took a sip of ale. "All right, be honest. Do you want to wed him?"

Maddie hesitated.

"Ah-ha!" Ashley crowed. "You do!"

"How did we go from kissing to marriage?"

Sera chuckled. "The heart wants what the heart wants."

Truer words were never spoken. "Is that greedy?"

"Greedy is wanting *three* husbands," Sera said. "You're fine."

"But he hasn't said anything since," Maddie went on. "He's polite and present and entirely himself, but—no declarations."

Charlene drained her tankard. "So he hasn't read you any horrific poetry."

"No, and I don't need such things. I just want… something. Anything. A clue. A glimmer."

Ashley leaned in. "You can always do the reading of poetry."

"No. Absolutely not."

Her friends laughed.

"Honestly," Charlene said. "He's a man, Maddie. They rarely *have* the words. They have gestures."

Ashley nodded sagely. "And beer."

Maddie hesitated again. Then: "I'm not against gestures if it's… his way of saying he couldn't find the words."

"Gestures go both ways," Sera pointed out.

Maddie considered. "Gestures from ladies would be wildly inappropriate."

Charlene grinned. "Which makes it *perfect*."

Maddie leaned back in her seat, heart a little lighter, and said quietly, "I hope it is perfect." She looked to Ashley's belly. "How are you feeling?"

"Oh, I'm barely eating, casting up what I do, and my feet are swollen like sausages. I'm in heaven."

Ashley's dry smile made the rest of the table burst into laughter.

"You truly have a way with words," Charlene said, grinning.

"I *was* a poet in another life," Ashley replied. "A tragic one. Died of scandal, naturally."

Maddie smiled, though her fingers were curled around her tankard like it might steady her very soul. "So what am I meant to do now? Wait for him to decide what he wants?"

Charlene tilted her head. "That depends, I suppose. Do you want to be courted like a lady in a novel? Grand declarations, letters folded into handkerchiefs, wildflowers delivered to your doorstep?"

"Saints, no," Maddie said quickly. "I'd die of embarrassment. Besides, I like things to be… real. Practical. Real."

"Then why are you waiting for him to take the lead?" Sera asked gently.

This again. Well, she didn't know how to take the lead, honestly.

"You kissed him," Sera pointed out. "You made the first move. Besides, the way I see it, you are already in courtship."

They were?

"That was… impulse."

"Darling," Charlene cut in, "if you think the rest of us operate on anything *but* impulse, you haven't been paying attention."

That was… so true.

"She's not wrong," Ashley muttered. "I practically threw myself at Thomas."

"For diabolical reasons," Charlene muttered. "Not impulse."

"The first time was diabolical." Ashley smirked. "Not the second time."

"Yes, well, you are indeed lucky that he caught you," Maddie said with a small smile.

Ashley nodded, then looked at her meaningfully. "And maybe Sebastian's waiting for you to trust him enough to throw yourself again. Just once. Fully."

"Normal gentlemen don't wait for that."

Maddie's brows pulled together. "But what if he's hesitating because he doesn't want the same thing I do?"

"What *do* you want?" Sera asked.

Maddie swallowed. That was the real question, wasn't it? And it had taken Sera to come from Transylvania and her tour of the Continent to ask it.

Come to think of it, Maddie had an answer. "I want someone who sees me. Who doesn't think I'm simply convenient or clever or a good match on paper." Her voice dropped. "I want someone who wants *me*. The messy bits. The stubbornness. The parts that don't fit into debutante expectations." The kind her mother tried so hard to mold her into.

Charlene gave a little shrug. "Then it's Sebastian. You know it is. We all do. I'd wager he sees a lot more than that."

Maddie stared into the golden swirl of her ale. "But I'm afraid of wanting more than I should."

"You mean you're afraid of being disappointed," Ashley said softly.

Maddie met her friend's eyes. "Yes."

"Let me tell you something about men," Charlene said. "Most of them, especially the good ones, don't always have the words. But when they want you, they'll show you. Even if they don't realize they're doing it."

Maddie exhaled. "So… I just need to look for the signs? While being swept off my feet?"

"No," Sera said, laughing. "You need to decide if you're brave enough to *give* a sign. Something small. A gesture, like you said. Something that tells him you're open to more."

Maddie tapped her fingers on the table. "What kind of gesture?"

Ashley's eyes lit with mischief. "Do you still have that book we gave you?"

"Yes."

"Read a passage from it to him." Charlene grinned. "Now *that's* romantic."

Maddie rolled her eyes. "You're asking me to send him running for the mountains."

"Well, he could comment on the advice." Sera raised her tankard. "To bold gestures."

The others echoed her, tankards clinking. Maddie clutched hers, a spark of certainty blooming beneath her ribs.

But certainty was a fragile thing, wasn't it? A single glance, a poorly timed silence, and it could crack like porcelain beneath the weight of doubt.

Maddie looked down at the frothy swirl of her drink, her thumb running absently along the tankard's handle. Her friends made it sound so easy—boldness, gestures, daring declarations. And she loved them for it, their fire and chaos and strange, glittering courage. But she wasn't like them. Not quite. Not yet.

She'd spent her whole life being careful. Measured. Making sense. She was the one who carried lemon drops in her reticule in case of nausea, who always had a spare handkerchief, who remembered names and allergies and who hated gooseberry jam. She knew how to tend a fever. How to pour tea. How to keep herself from wanting too much.

But now she wanted too much.

And it wasn't the kiss that had undone her. It was the way Sebastian looked at her after. Like he didn't want to let go. Like he saw her... and still stayed.

She pressed her palm flat against her chest, steadying the drum of her heart.

What if she gave him a sign... and he missed it? What if she gave herself to the moment, completely, and he hesitated again? Not out of indifference, but fear?

Would she be strong enough to survive the ache?

But what if... he met her there?

What if, just once, she chose to believe the glimmer instead of burying it? To step forward and offer something of herself not out of duty but desire?

Maybe that's what falling in love was. Not a grand gesture. But a thousand quiet choices.

And maybe, she could make the next one.
Perhaps she wasn't panicking after all.
Perhaps she was simply still falling.

Chapter Eighteen

SEBASTIAN STIRRED FROM an uneasy awakening, a chill skimming along his skin. His room was cloaked in a serene stillness that tugged him fully from slumber, the sort of quiet one only heard after a snowfall. He blinked, his breath fogging faintly in the cool air as he pushed himself upright. Across the room, the hearth had fallen dark, though the scent of last night's fire lingered faintly, earthy and comforting.

The pale light filtering through his curtains spoke of dawn, though it carried an unusual softness, muted and whitewashed. Sebastian swung his legs over the side of the bed, raking his fingers through the disheveled waves of his hair. He strode to the window, tugging back the heavy drapes.

The world was transformed.

Snow blanketed the grounds in a pristine layer, unmarred by footsteps or carriage wheels. It was a canvas untouched, a future uncharted. The dazzling white expanse before him seemed to mirror what his life had become since Maddie had taken up residence in his heart. A fresh start, an invitation to rewrite what had been cold and empty and paint it with warmth instead.

He had never cared for winter before, always finding it a dreary, slushy nuisance with its biting winds and damp chill. Yet now, standing here in this crystalline morning, it was as though the season itself had shifted. The snowflakes looked less like a burden to trudge through and more like tiny miracles scattered across the earth, delicate and fleeting. Everything felt different because of her.

Maddie had transformed the bitter into something bright.

His heart beat a little harder as he exhaled, fogging the glass. Like this snow, his future was untouched, unspoiled, and full of potential. And she, this impossible woman, had changed him in ways he hadn't even realized he needed. Maddie had changed his heart.

The pristine silence outside mirrored the stirrings in his chest, fragile yet brimming with something beautiful. His jaw tightened, the faintest lift curling the corner of his mouth as his eyes wandered… then caught. His gaze snagged not on the snow or the glistening trees but on something far more captivating.

It was Maddie, her dark-green cloak standing vivid against the canvas of white.

His breath hitched as his fingers flexed against the window frame. She moved with ease, her scarf slightly askew, the wind toying with its ends like a playful conspirator. She turned, laughing, the sound too far to hear but impossible not to imagine. That laugh had haunted his dreams, warm and unrestrained, the echo of it still tugging at his senses.

But she wasn't alone.

A sharp twist jerked through his chest when his eyes followed her companions. Ashley. Thomas. And a blackguard.

The Duke of Paisley.

Sebastian simply loathed the man.

It wasn't just the impeccable tailoring or the air of effortless charm the duke carried like a birthright—it was the history. The kind of man Paisley had always been. The kind of man everyone pretended he wasn't. Refined on the outside, yes. Polished to a fault. But beneath the sheen of nobility lurked a predator with a practiced smile. And everyone knew it. They all knew it.

And still, there he was, standing beside Maddie like he belonged.

A bitter taste rose in Sebastian's throat, the kind that came when one knew he was watching something wrong unfold and yet felt powerless to stop it. The duke leaned a fraction closer, too close. Maddie tilted her head toward him, laughing, her eyes sparkling with some secret delight. She swayed as though the moment had carved out a world just for the two of them.

Sebastian's breath stalled, trapped in his lungs like a held confession. His fingers curled into fists at his sides, blunt nails biting into his palms. That laugh, that free, sun-drenched laugh, he had earned that. He had watched her bloom into it, one day, one stubborn smile at a time. And now she gave it away so easily to someone who had no right to it.

He knew, logically, that she didn't belong to him. That no one owned a moment like that, let alone a woman like Maddie. But logic had never stood a chance against the look in her eyes when she smiled up at Paisley.

That should have been his smile to return.

He had seen the layers she kept hidden, the loneliness tucked into her laughter. He had felt her shiver beneath his touch, had breathed in the trust when she leaned into him, uncertain but willing.

She was not simply kind or clever or beautiful. She was his beginning. The first note in a song he hadn't known he was waiting to hear. And the thought of another man stepping into the melody before Sebastian had even sung a verse tore at something primal inside him.

He hadn't meant to fall this hard. Hadn't meant to hope.

But Maddie had ruined him for indulgence.

Now every brush of her hand, every shared glance slid inside him like a vow half-formed. And though he hadn't spoken the words aloud yet, he carried them like a sack of bricks he could barely manage to hold: I would choose you, every time. In every life.

And wasn't that the heart of it?

She had made him want things. Dangerous, thrilling, terrifying things. A future. A partner. A love built on stolen smiles and stubborn arguments and shared silences.

He wanted her. Not just for tonight or tomorrow. He wanted her always.

And if she didn't know that yet, she would.

A pulse of something darker—jealousy, fear, maybe both—tightened across his body. She had changed everything inside him, had turned winter into wonder, silence into longing, and now she was looking at another man like that?

He hated the heat curling beneath his skin. Hated that it made him feel like some petulant fool of a schoolboy, but he couldn't help it. Because beneath the flash of jealousy was something far more treacherous.

No.

The word formed in his chest, low and forceful, a challenge to the scene unfolding before him. Maddie with the duke next to her was something he could not stomach. For years, he had lived as though it didn't matter, as though women and marriage were games best avoided. But Maddie had rewritten whatever logic had bound him. This was different.

This was her.

Sebastian wrenched his gaze away from the window, his shoulders squaring as he made for the bellpull. His hand gripped it tightly, his knuckles whitening as he gave it a single, sharp tug. His valet would arrive soon, and that was good. Propriety, be forgotten. He wouldn't stand idly by while the duke attempted to charm Maddie in the snow.

He dressed quickly, ignoring the stiff chill of the room. Every button, every lace, every deliberate movement seemed charged with purpose. He wasn't a man prone to the reckless indulgence of passion, but perhaps Maddie had changed that, too.

Because if this fresh snow outside was the promise of a new future, he wouldn't allow another man to cross it before him. Maddie belonged to herself, of course, but Sebastian vowed to make clear where he stood. She deserved nothing less than his heart laid bare.

His boots hit the hall without a moment's hesitation. Whatever unspoken war was to unfold in the snow below, Sebastian would make sure this morning belonged to him and Maddie, untouched and uncharted.

With me.

MADDIE ACCOMPANIED ASHLEY in the snow, her boots crunching lightly against the frosty ground as servants bustled back and forth, readying the sleds for their morning ride. She pulled her cloak tighter around her, but the chill seemed determined to find its way through. Or maybe something else entirely made her shiver, something that had to do with the fourth window on the second floor. Or was it the fifth?

She squinted up at the grand castle again, trying to remember exactly which one was his. It had seemed so obvious last night. Surely, it had to be the one with the heavy blue curtains. Or perhaps the one slightly to the left...

"Maddie?" Ashley's voice sliced through her thoughts. "What are you doing? You've been staring up at the windows like you expect something to fly out of them."

"What? Nothing," Maddie said, blinking quickly. "Good morning. Lovely weather for sleighs, isn't it?"

Ashley raised a skeptical brow. "Lovely weather for frostbite, more like. Are you certain you're all right? You've been squinting at the eaves for a solid five minutes."

"I was... I thought I saw movement up there." Maddie's gaze darted upward again, frustration prickling. By now she couldn't be sure if it was the third window, the fourth, or if she had imagined the entire idea and none of them were Sebastian's at all.

Before she could reassess for the hundredth time, the Duke of

Paisley's clipped tones interrupted. "Ah, the sleds are nearly ready!" He stood with his hands clasped behind his back, surveying the scene like a general inspecting his troops. Though with all the air of command, Maddie noted, he hadn't so much as lifted a finger to help, unlike Thomas, who was busy adjusting harnesses and checking blankets. There was just something about this man... she couldn't quite place it, but all the grandness surrounding him had long since disappeared. He was not a good man. But Maddie would smile, keep up appearances, and not cause a scene while he was at the castle.

"Maddie!" Thomas called from the front of the nearest sleigh, his breath visible in the crisp air. "This one's ready!"

"Excellent." Paisley turned toward Ashley but then paused, his sharp gray eyes flicking to Maddie instead. "Miss Madeleine, I believe it would be most appropriate for us to share this sleigh. Don't you agree?"

Maddie's spine straightened instinctively, the ornate gloves on her hands suddenly feeling too tight. "Shouldn't we wait for the others? The party isn't complete yet." She shot what she hoped was a disarming smile, though her discomfort made her rub her gloved palms together.

"Oh, nonsense. Time waits for no one, and neither do sleighs," the duke said as he strode forward and climbed into the sled. First. Without offering her so much as a hand. Maddie frowned. Wasn't the lady meant to go first?

"Come along, my lady," Paisley called, extending a hand to her like an afterthought as he settled himself in the sled. "It's quite comfortable."

Maddie hesitated, her feet rooted to the snow. By all accounts, this should have been ideal. A slow ride through the snow with a respectable gentleman of status, the kind her mother would no doubt approve of. But as she stared at the duke's perfectly polished demeanor and the outstretched hand waiting for hers, her entire body resisted. Every fiber bristled against it.

Perhaps she could make some excuse, or...

Her thoughts scattered at the sound of heavy, purposeful steps crunching across the snow. Then came the voice, low and firm, its timbre like the heat of a roaring hearth after a day in the biting cold.

"She's with me."

Maddie spun around, her heart leaping and flipping like a startled rabbit in a snowdrift. Sebastian stood a few paces away, his coat open as though the chill couldn't touch him, his dark gaze fixed firmly on hers.

For a brief second, everything fell away—Ashley's curious look, the duke's stiff propriety, and all the bustling servants in the background. There was only him, standing there with a heat in his expression that warmed her more thoroughly than any fur-lined cloak could manage.

And then, because maddeningly it wasn't enough that he looked this handsome, he smiled. Oh, it wasn't an ordinary smile. No, this one blazed hot and bright, enough to melt snowbanks in its path.

"We ought to make good time," the duke interrupted, extending his hand again. "Come on, Miss Madeleine."

Maddie couldn't even turn toward him. Her face was too warm, her pulse too quick.

Sebastian's smile curled wider, the edges positively wicked now. He shifted his stance slightly, and then, with a sharp whistle that pierced the crisp morning air, the sled jerked into motion.

The duke, scrambling with both hands to hold on to his hat and his seat as the horses surged forward, shouted something less than dignified.

Maddie gasped, her gloved hand flying up to her mouth as laughter bubbled free, unrestrained and bright. Sebastian chuckled, clearly pleased with himself. "I grew up here," he said, a note of boyish pride in his voice. "I know all of Thomas's horse commands. Sorry. Most of them."

"Oh, most of them," Maddie repeated, trying and failing to keep the grin off her face. "That poor man will barely make it to the end of the meadow."

"Serves him right," Sebastian said lightly, straightening his coat against the cold. He turned as one of the footmen approached, a thick scarf wrapped so tightly around his face he was barely recognizable. "Milord," the man said, his voice muffled through the layers. "The earl has reserved the four sleds for his guests."

Sebastian didn't so much as blink. His grin widened, dazzling in its defiance. "How fortunate, then, that I'm not a guest here." He turned back to Maddie, tilting his head slightly as he extended his arm. "Shall we?"

Her heart raced as she looked up at him, but this time, it wasn't due to propriety or hesitation. There was a spark in his eyes that matched the fluttering thrill in her chest. She slipped her arm through his, her fingers lightly gripping his sleeve.

"Yes," she said, as they began to walk. "Yes, we shall."

Sebastian plucked the reins from a stable hand and gave the horse's glossy neck a fond stroke. "This is Swan," he said proudly. "She's an Irish draft horse, the only one Thomas has. Beautiful, isn't she?"

Maddie tilted her head, studying the mare. Swan's coat was a pale, almost gleaming silver-gray, dotted with black spots that seemed to shimmer when the sunlight caught them. Her mane and tail were a striking contrast, jet black and thick like winter velvet. Shorter legs than the other stable horses gave her an almost compact, determined air.

"She's stunning," Maddie admitted, stepping closer. "I don't think I've seen a horse like her before."

Sebastian gave a boyish grin. "She's practically made for the snow. Sturdy and strong, built for this terrain." He took a small stool from the stable corner and rested it beside Swan. "Now, after you."

"Oh, that's all?" Maddie teased, her brow arching. "Just climb aboard with no experience?"

He laughed, rich and low, as he offered his hand. "I'll help you."

She placed her gloved fingers in his. "If I fall," she said, only half-joking, "you're catching me."

"Without hesitation," he said, his voice suddenly earnest, though there was a glint of amusement in his eyes.

True to his word, Sebastian's hand was steady as he guided hers to Swan's mane. Then his other hand pressed gently against her waist, sending warmth through her even through the thick layers of her cloak. She swung a tentative leg over with more grace than she'd expected, though Sebastian steadied her shoulder the entire time.

"See? You're a natural," he murmured, his hands lingering just long enough to make her breath catch.

"A natural at not falling off? Very high praise," Maddie quipped, trying to mask how her pulse had begun to race.

Sebastian chuckled, and before she could fully adjust herself, he swung up behind her in one fluid motion, the movement so effortlessly athletic that Maddie couldn't help but turn to look at him. His dark coat brushed against hers, his arms reaching around to take the reins.

"You're very close," she whispered, suddenly all too aware of the solid warmth of his chest against her back.

"Yes," he said, his voice calm and sinfully deep. "I am." And he placed a gentle kiss on her shoulder, right over her scarf. But it didn't matter for it burned down to her skin.

A path straight into her heart.

His arm pressed lightly against her side as he steadied both her and the reins. The faint scent of leather and pine clung to him, mingling with the cool, heady freshness of the snowy morning.

"Hold here." His gloved hands briefly covered hers, showing her where to grip the saddle for balance. The gentle weight of his palms made her head swim, her chest tightening as though her corset had suddenly shrunk.

She couldn't decide if she wanted to sigh or bolt from the saddle entirely. "Well, you've certainly made me feel... secure."

He chuckled again, the rumble of it deep in his chest. "Good. You'll need it."

Before she could ask what he meant, he gave a low, confident command to Swan, and the mare's powerful legs pushed them into a steady trot. The rhythmic crunch of hooves in the snow filled the air as the stables fell behind them.

Maddie glanced over her shoulder. "We're going in the wrong direction," she said, though her tone lacked the conviction to stop him.

"Is that so?" Sebastian asked, his tone playfully innocent. "Wrong by whose standards?"

"By everyone else's," she replied. "The sleds are going that way."

"Yes," he said simply, guiding Swan left toward a path lined by snow-draped trees. "And we're not."

"And where, pray tell, are we going?"

He leaned closer, his breath warm against her ear despite the chill brushing her cheeks. "Sledding."

Maddie blinked, turning her head slightly toward him. "Sledding. Without a sled?"

A glimmer of mischief danced in his dark eyes. "There's a sled," he said, his lips turning upward in that maddeningly confident smile. "Where I intend to go."

She narrowed her eyes at him, or at least she tried. The way his words drew out, low and teasing, made her lips twitch against her will. "Is this one of those things you won't explain until we get there?"

"Precisely," he said, clearly delighted.

"You are impossible," Maddie muttered, but even she could hear the underlying amusement in her voice.

"Impossible?" Sebastian said, as if deeply offended. "You wound me, Miss Madeleine."

"I doubt anyone could manage that," she shot back.

"Anyone?" he echoed, soft and amused, his voice curling around the word like a challenge.

Her reply caught in her throat, betrayed not by his words but by the way his smile hovered just on the edge of boyish and dangerous. Maddie turned her gaze to the snowy path ahead, hoping he didn't notice the way her cheeks deepened in their warmth, or that her fingers gripped the saddle just a little tighter.

"Well?" Sebastian prompted after a beat, his voice bright. "Trust me?"

"You've left me little choice."

"Good," he said, sounding entirely too pleased.

And with a soft click of his tongue, Swan quickened her pace, carrying them farther into the snowy white unknown.

And she'd follow him anywhere, Swan or not, known or unknown.

⟫⟪

SEBASTIAN DISMOUNTED SWAN with practiced ease, his boots crunching audibly against the packed snow as he turned to help Maddie down. She was marvelously pliant in his arms, her small gasp as she slid from the saddle sending an irrational burst of pride through his chest. He steadied her as her feet touched the ground, letting his hands linger a fraction longer than necessary on her waist.

He had meant to plan out a moment to bring her to the lodge, but seeing her with Paisley, he thought better of it. What he needed was not a plan but to act.

"What is this place?" she asked, breath curling in the frigid air as she took in the modest stone lodge nestled against the crest of a wide hill. Snow clung to its slate roof and ivy-framed windows as if nature had claimed it for her own.

"It's an old hunting lodge. Only for private family use," Sebastian said, taking Swan's reins and looping them lightly around a nearby post. Stroking the mare's neck in thanks, he added, "Thomas's grandfather used to bring us here when we were boys.

It's full of supplies and old memories." He turned to Maddie with a rakish smile, "And, as it turns out, perfect for us."

He drew a ring of keys from his pocket, the metal tinkling like frost in the still air, and selected one with a worn, etched handle. "Watch this." He inserted it into the rustic door's lock, gave it a sharp twist, and pushed. The door creaked open, releasing a faint, woody scent mingled with stale smoke.

The room inside was small but cozy, with rough-hewn furniture bathed in the dim light coming in through the frosty windowpanes. A stone fireplace sat unused on one wall, and mounted antlers hung above it like silent sentinels. But Maddie's gaze went immediately to a brightly painted object propped near the door.

"There's a sled," she murmured, taking a careful step inside and eyeing the low, gleaming contraption with unveiled skepticism.

Sebastian followed her gaze and grinned. "Technically a toboggan," he corrected, brows lifting impishly. "Big enough for two, though." He strode to the sled, running a hand over its simple wooden base as though assessing it.

Maddie tilted her head, eyeing him. "It's a children's sled."

"All the better," Sebastian replied, crouching beside it and pulling a stubby candle from the mantel. "Lighter, faster… and infinitely more thrilling."

"What are you doing?" she asked as he ignited the candle briefly with a nearby flint and lit the wick before blowing it out. The flame gone, he rubbed the wax stub across the sled's base with meticulous care, the strokes deliberate and sharp.

"Improving speed," he explained, tossing her a glance over his shoulder. "Because if we're doing this, we're doing it properly."

Maddie smirked, arms crossed. "And by properly, you of course mean dangerously?"

"Precisely," he said without missing a beat, giving the sled a final swipe. He straightened, his black coat pulling with the motion, and gestured toward the door. "Shall we?"

She gave him an exaggerated sigh but followed as he carried the toboggan outside, its painted surface shining gaily even in the muted light. He set it carefully at the hill's peak, then turned to Maddie, who was eyeing the steep, snow-covered slope with cautious amusement.

"Well?" she asked, glancing between him and the sled. "Are we walking it down instead?"

Sebastian chuckled, stepping back to pat the sled invitingly. "Not a chance. Now, sit here, in front."

"You're assuming I trust you," she teased but stepped forward nonetheless, even though he knew she did.

"You're already here, aren't you?" he countered, helping her down onto the sled's small seat. He swung himself behind her, his taller frame neatly enclosing hers, and grasped the rope handles to steer.

Maddie stiffened slightly at the proximity as his arms bracketed her sides, their breath mingling in the chill air. "I don't need both a rider *and* a blanket," she protested, but her voice betrayed more laughter than reproach.

He leaned closer, his chin just above her shoulder, and murmured, "The speed's better with two. Physics."

"You're impossible," she said, and he could feel her smile, not merely see it. "Science?"

"Yes. And yet, here you are," Sebastian returned as he gave the sled a resolute push off the crest of the hill.

The toboggan shot forward immediately, the wax on its base sending it gliding smoothly over the icy snow. Cold wind whipped their cheeks, tearing at Maddie's scarf and tossing loose wisps of her hair back into his face. The rumble of the runners echoed loudly and cheerfully in the otherwise silent white landscape.

"Sebastian!" she cried, her hands clutching the sides of the sled as the hill steepened. "This is much faster than I expected."

"Not too late to jump," he teased, keeping a steady grip on the rope. He leaned into her ear and added, "Though I wouldn't recommend it."

"You're enjoying this!" she accused, but her bubbling laughter made the words hollow.

"Thoroughly," he admitted, grinning against the wind. "Especially since you've stopped listing all the reasons this was a terrible idea."

He heard her scoff but didn't miss the unrestrained joy in her voice as the sled darted over a rise, lifting briefly into the air before settling back down with a thud. Her laughter rang out freely now, and it was sweeter than any melody he'd ever heard. By the time they reached the bottom, their cheeks were flushed, eyes bright, and the sled finally slowed to a halt in a drift near the trees.

Her laugh was a bright melody that tangled itself in his chest, making it impossible to breathe, to think, to do anything but adore her. The way she tilted her head, just so, as if she were daring him to keep up with her wit, made his world spin. Maddie glanced at him, her wide eyes sparkling with a mischief that sent his heart tumbling. She owned him, utterly and completely, and every time she said his name, it wasn't madness he felt; it was Maddie. She was his every rational thought undone, his every certainty rewritten just to include her.

She laughed, and the sound carved through him—it almost hurt. How had he lived before this? Before her? Before her voice, before her eyes, before this kind of joy? Unfettered, simple, and impossibly real?

Sebastian had lived a life of measured steps and controlled edges. Of knowing what he should do, who he should be, how not to want too much.

And then she arrived with her honey-sweet voice and skeptical frowns and the kind of laughter that broke rules just by existing.

This… this… was not what he had expected when he started to fall for her. He hadn't prepared for a world in which sledding through snow could feel more intimate than the waltz. But she had given him something far rarer than this.

She had given him belonging.

There was no mask here. No title, no expectation, no legacy chasing his heels. Just two people tumbling toward something remarkable.

He hadn't asked her to come with him as part of some grand scheme. He'd acted on impulse, on the gut-level panic that Paisley might charm her out from under him. But now, watching her, flushed and grinning and beautiful beyond belief, he realized he didn't want to win her. He wanted to deserve her.

She made him want to be the kind of man who could make a life with her. Someone who could give her more than reckless rides and almost-kisses. Someone who could hand her his heart and mean it.

And he would.

Maddie twisted to face him, still breathless. "I can't decide if that was exhilarating or utterly reckless."

Her radiant smile, however, left no room for doubt about her true sentiments.

Sebastian gave her a rakish grin, brushing flecks of snow from his coat. "Why not both?"

And then, without asking, he stood, extending a hand toward her. "Again?"

"Do I have a choice?" she asked cheekily.

He tilted his head, eyes sparkling. "No, not really."

Maddie laughed, taking his hand. "Then lead on, my lord."

And lead he did, back toward the hill, back toward the snow, back toward everything he already knew he never wanted to live without.

Chapter Nineteen

THE ROAR CAME suddenly, a thunderous crack that echoed across the white-capped hills, making the earth seem to tremble beneath them. Sebastian's head snapped up at once, his gaze falling on the ridge above the valley. Snow peeled away like a shattering pane of glass, spilling over itself in an elegant, devastating rush. Maddie, who had been mid-laugh, froze in place beside him.

For a brief moment, neither of them spoke. The avalanche tumbled downward, its movement hypnotic as it carved a powerful path through the trees and blanketed the lower slopes with pristine white once more. The air crackled with sound, a distant echo of thunder and cascading force.

"Does this…" Maddie's voice was unsure, almost tentative as she tore her gaze from the sight to glance at him. "Does this happen often?"

Sebastian's lips tilted into a faint, reassuring smile as he folded his arms, watching the valley stilling after the chaos. "It's rare enough, though predictable under the right conditions."

"Predictable?" she echoed, her brows lifting.

"Physics," he explained, the satisfaction of her curiosity bringing out a smug glint in his eye. "Snow accumulates, of course, and it settles in layers, some denser than others. A sound or a shift in weight disturbs the delicate equilibrium." His tone softened, and he gestured toward the ridge. "The force it released just now was inevitable."

Beautiful, but inevitable.

Maddie turned her head slowly back to the scene. "You make terrifying things sound rather poetic."

"Perhaps terrifying things have their own kind of poetry," Sebastian said lightly, though her words lingered with an unexpected weight in his chest.

Just as the last echoes of the avalanche faded into the brisk air, a loud snort and a startled shuffle reminded him of something infinitely less poetic. "Swan," he said sharply, just as the mare reared back, her ears flat against her skull. The thunder, the chaos, and the quaking ground were too much for her. Swan's hooves scraped against the frozen earth before she bolted, dashing back toward the hills at a breakneck pace.

"Sebastian!" Maddie cried, clutching his arm. "The horse!"

He drew a breath, steadying her with one hand while his gaze followed Swan's retreating form. A pang of frustration hit him, but it was tempered by a flicker of regret—not for the horse, but for Maddie's startled expression. "I see her," he murmured. "She'll be fine. She knows these paths better than either of us."

"But she ran," Maddie pressed, her tone uncertain. "Why didn't you tie her up?"

Sebastian met her gaze, his own calm and unshaken. "Because I wanted her trust, not shackles," he said simply. "A horse bolts when it feels trapped. She'll come back when she's ready."

For a moment, Maddie said nothing. She studied him with a searching expression, her lips parting as though words were on the tip of her tongue. But then she surprised him with a soft laugh, shaking her head. "Trust, not shackles," she echoed, almost to herself. "I suppose that should apply to more than just horses."

The rumble at first was faint, so low she almost convinced herself it wasn't growing louder. Maddie barely noticed it over her laughter, but Swan did. The horse reared her head, ears flipping back. A sharp whinny echoed across the hills as Swan darted off through the snow, her hooves kicking up powder as she vanished down the slope.

Maddie turned instinctively, catching the concern etched in Sebastian's face. The sound returned, louder now and closer, rolling through her chest as if the earth itself groaned with effort. Her eyes traced the hills in the distance, and she froze, her breath shallow. A sheer patch of snow slid away from a ridge, swift and smooth as a wave breaking on a shore. It couldn't be dangerous, could it? But then another slab broke free nearby. And another.

"Maddie..." Sebastian's voice was low, tight, shaking with something she couldn't place.

She tore her gaze from the hills to him, alarm building as his posture stiffened. His hand raised slightly, as if to halt her from moving even though she hadn't dared to yet.

"What's happening?" Her own voice sounded fragile in the frigid air.

"A rockslide. Snow on top." His words came so clipped it barely registered.

Her brows knitted together. "You mean like an avalan—"

But her voice faltered when his eyes darted behind her, the sudden shift in focus pinning her in place. Her stomach dropped. She turned slowly, her heart hammering in her chest, and saw it. A great white cloud burst outward like a ghost clawing its way up the hill. Snow rolled sideways and upward, billowing higher as it swallowed everything in its path. Beneath it, rocks trapped beneath the snow churned forward with a grinding, hollow roar.

The air wasn't air anymore. It thickened with the sound, the sheer power growing louder and closer until her knees locked, unsure where to go. The cold grew sharper somehow.

"Maddie!" His shout came a second before his hand caught her shoulder and pulled. She would've screamed if she had breath to spare, but all she felt was the sharp burn of impact as her body crashed into the snow.

Her face hit first, the icy sting clawing at her skin. For a moment, the world was an endless smear of pale frost and blinding white. Then something warm barreled into her, heavy and solid.

Her lungs fought for air as the snow pressed cold against her lips, seeping through her gloves and the hem of her coat, freezing her to her core. She shifted slightly, trying to raise her head, but the weight on her back crushed her farther into the endless frost.

Maddie tried again to breathe, but nothing came. Her chest flared in panic, an aching vacuum where air should have been. She blinked furiously, desperate to see more than the endless darkness pressing against her.

Suffocating.

Cold.

Her heart thudded wildly, a frantic beat that seemed to mock her helplessness. She clawed at the snow with trembling fingers, the icy compactness denying her every effort. Between the numbness spreading through her body and the crushing pressure above, she couldn't tell where she ended and the snow began. And Sebastian? Was he still keeping the worst of it from her, or had he been buried, dragged down into the weight of it all?

She tried to speak his name, but her throat felt tight, dry, as though the snow had filled every space inside her. Panic churned in her stomach. If she couldn't see him, didn't feel him move soon, then surely... Her mind reeled with possibilities she couldn't bear to finish. Was he just inches away, struggling as she was? Or—as dread pushed at the edges of her fraying thoughts— had he been crushed beneath the merciless weight?

"Sebastian," she managed, her voice weak and hoarse. It barely broke the cold silence. The only sound in response was the faint, unrelenting hiss of her shallow, ineffective breaths.

Snow.

Everywhere.

Heavy and relentless. Maddie wanted to move, to claw at it, to fight it off of her body, but her muscles refused. Her back burned under the cold press of soaked fabric, and her cheeks raw from contact with the freezing ground. Blinking hard didn't stop the flickering streams of white that seemed fixed in her view.

Then something shifted slightly above her, and her awareness zeroed in on the faint scrape of his breath brushing the nape of her neck.

Sebastian.

He wasn't fully collapsed, propped up somehow by sheer will and trembling arms just above her.

"Maddie," he rasped.

She tried to respond, tried to turn her head to look at him. But the snow didn't allow it, and her body stiffened with the effort. It took too long, every motion sluggish and wrong as though her mind had detached from her limbs. "I'm…" It came out broken, weak, and unfinished.

Her chest clenched again, and this time, panic joined the growing numbness creeping through her fingers and toes. The cold wasn't just biting anymore. It gnawed. Stole heat, stole strength. Her hand shifted weakly, trying to brush at the snow weighing her down, but it was useless.

Sebastian shifted again, his breath a little louder now, labored. Fear flared in her stomach. Not just for herself but for him.

She'd always thought her fears were logical. Sensible. Fear of disappointing her mother. Fear of being too much, too loud, too independent. Fear of wanting more than society said she ought to.

But this… this was real fear. A raw, soul-deep terror that she might never hear his laugh again. That she might never see the way he softened when he looked at her like she was the only thing worth protecting in a chaotic world.

Sebastian.

She had wanted to believe she had time. Time to sort through her feelings. Time to figure out what came next. But time had vanished the moment that second avalanche tore through the hills, and now all that remained was the sound of his breath and the weight of his body keeping her from being buried completely.

If he was hurt because of her, if he had shielded her and paid the price, she would never forgive herself even though she had no control over nature.

A sob built in her throat, dry and aching, and she swallowed it down. Not now. Not yet. They weren't dead. They couldn't be.

She had fallen for him faster than sense allowed, and still she'd hesitated—held back, waiting for certainty, for signs. But here, under this brutal cold, she realized she didn't need signs.

She just needed him.

She didn't care if he never wrote a poem or brought her flowers or declared anything with fancy words. She just wanted more mornings. More stolen glances. More rides. More everything, so long as he was there beside her. To kiss her after. To tell her, in his way, that he'd do it all again.

Please, she begged silently, pressing her heart into the dark.

Please don't take him from me.

THE WEIGHT PRESSED against Sebastian's arms, trembling now, despite his stubborn attempts to keep steady. The weight was immense, relentless, crushing down on him with an unforgiving force.

How much did snow weigh? A ton? It certainly felt like it, pressing on his back, on his shoulders, grinding his body into the cold abyss. Suddenly, his arms trembled violently against the burden, every muscle in his body alight with searing pain. His instincts screamed at him to drop, to collapse into the suffocating white, anything to make the agony stop. But Sebastian knew if he gave in, the fragile chamber of air he'd created over Maddie would vanish. The snow would claim her completely, seep into every inch of what lay beneath him, leaving no space to breathe, no space to survive. If he fell, they would die.

He roared and pushed himself farther up, trying to see if

Maddie was alive. Was she safe? Breathing?

The realization hit him like another avalanche, heavier than the one that buried them. It wasn't just his strength fighting gravity now; it was his will, forcing his body to endure past its limits. He had thrown himself over her in those frantic moments, instinct taking over before fear could paralyze him. His arms had locked, forming a barrier, and for all he knew, it was that thin, trembling shield that stood between Maddie and death. The snow weighed so much more than he'd imagined. Every second dragged through him as though the icy mass above grew heavier, testing his resolve. His muscles burned with each breath he took, threatening to give way, to betray him. His knees were pinned beneath his twisted body, trapped so firmly he barely had feeling left in them, yet even that unpleasant numbness was a gift compared to the screaming ache across his shoulders.

And still, he held.

Because if he didn't, Maddie would disappear beneath the snow, suffocated by the same icy void clawing at him now. Giving up wasn't just failure. It was a death sentence—for both of them.

How long had it been since the stifling silence had washed over him after the roaring of the rockslide?

Seconds?

Minutes?

Sebastian shifted slightly, his torso burning from the strain of keeping himself aloft. Snow had crept into every space it could find, chilling his body to the core, soaking through his coat to claw at his skin. His legs were twisted beneath him, trapped awkwardly by the force of the avalanche, but he ignored the sharp protests of pain racing through his muscles. Pain meant he could still move. Pain meant he was still alive.

"Maddie," he rasped, her name escaping him in a voice he barely recognized. His breath clouded the pocket of air above her, his mouth close enough to see the faint tremble of snowflakes on her hair. She didn't answer. Her silence was worse than the crushing cold, worse than the suffocating darkness encompassing them.

"Say something," he murmured, his voice breaking. "I just… need to know you're alive." He adjusted his posture to shield her more fully. The motion sent a stab of agony through his shoulders, but he bit down on it until his teeth ached. He couldn't move too much, not without risking further collapse.

"Maddie?"

The memory of the avalanche flashed through his mind. He had seen it before she had, the first shift of snow on the ridgeline, like sand tumbling from an hourglass. The terror swallowed him whole, not for himself, but because she had been so still, so unaware. She'd barely started to turn before he acted, instinct taking over as he shoved her down, throwing his body over hers. He hadn't even stopped to think. There hadn't been time.

Above her now, he closed his eyes for a moment, forcing out the thoughts that clawed at him. He hadn't been nearly fast enough. If he had pulled her further… If he had done more… His jaw clenched painfully. The what-ifs threatened to drown him almost as much as the snow.

Sebastian leaned closer to her ear, forced to shift precious inches down as his strength faltered. "Maddie," he said again, more desperate now. His voice cracked like a brittle branch underfoot. "You… you have to hang on for me. Just for a little while longer." A pause. The silence around them was too heavy, a reminder that they were both buried in something much too large to fight. "It'll be alright. It has to be."

Still no reply. His breath hitched, but his determination didn't waver. He wasn't going to lose her here. Not like this. Not under this frozen grave. "You're not allowed to give up," he said, his words jumbled and rushed. "That's not who you are, Maddie. And I need you. I need you to fight with me."

He hadn't prayed since he was a boy.

Not when his father fell ill. Not even during those empty years where he'd lost the ability to want anything at all. But now, with Maddie buried beneath him, her life balancing on the strength of his arms, he prayed.

Not for miracles.

Just for her.

Let her breathe. Let her wake. Let her laugh again and argue with him over absolutely everything. Let her glare at him the way she did when she was hiding a smile. Let her live.

He would take the pain, the frostbite, the collapse of every part of him that still worked if it meant she would live.

And the truth? The thing he hadn't dared speak, even to himself?

He didn't know how to go back to a world without her in it.

She'd marched into his life in that green cloak and unsettled everything. Challenged every belief he had. Every line he'd drawn to keep others out. And he hadn't just let her in, he'd wanted her there. He needed her there.

The thought of failing her, of this being the last moment they shared broke something in him.

And yet... if this was the end, he would meet it like this. Holding the line. Protecting her. Loving her.

Even if she never heard the words.

Even if she never got the chance to say them back.

The snow pressed tighter against his body, his weight sinking against it as his strength drained. He wracked his mind for something else to tell her, something to keep her with him. "I..." He hesitated, his chest tightening in a way that wasn't caused by the cold. His voice softened, barely audible. "I couldn't bear it, you know, if..." He stopped again, feeling the words scrape at him, raw and exposed. "I'll get us out of here," he promised, reaching as deeply into himself as he could muster. "Even if you hate me for shoving you like that, I'll make sure you're all right."

His arm trembled uncontrollably, and he gritted his teeth again. "I'll bring you home. I don't care about the rest." He gave a hoarse chuckle as if any of this could be lightened. "Wouldn't be the first time you've been repulsed by me."

And still, he propped himself up, the weight of endless snow pressing down, the cold gnawing into his very bones. Because it didn't matter what it cost him. Maddie was beneath him, alive, barely moving but still his. And so long as she drew even the shallowest breath, he'd fight for both of them. If she didn't hate him now, he reckoned she might once they escaped, especially when she realized what he had done. But he'd bear that too, gladly. With Maddie safe, he'd bear anything.

Would she respond?

Chapter Twenty

T HE SNOW SHIFTED above her, weight grinding down in a slow collapse, and Maddie's chest seized with panic. Then there was a tug, firm and deliberate, cutting through the suffocating cold. Air rushed back into her lungs as she was dragged free, coughing violently against the damp chill clinging to her face. She blinked rapidly, her snow-laden lashes stinging with the effort, until his face appeared above her, pale and stark against the icy void around them.

"Maddie," Sebastian breathed, his voice hoarse with strain. His hands didn't leave her shoulders, as though ensuring she was fully out of danger. His lips moved again, murmuring something she couldn't catch over the ache in her ears and the frantic rasp of her own breathing.

She coughed once more, sharper this time, and finally managed words. "Sebastian…"

"You didn't answer! Do you know what I was thinking?" She'd never seen him sound so scared.

Her voice cracked, weighted with the enormity of what had just happened. "You… you saved me."

His jaw tightened, and he looked away, almost embarrassed. "It wasn't much," he said gruffly, shaking loose snow from his sleeves. "Anyone would have done the same."

"No," she said, blinking up at him. Air was still barely coming to her, but she could see him clearly now, his hair plastered to his forehead, his usually precise cravat beginning to get soaked through by the snow that had melted on his neck. His coat hung limply. He looked utterly undone, raw and unguarded in a way she'd never seen. "It was everything, Sebastian."

He ducked his head, brushing her face, her arms, checking for injuries while avoiding her eyes. "We're safe now," he muttered. "Just breathe. You're all right."

Safe.

In his arms.

Her fingers twitched against his chest as she leaned up, struggling into a sitting position. He offered his arm for balance, even as she felt the tension in his body. Snow clung to him as though it had tried to pull him under too. She glanced at his trembling hands, red and raw, and it struck her like a blow. He had used every ounce of strength to shield her, an act so selfless it stole the breath she had just fought to reclaim.

"You didn't have to…" Her throat tightened, and she tried again. "You could've been killed."

"And you could've been," he said sharply, his gaze flicking up to meet hers. For a moment, she saw the depths of his fear, the fury barely stifled by relief. Then he softened, taking a breath. "Don't waste your strength thinking about it. Let's get warm."

She opened her mouth to argue, but he pressed a hand against the snow beside her, readying himself to move. "Come on," he said, his voice gentler now. "We've got to get out of this. Can you stand?"

Shivering, she nodded, her muscles protesting every inch she hauled herself forward. The snow shifted against her every effort, compacting and heavy, as though it wanted to drag her down again. But there he was beside her, pushing through with a determination that seemed impossible given what he must've endured.

Sebastian reached back once with surprising patience, steadying her as though she were made of porcelain. "That's it, Maddie," he murmured, his voice closer now, the encouragement threading warmth through the blistering cold. "Just keep going."

She could barely see through her exhaustion and the endless white ahead of them, but he never faltered. His resilience didn't just drag himself forward; it lifted her, carried her through the impossible until they broke free from the snow's crushing hold.

When they finally collapsed onto firmer ground, panting and shaking so violently they could barely stay upright, she turned to him, her chest tight with more than just the cold. "You risked everything," she whispered, her voice trembling. "Why?"

The faintest smile flickered across his cracked lips as he sat back, leaning heavily on his arms. "Because you're worth it." His voice dropped to something softer, private. "Always will be to me."

It shouldn't have undone her.

Not after everything they'd endured, not after the way she'd seen him throw his body over hers without a second thought. But those words, soft, quiet, as though they didn't carry the weight of the world, destroyed her.

Always will be to me.

Not a declaration. Not quite.

But not nothing either.

It settled over her more deeply than the snow ever had. Not cold. Never cold. It was warmth in the sharpest place. Maddie's fingers clenched into her skirts, her eyes fixed on his profile. His jaw was tight, lips pale, but his voice had held a truth she didn't think he meant for her to carry home.

She swallowed hard, her throat dry despite the meltwater still clinging to her lashes. No one had ever said she was worth it before.

Not truly.

Not like this.

Sebastian wasn't a man who flung words for show. He guarded himself like a fortress, and still, somehow, she had slipped through the cracks. And he had let her. Protected her. Cherished her, even now, while pretending it meant less than it did.

A single thought blossomed in her chest, wild and unwanted.

If he dies of frost or exhaustion, and this is all I ever get of him… I will never forgive the world for letting him go.

She blinked the thought away and drew a breath.

Her heart thudded harder against her ribs as she stared at him, unsure whether her breathlessness was the cold or the sheer weight of his words. He tipped his head forward, tapping snow from his hair, clearly uncomfortable under her gaze, but she didn't look away. She couldn't. This man, drenched and trembling beside her, had given more than she'd thought any person could. And he dismissed it as though it meant nothing, even when it was everything.

SEBASTIAN'S FACE WARMED, though whether it was from the sentiment or the way her words hung in the frosty air, he wasn't sure. Either way, he straightened, clearing his throat briskly. "Come," he said, offering his hand. "The lodge isn't far. We won't be able to walk back to the castle. I'll make a fire."

"How are we going to get back?" Maddie looked around. The pristinely white landscape, the moments alone she'd cherished with Sebastian now twisted her stomach. This was no longer proper.

"Someone will have to come for us." Sebastian lifted the sled with one hand and offered his other to her. "Are you coming?"

"This is hardly proper."

"It's an emergency. Where do you want to go?" Sebastian gestured grandly around them. "Nobody can see us, hear us."

"Find us? Oh, they'll find us. Thomas knows where we are."

"Did you tell him?" Maddie's eyes grew wide for she couldn't hide the surprise, shock, embarrassment—or a strange combination of the effects of the scandal she was about to suffer. An avalanche could unleash much, but the Ton's scandals left avalanches much to learn.

"Nobody knows where we are. I didn't say a word. But Thomas will know when he realizes which horse was gone and came back without the rider or the keys to the lodge. Don't worry; he'll know how to be discreet."

"So you do this often?"

"Getting stuck in avalanches because Swan runs off? No, can't say I've ever done that."

"But seducing women in secluded lodges?"

Sebastian stopped and gave her a once-over. He pressed his lips into a flat line as if he had to suppress a laugh and quirked a brow. "Would you," he cleared his throat, "Miss Madeleine, like me to seduce you in the lodge?"

Maddie forgot to breathe. She couldn't tell if he was jesting or offering to make this... this... absurd suggestion reality. She ought to be scandalized. That was for sure.

Except that she wasn't.

This is what I want.

She shouldn't; it wasn't proper. *Yes, yes.* The handbook would go up in flames if it knew what she was about.

And yet, there was plenty of snow to put that fire out.

Except not the one in her chest.

She was burning for Sebastian, and there was no denying it.

Maddie glanced behind her, at the distant trail Swan had taken, before placing her gloved palm in his. Her steps blended with his as they began the walk back up the hill.

"You do know," Maddie said as they crunched uphill, "that if the lodge isn't actually nearby, I shall stage a dramatic collapse in the snow and make you carry me the rest of the way. It might not even be dramatic because it will be true."

Sebastian glanced at her. "Please don't. You've already collapsed once today. My heart won't survive another one."

"Oh? This will be a survival strategy. I heard men can't resist a woman fainting into their arms."

"Careful, Maddie," Sebastian teased. "That sounds suspiciously like you've been thinking about falling into my arms."

She sniffed. "I think about a great many things. Bread. Books. Potions. Doesn't mean I'm about to swoon over one."

"A book has never kissed you senseless."

"That," she said, slightly breathless, "is an unverified claim."

"You should be worried," she said pointedly, "that if we're found out here alone together, my reputation will be toast."

He stopped walking and turned toward her. "Then let me be clear. I am the sort of man that takes responsibility."

Her steps faltered. "Good. But let us hope it doesn't come to that, because if I'm going to be ruined, it should be for something glorious. Not a cold walk and a lost horse."

"Glorious?" he murmured. "That sounds dangerously like a challenge."

"Only if you're the sort to rise to it."

"Oh, I do rise—"

"Sebastian!"

"—to challenges," he finished smoothly, entirely unrepentant.

She huffed, but her cheeks flushed and her smile betrayed her. "You're insufferable."

"And yet," he murmured, his hand brushing hers, "you haven't let go."

By the time they reached the lodge, the distant sunlight gave way to shadows, and the cold air had grown sharper. Sebastian led the way inside, immediately heading for the hearth.

"It'll be warm soon," he assured her, crouching to stack wood from the corner pile. Within moments, the beginnings of a fire flickered to life, and he carefully fanned the flames until they grew strong, their glow casting soft light across the room.

Maddie, who had been untying the ribbon beneath her chin, shrugged out of her cloak and set it aside. "I don't think I've felt my toes in half an hour," she admitted with a small laugh, already tugging at her damp boots.

Sebastian turned just as she slipped the first one off, exposing her stockinged foot to the warmth of the hearth. For a moment, he watched her, the sight strangely intimate. The act was unadorned, completely natural, and yet something about the way she unfolded her movements drew him in. She leaned back slightly on her hands, angling her feet closer to the fire with a soft sigh.

"I'm not saying this was your plan all along," Maddie said, stretching her legs with a satisfied sigh, "but if it had been, I would be impressed."

Sebastian glanced over from where he was stoking the fire. "What, get stranded in an avalanche with you and risk frostbite for the pleasure of your company? Sounds exactly like something I'd arrange."

She gave him a sidelong look. "Oh yes. Nothing screams romance like damp stockings and nearly dying."

He leaned back against the wall, one knee raised lazily, his shirt slightly askew from his rushed dressing. "You know," he said, voice low, "you could sit here sulking about propriety and scandal and your snow-ruined plans…"

"Or?"

"Or you could admit that part of you is glad the horse ran off."

Her brow arched, but her lips curved too. "That's an outrageous accusation."

"Is it?"

She turned her face toward the fire. "I should be scandalized. Appalled. Marching back to town with righteous fury."

"And instead?"

"I'm warm. You'll have to revive me if I fall asleep," she teased lightly, her head tilting toward him.

Sebastian, rooted where he stood, found only one response necessary. "I trust you'll manage to stay awake, Maddie."

Her smile, framed by the firelight, flickered briefly up at him before she turned her eyes back to the flames. And Sebastian, for all his effort to think of something practical or useful, found himself sitting back on the hearth's edge. Close, but not too close. Or just close enough.

For the first time since entering the lodge, silence claimed them—not out of awkwardness, but because neither wanted to disturb it. It was, as the snow, something simultaneously inevitable and more powerful than either of them alone.

Chapter Twenty-One

MADDIE'S FINGERS FLEXED slightly against the rug as she leaned back on her hands, the fire coaxing heat into her chilled toes. Her limbs still ached from the cold, but there was a peculiar comfort in this lodge—one she hadn't anticipated. Maybe it was the low glow of the fire. Or maybe it was the man sitting a breath away.

She risked a glance at Sebastian. He sat beside her now, not touching, not speaking, just close enough to stir the air between them. His profile was softened by the flickering light, shadows playing across the sharp angle of his jaw, the stubborn slant of his brow.

He looked like temptation.

Unfolded. Relaxed. A little tousled in the most dangerous way.

And entirely unaware of the havoc he caused simply by existing.

But that was the trouble, wasn't it? He didn't even know what he did to her. Or maybe he did, maybe he did and he still chose to sit this close, still let the firelight dance across that maddening jaw and let his knee rest just inches from hers.

It wasn't just that he was beautiful. It was his steadiness. The patience. The unexpected softness that had slowly been peeling

195

away her defenses, one moment at a time. When he wasn't looking, she looked. And when he was looking, she pretended not to.

Because she wasn't the sort of girl who did this.

She followed the rules. Or at least… she followed the right ones. The ones that let her keep her freedom, however narrowly. She didn't stay in lodges with men and allow herself to dream of what if.

And yet here she was. Sitting beside a man who had just risked his life for her. Who had called her name beneath the snow like it meant something. Who hadn't tried to charm her, or flatter her, or coax her into anything she didn't offer freely, but who still managed to unravel her with a single glance, a single breath.

And the worst part?

She liked it.

No, craved it.

The attention. The safety. The maddening, impossible temptation of being seen for more than her breeding or her usefulness. Just… her.

He looked at her like she wasn't a problem to solve or a daughter to marry off. Like she wasn't a scandal waiting to happen. And that was why this moment, this warmth, this closeness, felt less like a dream and more like a revelation.

Maybe that's why she didn't pull away. Maybe that's why she didn't want to.

Because deep down, she wasn't afraid of Sebastian's attention.

She was afraid of how much she wanted it.

"This feels like a dream."

He tilted his head toward her. "Oh? A dream? How so?"

"I'm not sure," she admitted. "I mean, it was rather terrifying, but now it's just… dreamlike. I shouldn't feel so at peace. I should demand you build me a sleigh and whisk me home like a proper gentleman."

He smiled, slow and lazy, like he wasn't in a hurry to be anything except right here. "You'd freeze before we made it down the hill. And besides, I'm not certain I qualify as a proper gentleman after this."

"No," Maddie agreed. "You're something worse."

He raised a brow. "Worse?"

"Infinitely more dangerous."

A beat passed. The fire snapped between them, throwing golden light against the walls.

Sebastian leaned back on his elbows. "That sounds suspiciously like a compliment."

"Of course a man would think dangerous is a compliment."

"It definitely is."

She laughed, the sound surging up from her throat before she could stop it. And he grinned at that, unabashed and boyish, and so different from the Sebastian she'd known when this all began. The broody sneezy man.

Or perhaps, not so different at all.

Perhaps she was just seeing what had always been there, beneath the surface. Beneath the careful distance he kept, like a man who'd never expected to want someone close.

He wanted her close.

And, heaven help her, she wanted to close the distance between them too.

Her laughter quieted. Her gaze lingered.

And something in the air shifted.

Sebastian's smile faded, replaced with something else. "Maddie," he said, her name almost a whisper. "If this is improper, say the word. I'll walk back out into that snow and go find help."

She looked at him, really looked—at the worry in his eyes. He wasn't playing games with her. Not now. Maybe not ever. He was offering her a choice. And it wasn't a game. It was a risk. For both of them. "Just because you're a man, doesn't mean you're invincible. You'd freeze to death, too. Besides, there is nothing I'd change about this moment."

He didn't move. Didn't speak. But something shifted in his posture, the tension in his shoulders easing, as though her words had settled something inside him too.

Maddie reached to feed another small log into the fire; the flames crackled their approval. The sound was oddly soothing, like a heartbeat. Steady. Alive.

"You say this feels like a dream," Sebastian murmured, his voice low and thoughtful. "But what would your real one be? If you could choose. No rules. No scandal. No society."

She blinked, caught off guard. "You mean… what I'd want? If there were no expectations?"

"No expectations," he repeated. "Only the truth."

Maddie wrapped her arms around her legs, resting her chin atop her knees. This was what her friends had asked her too. Not exactly. But about what she wanted. "I don't know if I've ever said it aloud."

"Say it now."

Her throat tightened a little. It was easier to laugh. Easier to spar. But this… this was uncharted terrain.

"I suppose," she said slowly, "I'd like a place of my own. A home of my own. Outside the influence of my mother and sharing the space with someone I love. No balls if I don't want to, no calling cards if I'm not in the mood. Just my little world."

Sebastian studied her. "You forgot to list a greenhouse for your herbs."

"That's a given." She glanced over at him, her lips tugging up faintly. "And what about you? What's your dream?"

His gaze slid toward the fire. "I never had the luxury of dreaming. Not really."

"You've never wanted anything for yourself?"

He exhaled. "Study. To be useful. And lately…" He looked at her then. "To matter. To someone."

The words landed somewhere soft and deep in her chest, right between the ribs.

"You matter," she said quietly. "You already do."

Sebastian shifted a little closer, his thigh brushing hers. The silence that followed wasn't awkward. It was full. Heavy in the best way.

The fire danced, their joined hands resting between them, and the snow outside pressed soft and silent against the windows. It was, Maddie thought, the sort of moment that would linger long after the world returned to normal. A moment suspended in snow light and secrets, and hopeful, even if unspoken, promises.

A dream, perhaps. But one she'd finally allowed herself to want.

To fight for.

SHE WAS BEAUTIFUL.

So very beautiful.

Not just in the obvious way. Not just because she made his chest ache and his breath stutter. But because she was real. She hadn't fallen apart after their ordeal. She hadn't complained about the hike to the lodge or the scandal they were inviting by being here together. Instead, she'd laughed. Joked. Shared something sacred with him.

Her dreams.

Sebastian's jaw tightened as he watched the firelight flicker over the curve of her cheek. No one had ever asked him about dreams before. People didn't ask things of Sebastian unless they wanted a problem solved, a decision made, or a door quietly shut. With the exception of Thomas. Otherwise, he was the man who arranged, who ensured, who fixed. Not the man anyone looked at and wondered, what does he want?

They assumed he already had it all.

And yet, Maddie had asked. Not in passing. Not to be polite. But like she wanted to know.

And when she'd told him her dream? A quiet life, a place of her own, a space filled with love… he'd felt something shift in his chest. Something subtle. Dangerous. Irrevocable.

Because he wanted to be part of that dream.

Not in theory. Not as a passing flirtation or a snowstorm memory. But truly.

It terrified him.

It excited him.

And there it was. The truth, stark and sudden, like a gust of wind, or an avalanche, that stole the breath from his lungs.

He wanted a place in her world. Not as a footnote, not as a passing fancy whispered about behind fans and closed doors, but as something solid. Present. Lasting.

That terrified him.

Because Sebastian had never believed himself capable of that kind of role. His life had always been defined by function, by duty and the expectation that he would be the one to carry burdens without complaint. The capable one. He had never resented it. Much. It had been easier, in many ways, to escape behind duty. To avoid being noticed all that much.

Until Maddie saw him.

Not just the polished man or the titled man. She saw the parts of him he kept tucked beneath his spine, the yearning, the loneliness, the hunger to be… wanted. Not needed. Wanted.

That kind of exposure should have made him retreat.

But instead, here he was, sitting beside a woman who had very nearly died in his arms, who had laughed with him not an hour later, who spoke of dreams like they were visible things, and he wanted to reach out and wrap himself in every single one of hers.

He wanted to be the one she leaned on. The one she let into her greenhouse. The one she let make the tea while she concoct-ed strange potions that filled the house with the scent of vinegar and fish and whatever else made her nose crinkle.

He wanted a life with her.

And that want ran so deep it scared him.

What if this was just a dream? What if she woke tomorrow and he had no place in her life? But she had leaned on him. She had rested on him. And that, more than anything, felt like truth.

He glanced over at her again. And in that moment, Sebastian realized…

He didn't want to go back to the life he'd had before Maddie.

And if she'd let him, he'd never leave her side again.

He turned slightly, watching her with the kind of scrutiny that only came when a man knew he stood on the edge of something that could change everything. She was hugging her knees still, her profile soft, lost in thought.

He found himself speaking before he had time to think better of it. "You're not cold anywhere anymore? All warm?"

Her eyes flicked to his, surprise blooming across her features, chased quickly by a smile. "Mostly," she said. "My toes still have questions."

Sebastian exhaled a low laugh. "Stubborn things, toes. Not easily convinced."

"I think they're holding out for better company," she said, wiggling them toward the fire. "Or perhaps an apology."

He arched a brow. "An apology?"

"For subjecting them to an avalanche and a snow-laden trek, naturally."

"Then allow me to speak directly to the aggrieved parties." He shifted closer, gaze fixed pointedly on her feet. "To Maddie's toes: I deeply regret the aforementioned trauma and promise to make amends in the form of warmth, comfort, and if necessary… hot cider."

She laughed again, a soft sound that made a home in his chest.

"Is this how you handle all crises?" she asked, tilting her head. "Charm and negotiation?"

"You are so silly."

"Happy to oblige."

"You know," she said, voice quieter now, "I meant what I said earlier."

"About the sleigh?" he teased.

"About not changing this moment," she replied, her gaze steady. "I've spent so long avoiding anything that might ruffle feathers or invite whispers. I've been the good daughter, the proper lady, the quiet observer. And now, here, I feel like I can just be."

Sebastian's chest tightened. "You can."

She looked away then, into the fire, and he let her. Some things were easier said when you didn't have to look the other person in the eye.

"I think," she said after a long pause, "that's what I've wanted all along. Not grand passion. Not fairy tale ballrooms. Just... someone to sit beside. Someone who listens. Someone who stays no matter what."

Sebastian couldn't speak for a moment. Not because he didn't know what to say, but because what he wanted to say felt too raw. Too revealing.

But he forced it out anyway.

"I'll stay."

She turned, startled.

"No matter what," he reaffirmed. "I know you weren't asking for promises. And I know this," he gestured around the lodge, the snow, the flickering fire, "this feels like something outside of time. But if you want someone who stays... Maddie, I would."

Silence. But not empty. Never empty with her.

Then she whispered, "Even when I'm difficult?"

He let out a breath of laughter. "Especially when you're difficult."

"Even when I make potions that smell like vinegar and smelly fish?"

"I'll breathe them in like perfume."

And then she shifted, slowly, carefully, until her head rested lightly against his shoulder.

Sebastian didn't move. Didn't dare. He only breathed her in and let her settle into the crook of his body like she belonged there.

They sat like that for a long time, the fire crackling and the snow pressing close against the windows. Time didn't move. Not in the normal way. It moved almost in the way that dreams do.

Eventually, she whispered, "You're very good at this."

"At what?"

"Making me feel safe."

He closed his eyes briefly. "I've never wanted to be good at anything more."

A pause.

Then, very softly, "Are your toes still being stubborn?"

She shifted, just enough for her cheek to brush against his shirt. "Yes."

He turned his head, kissed the top of hers. "So stubborn."

He knew they would leave this place eventually. That someone would come or the snow would clear, and reality would reclaim them both.

But for now, she was in his arms. And that was enough.

He didn't need dreams anymore.

He had Maddie.

Chapter Twenty-Two

MADDIE WATCHED AS Sebastian crouched near a low shelf, his broad shoulders blocking her view of whatever treasure he was after. The lodge was warm now, the fire casting shadows that danced along the rugged beams of the ceiling. She watched him curiously as he pulled out a wooden crate, his fingers brushing away cobwebs and dust with care. The motion sent a faint, earthy scent into the air that mingled with the crackle of burning logs.

"What are you doing?" she asked, unable to keep the smile from her voice.

He didn't answer immediately, instead blowing a gentle breath across the top of the crate, sending a fine puff of dust swirling in the firelight. "Finding the right way to end our evening," he said at last, glancing back at her, his lips curved into a boyish grin that made her pulse do a ridiculous little stutter. "And hopefully begin our courtship." His eyes met hers. "Officially, if I may."

Maddie felt that familiar heat rising and sat up straight.

Her curiosity deepened as he lifted the lid and reached inside with deliberate care. After a moment, he stood and turned to face her, holding a dark green bottle in one hand and a well-loved corkscrew in the other. "This," he announced softly, tilting the bottle toward her, "is from my parents' wedding. We have only four bottles left."

Maddie's breath caught, her teasing smile faltering. The firelight played off the glass, illuminating the deep red liquid inside and the faded label on the front. "Sebastian," she said, her voice lower now, more tentative. "You can't mean to open it."

He arched a brow at her, his expression equal parts amusement and resolve. "Why not?"

"It's too precious!" she protested, standing and closing the small distance between them. She searched his face, hoping to find even a flicker of hesitation. Instead, what she found was warmth, unwavering and entirely directed at her.

"Nothing is too precious for you," he said simply, the words so soft yet so sure that they stole the air from her lungs. "And this leaves three, one for the christenings of each child?" Maddie snorted at that but caught him smiling.

Again, she didn't know if he was jesting or not.

Hopefully not.

He turned toward the cabinet, retrieving two delicately etched glasses. "These have Thomas's grandfather's initials." The lodge might have been rustic, but clearly, sentiment had nestled itself in every corner.

Before she could argue further, he inserted the corkscrew into the bottle with practiced ease, drawing it out with a gentle pop. He tilted his head slightly, like a silent toast to the room's quiet history, then poured a measure of the deep, ruby-colored wine into one of the glasses.

"Here," he said, extending the glass toward her. "Try it."

Maddie hesitated, her hands clasped tightly in front of her. She shouldn't, she told herself. Not with something that carried so much meaning. But the way he was looking at her—with that quiet mix of hope and intensity, as though sharing this moment with her mattered more than the wine itself—left her powerless to refuse. Slowly, she took the glass, the stem cool against her fingers.

Sebastian filled his own glass, then paused. He held the wine up to the firelight, swirling it gently until the rich liquid caught the flickering ruby glow. "Just… let it breathe a little," he murmured, his voice slightly hushed, as if they were standing in a cathedral rather than a quiet lodge. When he tilted the glass to his nose and inhaled, his eyes fluttered shut for the briefest of moments. "This is the same wine my father poured for my mother the day they were married. If I can share it with you, Maddie…" He opened his eyes, and there was something raw and unguarded in his gaze. "It means a small piece of them can be here with us today."

Her chest tightened, that maddening ache that always came when he veered from his playful flirtations to something honest and unvarnished. She raised her glass to her lips, unsure whether she could trust her voice to form coherent words.

"I know what it means that we're here alone tonight. And I want you to know that I am not taking it easy. Nor will I do anything you don't wish."

Understood.

She nodded more with gratitude than she dared.

The first sip was warmth and richness, tangy on her tongue yet smooth as it settled. Hints of dark berries and something faintly floral lingered after she swallowed, and the sensation was so vivid, so unexpectedly intimate, that she couldn't help but glance up at him.

"Well?" he asked, his lips curving into the gentlest of smiles.

"It's…" She paused, her eyes flicking to the glass in her hand as she struggled for words. "It's extraordinary."

Sebastian's smile deepened, and he lifted his glass. "Cheers."

Maddie tilted her own glass toward his but narrowed her gaze playfully. "Cheers to the disaster or the scandal?"

He paused mid-motion, his brow knitting slightly, though his grin never fully disappeared. "Neither. Cheers to us and what we make of it."

Maddie didn't sip right away. She simply stared at the man

before her, the man who had just handed her a piece of his past as though it were no burden at all. A bottle of wine from his parents' wedding. One of four. One of four, and he chose tonight. Chose her.

Her fingers tightened slightly around the stem of the glass. Her heart gave a quiet, dizzy lurch, not because of romance or scandal or the impropriety of the moment, but because something inside her recognized the intention behind it. It wasn't grand. It wasn't flashy. It was real.

Real was infinitely more terrifying.

She'd been courted before. Flirted with. Admired. But those attentions had always come with caveats. With expectations. With the unspoken understanding that she was being weighed and measured—her dowry, her connections, her usefulness as a wife.

But this?

This was something altogether different. Sebastian hadn't asked anything of her. He'd simply given. Offered. Without condition.

And that was what made her chest ache the most.

Because it meant something.

Because he meant something.

She let out a slow breath, watching as he turned away, casual and composed, as though he hadn't just made her heart pound. He didn't press her, didn't chase her gaze, didn't try to dazzle her with compliments or clever quips. He simply was.

Solid. Present.

He had a way of making the world shrink until it was just the two of them in a snowbound lodge with too much heat between them and not enough distance to cool it.

And Maddie, for once, didn't want distance.

She wanted to savor this, this man who listened, who remembered, who didn't treat her like a passing fancy but like a partner.

She raised her glass, barely a breath behind him, and whispered so low only the fire might've heard her: "To what we make of it."

He smiled and turned and strode to the fireplace.

The quiet confidence of his movements drew her in, the set of his shoulders and the way his profile softened in the firelight. She watched as he crouched, picked up a few logs from the basket, and laid them carefully among the glowing coals, the air filling with the faintest hiss of sap.

"You didn't answer," she said, stepping closer, her glass still in hand.

He spoke without turning, his voice low and rich as the wine itself. "Some moments don't need answers."

The words held weight, as if something unspoken lingered just beneath them, but Maddie wasn't ready to press. Instead, she sank back into her chair, her legs folding beneath her as the fire's warmth enveloped her.

Sebastian, who had straightened to stoke the fire, turned just enough to catch her in that unguarded moment. He paused, the poker still in his hands, his expression unreadable in the half-light. But Maddie saw the way his gaze softened as it passed over her, lingering on her hair that caught the glow of the fire, the curve of her shoulders relaxed in the chair.

For a moment, neither of them spoke. And in the stillness, in the way the flames crackled and the wine glistened in their glasses, Maddie realized that sometimes, words weren't needed at all. What was needed was closeness.

SEBASTIAN LEANED BACK in his chair, one ankle resting casually atop the opposite knee, as the flickering firelight painted warm shadows across his sharp features. Maddie sat opposite him, perched on the edge of her seat as though the world itself hinged on their conversation. Her nervous energy amused him, though he dared not admit it aloud. Instead, he offered her one of his impossibly charming smiles and said with a teasing lilt, "I don't remember agreeing to a courtship."

"You didn't disagree, either," she countered, and her eyes narrowed slightly, though he noticed the faint pink creeping up her cheeks.

"Do you do this often?" she asked, her voice carrying just enough accusation to make him chuckle.

"Courting?" he replied, and his lips pulled into a grin that was far too confident for someone under such scrutiny. "No. Why do you keep asking me these questions?"

"Because I just… can't explain it," Maddie said, her hands fluttering briefly before settling in her lap.

His brows lifted, intrigue sharpening his expression. He leaned forward slightly, studying her. "Explain what, exactly? That I like you? Why is that so impossible to comprehend?"

"It's not… impossible," she said, hesitating. "It's just that it's supposed to be difficult. Complicated. That's why they write books about it."

Sebastian tilted his head, genuinely entertained now. "Books?"

"Yes," she said, a little defensively. "I have one. Well, ahem… I share it. I don't actually own it. We all do."

"By we all," he said slowly, his grin widening, "are you referring to the Bible?"

"No!" she exclaimed, clearly flustered. Her hands twisted together in her lap. "I mean the handbook."

That got him. "The handbook," he repeated, his brow arching as he leaned back just enough to signify his intrigue.

"The Handbook on Seduction and Matters of the Heart." She nodded primly, but he wasn't buying it anymore—there was more to this façade of propriety than she let on. There was fire! And he wanted to stoke it so badly.

But to her credit, she tried to maintain her composure despite the heat creeping up her neck. "It's thick," she said, grimacing at the admission.

"I'm sure it is," Sebastian replied, struggling to keep his tone even. He rested his fingertips against his lips for a moment, feigning thought, though in truth it was to hide an inevitable smirk.

"And yet," she continued, with all the sincerity of someone revealing a state secret, "I don't know what to do. I've read every page. Multiple times. Even... even the ones my friends added. And I still don't know what to do."

Sebastian stilled.

Of all the things she could've said, he hadn't expected that. Not from Maddie, who wielded wit like a rapier and marched into every conversation with her chin lifted and her arguments prepared. She always knew what to do, or at least pretended to, which was almost the same thing.

But this... this honesty?

It hit him square in the chest.

She looked so earnest. Flushed and fidgeting, a bit mortified, but she hadn't lied. She'd handed him a piece of her truth.

And didn't that make him want to kiss her. And want her.

Because he knew how hard it was to admit confusion, to not have the answer when the world expected you to. He'd spent his life filling silences with certainties, offering solutions before people even finished speaking. That was his role. The fixer. The composed one. The one who knew.

But she wasn't looking for someone who always knew.

She was looking for someone who understood.

His throat tightened. Because suddenly, all the teasing felt less like a game and more like a plea. Not for seduction, but for reassurance. For connection. For someone who didn't need her to have it all figured out to want her completely.

He wanted to tell her it was all right not to know. That desire wasn't meant to be neat or scripted or annotated in a shared volume of seduction wisdom. It was messy. Confusing. Terrifying. Beautiful.

And that she didn't need a handbook to be extraordinary at it.

Because she already was.

Already possessed him, and she didn't even know it.

He swallowed hard, dragging his fingers through his hair. His gaze dipped to her hands, still twisted tightly in her lap. Part of him wanted to cover them with his own, to steady the tremble, to offer her the certainty she seemed to be searching for.

But he didn't. Not yet.

"What? Did I suddenly stun you into speechlessness?"

Sebastian tried to stifle the laugh building in his chest, but a cough escaped instead. He wiped at his face, his shoulders shaking slightly from restrained amusement. "You've read the entire thick volume on… seduction and… matters of the heart? Including the 'addendums' your friends contributed?" He coughed, trying to maintain his composure. She was fun!

"Of course I did," Maddie said, her blush deepening as she straightened in her chair. "I'm twenty years old. I cannot afford to be unprepared."

I'd love to help in that regard.

"And yet," he said, tilting his head as though to make a very serious point, "you still don't know what to do?"

"Exactly!" She raised her hands in triumph, clearly believing she'd made her case.

Sebastian shook his head, his grin now utterly unrestrained. "I think, Maddie, that you've just managed to explain yourself and confuse me at the same time."

"What do you mean?" she demanded, her earlier triumph faltering.

"I mean…" He hesitated for dramatic effect, running a hand through his dark hair. "Is it the technical ways of things that have left you uncertain?"

Her blush deepened to a startling crimson. "No. There really wasn't much… on kissing."

"Kissing," Sebastian repeated, rubbing the back of his neck in what might have been mock contemplation. "And yet… you have kissed me?"

"Well, yes," she stammered.

"You did, if I might say, extraordinarily well with that particular skill or lack thereof, whatever you wish to call it to flatter the need for propriety."

She clapped her hands to her face, groaning softly. "Stop," she muttered. "You're being awful."

"Anything else in the handbook I should be aware of?" he teased, leaning forward now, clearly enjoying her discomfort far too much.

"Oh, no!" Maddie exclaimed, shaking her head so vehemently that a few loose curls danced over her shoulders. "You cannot read it! It's secret. What Ashley and Sera put in there… and most recently, Charlene… absolutely not."

He paused, an amused silence stretching between them. "Perhaps," he began, his voice low and warm, "we should try it ourselves."

She blinked. "Try… what?"

"Adding to it."

Maddie's mouth opened and closed before she swallowed hard. "P-p-perhaps," she managed.

Sebastian stood smoothly, his movements unhurried as he stepped closer. She didn't shrink back, though he could see her pulse flutter just beneath the delicate skin of her throat.

"I mean, the scandal or the courtship are inevitable, as you said," he murmured, his voice dropping just slightly, enough to fully captivate her.

"Y-yes," she whispered.

"So," he said, his lips curving into the faintest, most wicked of smiles, "shouldn't we pick the one skill we prefer to work on then?"

Her gaze darted to his, and for a moment, the only sound between them was the crackle of the fire. Sparks flew there too, bright and alive, a perfect echo of the charge that lingered between them, waiting for one of them to lean just a little closer.

But he didn't. Not yet. Instead, he waited for her to make the choice. And that, perhaps, was the most maddening part of all.

✦

Chapter Twenty-Three

S EBASTIAN'S GAZE LINGERED on her as the firelight painted soft, golden hues along her cheeks. Maddie was unusually still, her hands folded in her lap, her eyes fixed on the flames. Icy snow outside and fire inside—she felt like the lodge. And Sebastian was lighting the fire inside for her, too.

Beneath the sturdy beams of the lodge's oiled ceiling wood, with the rich scent of burning wood and the faint edge of wine still hanging in the air, the space between them crackled with something unspoken.

He leaned forward from where he sat on the hearth, his elbow resting casually against his knee. "You're awfully quiet. Shall I be worried?"

Maddie turned her head just slightly, her curls shifting on her shoulders. Her expression was caught somewhere between shy and mischievous. "No," she said softly, though her knee bounced just enough to give her away. "I don't know where to begin my exploration. Research, I suppose. For the book?"

"That sounds unconvincing. I think it's research for yourself."

"Why would I need it?"

"To decide whether this is a scandal or a courtship."

"I already know."

"Which is it then?" He arched a brow and gave that once-over that instantly made her feel as if she were naked.

"Find out for yourself."

"Hmm." He straightened, leaning back on his hands, the careless movement so at odds with the warmth in his eyes. "And here I thought you were concocting some new set of questions to interrogate me with to fill the pages of the handbook with notes."

Her lips parted in mock offense. "Interrogate? I'd hardly call it that."

"No? Perhaps you'd prefer the term cross-examine?" His grin widened as her blush deepened, the rosy hue creeping above the delicate neckline of her dress.

"I can hardly be blamed," she said, lifting her chin. "You've been very difficult to understand."

"Ah, delightful, and yet incomprehensible? The goal of every courtship," he teased with a wink. "What precisely is it about me that requires clarification?"

She hesitated, her teeth catching her bottom lip in a way that completely derailed his composure. The effect she had on him was absurd. Maddie didn't even realize she had all but rendered him a moth darting toward flames.

"Well?" he prompted, his tone deliberately light even as he tensed under her scrutiny.

"It's…" She sighed, her shoulders dropping as though she'd given up the fight. "It's just that when you look at me like that…"

"Like what?" he interrupted, shifting forward just enough to diminish the space between them.

"Like you do," she finished, her voice so quiet he had to strain to catch the words. "I forget all the rules. You make me feel as if I were posing for an artist in the nude."

As soon as the words left her lips, Maddie wanted to claw them back.

Saints, had she truly just compared herself to a nude subject?

The heat that flooded her cheeks had little to do with the fire.

Her heart thudded against her ribs, uneven and wild, because this wasn't her. She wasn't the girl who said brazen, ridiculous things aloud. She wasn't the girl who flirted or teased or bared herself emotionally or otherwise.

But he looked at her like he saw all of it. Every flustered thought. Every unspoken longing. And even more, like he liked what he saw.

For all his practiced charm, the confession made him falter. Sebastian stared at her, the weight of her honesty tugging something deep in his chest. He reached forward, his fingers brushing hers, hesitant at first but firm when she didn't pull away.

"Forget them then," he said simply.

Maddie blinked, startled. "Pardon?"

"The rules," he clarified, his thumb tracing slow circles along the top of her hand. "Forget them."

"You can't just…" She floundered, clearly unprepared for his boldness. "There are rules for a reason."

"Maddie," he said, leaning closer, his deep voice softening to a near whisper. "Would you like to know my opinion of rules?"

Her eyes narrowed, but there was no mistaking the spark of curiosity that danced behind her hesitation. "I suspect I will regret asking," she murmured.

"Likely," he agreed, a smile tugging at the corner of his mouth. "Rules are for the unimaginative."

She gaped at him, her indignation both immediate and wholly charming. "Is this why you're impossible?" she exclaimed, flustered. "Because you just make things up as you go?"

"Not everything," he countered, his grin broadening. "For example, I didn't make you up. You're better than anything I could ever imagine. Ever did imagine. So much better."

There was that once again.

Her expression softened, the teasing air between them shifting just enough to make her pause. "I'm not certain what to do with you," she confessed, her voice so quiet he almost missed it.

His hand tightened gently over hers, the slight pressure sending a current down her arm. "I'll tell you what to do," he said, his smile soft as he tilted his head toward her. "Kiss me."

Her inhale was sharp, her lips forming a small "O" before she caught herself. "You can't just… say things like that."

"Why not?" he asked simply, his fingers sliding to brush the inside of her wrist, where her pulse fluttered wildly against his skin. "You'd rather I say what's expected of me?"

She glanced toward the fire, her eyes catching the light in a way that made his chest ache. "I don't know what I'd rather," she admitted finally. "You… unsettle me."

"Good." The softness of his gaze tempered the heat in his voice. "Unsettling you might be the best thing I've done today."

Her laugh came unbidden, but she quickly stifled it with her hand, shaking her head. "You're infuriating."

"So I've been told." He cocked his head, his hand lifting hers as though testing her weight against his palm. "And yet, you're still leaning closer to me instead of running away."

Maddie opened her mouth to retort, but no words came. Instead, she held his gaze, the silence between them thick and charged, the air between breaths growing faint. His thumb passed over her knuckles once more, a deliberate, questioning motion that pulled her closer in spite of herself.

"What happens," she asked softly, breaking the silence, "when all this… unsettling leads to something we cannot undo?"

Sebastian smiled, slow and knowing, as though her words had given him precisely what he needed. "Then we'll call it a triumph instead of a disaster."

Her lips parted, the simplicity of his answer unraveling the knot in her chest. And when he leaned in, so close she could feel the faint warmth of his breath brushing her cheek, she didn't pull away. For once, Maddie forgot the rules entirely. She forgot the questions, the objections, and the nagging doubts.

And in that moment, there was only Sebastian, impossible, infuriating, and hers for the taking.

SEBASTIAN CARESSED MADDIE'S cheek, the softness of her skin under his touch leaving him breathless. Every detail of her was imprinted in his mind, but this moment was different. Her lips parted slightly, and the shallow rise and fall of her breaths beckoned him closer. That she didn't turn away, didn't shy from him, was a gesture that seemed to say, *Yes.*

Here.

Now.

He kissed her softly, reverently, letting their connection build like the flames in the hearth behind him, burning slow and steady. Then, with gentle confidence, he took her hand and guided it to the side of his neck. Her fingers hesitated against his warm skin, but when he caught her gaze, the trust in his eyes seemed to give her the courage to move. Slowly, her hand slid upward, her fingers threading into his dark hair. Her touch was unsure at first, light and experimental, but then she grew bolder, the tug of her fingers sending a pleasant shiver down his spine.

She was discovering him, bit by bit, and every moment of it felt like a revelation. He kicked off his boots carelessly, never breaking contact with her except to adjust, drawing her closer into his space. His hands skimmed her waist, feeling the dampness of her dress where the snow had soaked through. He stilled, leaning back just enough to look at her.

"Your dress," he murmured, his voice low and roughened by the heat between them. "It's wet."

Maddie blinked, as though waking from a dream. Then understanding dawned. "It needs to dry," she said, her voice no more than a whisper. "Melted snow…"

She turned her back to him and pulled the pins from her hair. Then she let her hair down, a dark mane of the softest curls. Her movements were deliberate, curling her arms slightly as she lowered her head. The mass of her hair shifted as she bent forward, and the line of buttons running down her back stretched taut before him like a challenge. He reached for the first one with a steady hand, his fingers brushing the fine fabric. One button came loose, then another. Each felt like a tiny victory, its release bringing him closer to unraveling the mystery that was Maddie.

The soft popping of the buttons filled the silence between them, echoing like the crackle of the fire. The fabric gave way under his fingers, bit by bit, revealing slivers of skin kissed golden by the flickering light. She shivered once, the barest trace of goosebumps rising beneath his touch, but she didn't pull away.

When the last button was undone, the gown sagged against her, no longer supported by its structure. His hands carefully slipped the fabric from her shoulders, and gravity took over. It fell in a gentle rush, pooling at her feet in a sea of deep hues. For a moment, he didn't move, watching the firelight play across the newly revealed contours of her figure, entranced by the unspoken grace in every line of her.

He reached out, and she confidently placed her hand in his. Together, they stepped her free of the dress, the cool air whispering over her skin. But the chill didn't linger long; the fire was steady, warming the room just as the weight of his gaze seemed to warm her core.

Sebastian stood back slightly, still clasping her hand in his, and began to work the laces of his shirt in silence. The air between them felt taut but not strained, charged yet comforting. He tugged his shirt over his head, discarding it carelessly. A light sheen of firelight played over his chest, his form strong yet softened by the vulnerability he allowed to linger in his expression.

Then came his breeches. His movements were unhurried, as though the moment stretched endlessly before them, full of quiet electricity. He unlaced them with steady hands, stepping free of all of his clothes.

Now they stood together, him bare and her merely in her shift in the warmth of the lodge, the fire crackling steadily, outside snow melting into nothing. The air thrummed with potential, unspoken but deeply felt. For an instant, they neither moved nor spoke, the connection between them saying all that needed to be said. Sebastian, steady and sure, couldn't help the slight, grateful smile that tugged at his lips. Maddie, wide-eyed but fearless, lifted her gaze to his, ready to meet him exactly where they were.

Sebastian held her gaze, his hand still clasped around hers with a steady, protective assurance. The fire cast a golden glow that flickered over the bare planes of his chest and across her delicate frame. She seemed almost weightless in his grasp, her breaths soft and deliberate yet unsteady in the way that made his pulse quicken.

His thumb grazed the back of her hand in a slow, thoughtful motion before he lifted it just slightly, pressing her palm flat against his chest. "You feel that?" he murmured, his voice low and uneven. Beneath her touch, his heart thundered, strong and fast, as though it had no desire to be subtle. "That's because of you."

Her lips parted as she stared at him, her expression a mix of awe and uncertainty. He stepped closer, drawing her hand downward until it rested against the center of his ribcage, her fingers trembling slightly but not pulling away. "Every beat," he continued, his tone soft but deliberate, "it's yours."

For a moment, they simply stood there, caught in the charged stillness of the room. She traced her thumb absently along the curve of his ribs, her movements faint yet deliberate, her hands discovering what words could not articulate. His breath hitched, heat unfurling in his chest as her touch grew surer.

Sebastian tilted his face toward hers, slowly, so as not to startle her. Every move he made felt measured, intentional, allowing her all the space and time in the world to meet him halfway. When her lips softly brushed his in return, he felt a spark strong enough to light every dark place within him.

It was in the tiny, hesitant press of her fingers against his skin, the way her breaths mingled with his, that he could feel her trust blooming. Maddie's fingers crept over his shoulders to anchor herself, and the tentative slide of her touch down his arms made his skin prickle with awareness. He caught her hands mid-motion, tangling his fingers with hers, and drew them to rest at his sides as he leaned his forehead against hers.

"Don't think about what you've read or what you think you don't know, Maddie. You're everything to me. You don't have to be anything but yourself," he murmured, his voice rough around the edges but gentle. "Do you know that?"

She nodded, just barely, her hair brushing the edge of his jaw as she tipped her chin upward. He could feel the strength of her gaze, unwavering now, locking him into her orbit. With a soft hum, he slid one hand along her waist, making a slow path upward until it settled at the nape of her neck, his fingertips playing lightly at the edge of her curls.

The fire crackled in the silence, filling the room with soft, rhythmic warmth, but what seemed louder to him was the measured rise and fall of her breaths. It felt as though the world had narrowed to just this moment, just her, the uneven pulse at the base of her throat marking time in a language they both understood.

Maddie's hands trembled when they landed on his shoulders again, steadying herself against his broad frame. She was light and hesitant at first, but his patient stillness seemed to unravel her caution. Her hands moved upward, brushing his jaw, tracing the stubble along his cheek, her featherlight touch sending sparks through his veins.

He leaned in again, capturing her lips with a fervor that was still restrained, holding back because this moment wasn't one to rush. It was one to savor. Her mouth answered his, unsure but eager, and their shared breaths grew heavier, their rhythm syncing without thought. He could feel the heat radiating between them, her warmth seeping into him like she was stitching herself into the cracks of his armor.

When her lips broke away, it wasn't to pull back but to hover. Her breath ghosted against his jaw, uncertain but close, and then her hand slipped higher, fingers threading through the unruly strands at the base of his neck.

"Maddie," he whispered, his voice catching somewhere between reverence and disbelief. The sound of her name filled not just the space around them but the space within him, solidifying what he hadn't dared to name.

Sebastian felt her breath skim his skin, each exhale light but deliberate, the simplest touch igniting a steady blaze deep inside him. Maddie's mouth lingered just beneath his ear, the warm softness of her lips pressing fleeting, ghost-like kisses along his jawline. Her hesitations seemed to melt away with every fraction of movement, each brush of her lips more purposeful than the last. He could hear the faint rustle of her breath, uneven but filled with a yearning that matched his own.

His hands rested at the curve of her back, the textured fabric of her shift cool beneath his palms. Gently, as though afraid his actions might startle her, he slid his fingers upward, tracing the length of her spine and committing its subtle curve to memory. The shiver that coursed through her body matched the way her fingers lingered briefly at his collarbone before drifting lower, exploring the steady contours of his chest like she had never dared to before.

Guided by instinct, Sebastian tipped his head to the side, planting a succession of tender kisses along the curve of her neck. Her breath hitched in a way that made his blood hum. He allowed himself to linger there, his lips grazing her skin, savoring every delicate sigh that escaped her until he made his way to her soft buds.

"So pink! So perfect!" He groaned with pleasure when he took each nipple in his mouth in turn beneath her shift. He could feel the tremor in her arms as she murmured something indistinct, something that wasn't a word but carried meaning all the same.

She shuffled so that she could pull her last garment off.

He pressed one hand to the small of her back to steady her, the shift of pressure bringing her closer until the warmth of her body fused with his. Slowly, with an almost reverent touch, his other hand traveled to her shoulder, tracing circles against her skin as though to map the points where she softened under his touch. The hum of the fire was the only sound between them, its heat paling in comparison to the way she seemed to unravel beneath his fingers.

Sebastian paused just long enough to lift his gaze to hers, a silent question passing over him like an unspoken vow. Her response wasn't in words but in the way her hands found his face, her palms cradling him with a strength she hadn't displayed moments earlier. Her movements were hesitant no longer; there was certainty in the way her lips sought his, a quiet but determined answer passed between them in the quiet press of her kiss. It wasn't rushed, wasn't demanding. It was patient but thorough, deeply grounding in a way that made the room dim and fade until there was no space left between them.

The rustle of fabric on the small bed in the lodge broke the quiet spell as Sebastian's hand ventured down to find her hip and position her safely under him. His fingers splayed wide, spreading possession and care in equal measure as he guided her closer still. Maddie followed his lead, her movements instinctively mirroring his, until there was no doubt that both of them had chosen to meet in this fragile, unbreakable moment. For an instant, she met his gaze, her eyes shining with emotion he wasn't sure he deserved to see reflected back. She said nothing, but her fingers tightened slightly in his hair. That was as much an answer as he needed.

He drew her closer still, warmth enveloping them as the fire softened the cold that lingered just outside. The world outside seemed a vague and distant thing, eclipsed entirely by the one they were building here in the quiet of this room.

And in some small, unspoken way, they both knew this wasn't just about the moment—it was about every moment to follow.

Chapter Twenty-Four

M ADDIE'S PULSE FLUTTERED, erratic and unsteady, resonating in her ears as though it were the only sound in the room. Her breath hitched, caught in her throat as Sebastian's hands moved against her back, firm yet careful, like he was learning the language of her body and speaking back in quiet, reverent gestures. There was a steady warmth in the room, not from the crackling fire alone but from the nearness of him, the overwhelming presence that filled every space inside of her she didn't realize had been empty.

She tilted her head, her lips brushing Sebastian's jawline, the texture of his stubble sending soft tingles down her nerve endings. She surprised herself with the movement, each small step forward dissolving layers of tension she'd held too long. Every moment felt magnified, every touch carrying a weight she hadn't expected. Her fingers shook slightly as they explored the breadth of his shoulders, tracing the strength beneath his skin, marveling at something that felt both unfamiliar and safe.

Her thoughts swam, disjointed and vivid, as though her senses were taking in too much at once. The faint scent of the firewood mixed with the musk of his skin, earthy and clean, grounding her even as her knees felt weaker beneath her. His breath warmed her temple, each exhale brushing her like a whisper she couldn't quite discern. She closed her eyes, letting every sensation overwhelm her one by one, giving herself permission to feel, to trust.

A low murmur spilled from her lips, unbidden, as Sebastian's hand found its way to her waist, his fingers pressing into the curve with a careful firmness, like he expected her to slip away. But no part of her wanted to retreat. She was barely tethered to herself, floating somewhere between uncertainty and exhilaration, her body responding to his touch with a depth she didn't know she possessed.

When his lips moved to her neck, the fleeting pressures of his kisses sparked sharp threads of warmth that spread outward in ripples. Her hands tightened instinctively on his arms, holding him in place as though she feared the moment would dissolve if she didn't grasp it tightly enough. Each press of his mouth felt deliberate, like a promise unspoken, folding layer upon layer over her reluctance until all that was left was him and the quiet certainty in his steady presence.

Maddie couldn't keep track of time, lost in the gentle rhythm they created together. She felt his grip shift, sliding down her back and settling on her hips, anchoring her with a tenderness that brought a knot of unexpected emotion swelling in her chest. Her breaths seemed to synchronize with his, falling into an instinctive cadence, as if their bodies spoke to each other in their own private language. She tried to focus on the patterns of movement, the delicate slide of his hand against her ribs, the way his touch seemed to anticipate her reactions before she even had a chance to process them.

Every nerve in her body felt alight, humming with a warm, vibrating energy that ebbed and flowed with each movement. Her skin seemed to come alive under the path of his hands, her sense of self shifting inward, turning entirely toward him. She felt exposed, not just physically, but in the soft way his gaze rested on hers, like he wasn't looking at her but into her. That realization sent her heart into a tumbling rhythm, and she wasn't sure if the heat she felt was from the room, his nearness, or the emotions cracking open inside her.

When his hands gently guided her hips, her breath caught again, the subtle motion more powerful than she could have prepared for. There was no rush in him, no haste to move faster than she was ready for. It was maddeningly patient, that deliberate care, drawing her into a trust she hadn't quite realized she was ready to give. Her body answered before her mind could catch up, leaning into the path his hands set for her, letting herself fall into the unspoken rhythm he created for them both.

Maddie's mind buzzed with the sheer intensity of the moment, sensations and emotions blending together so intricately she couldn't separate them. She felt the press of his forehead against hers, his warmth bleeding into her own, the small gesture grounding her in ways words never could. She was vaguely aware of the sound of her own breathing, heavier now, mingling with his in the quiet between the crackle of the fire. Somewhere in that quiet, she felt something change, her grip slipping from hesitation into something almost fierce, like she couldn't hold herself back anymore.

When her lips found their way to his again, it wasn't hesitation or uncertainty that guided her, but a confidence born of the trust he'd built in her. She kissed him deeply, wholly, pouring an unspoken truth into every movement, her heart hammering in her chest as though it might leap out entirely. She felt him steady her once more, his arms wrapping fully around her this time, enveloping her in a security that felt as fragile as it was unshakeable.

Her fingers moved of their own accord, slipping up the back of his neck and curling into his hair, the texture coarse yet familiar under her fingertips. She felt the muscles in his shoulders shift and flex with every subtle motion, a physical reminder of the strength he held and the gentleness with which he offered it to her.

He groaned a few times and then stiffened for an instant. He pushed into her with a vigor, squeezed his eyes shut and then let out a roar that surprised and flattered her in equal measure.

She was frightened, but not of him—not of this. It was the flood of raw, unbridled emotion shaking her to her core that startled her, the truth of her own feelings rushing forward faster than she could brace for. But even in her fear, she found stability in the way he slowed for her, his movements deliberate, his focus entirely on her.

"I love you," he murmured against her cheek, his voice steady but low, as if he already understood the chaos of emotions she tried to contain. The assurance in those words settled deep in her, rooting her to the moment and to him.

Her body responded as though it understood that everything he offered was hers to take. Each movement felt smoother, more certain, as though the quiet intimacy of their connection had eased away her reservations. Every touch, every brush of his hand, built a momentum that swirled through her until she felt utterly weightless in his arms.

There was a rhythm between them now, a synchrony that needed no words to define. Maddie felt herself sink further into it, surrendering pieces of herself she hadn't been able to imagine giving before. She wasn't sure when it had happened, when she had decided to open the locked doors of her heart, but with his hands on her, gentle and steady, it didn't feel like a decision. It felt inevitable.

Her world narrowed to just him, each breath, each soft caress tethering her more tightly to the moment. There was something freeing in it, her mind finally letting go as she felt confident in each choice he made, in each place his hands guided her. She didn't need to think, only feel—to trust that somehow he already knew how to catch her if she fell.

Her heart swelled as the words he'd said earlier lingered in the back of her mind. *I love you.* He'd told her, and she realized now, with a startling clarity, that all the pieces of herself she felt might shatter were held together now—with him beside her, filling the quiet spaces she hadn't even known were falling into place.

※※※※※

IF SEBASTIAN HAD known an avalanche might lead to this moment, he would have prayed for one sooner. He lay on his side, one arm curled under Maddie's shoulders, the other resting across the slope of her waist. Her breath warmed the space beneath his collarbone. Proof that this moment, this impossible, beautiful moment, was real.

And he was in it.

Still inside it.

Still inside her.

How many times had he imagined her like this? Tangled in his arms, flushed with trust, her limbs boneless and satisfied and draped over his like a sleepy cat who'd decided he made a fine piece of furniture?

But this was no idle fantasy. This was her. Maddie. Glorious, clever, maddening Maddie. In all her bold laughter and open expressions. The woman who challenged him without effort, who'd once called him insufferable and sneezed in his direction like it was a perfectly acceptable punctuation to conversation.

He adored her.

He *loved* her.

He wanted to tell her. Say the words again, louder, clearer, with the sort of recklessness bellow that belonged to men who didn't care if their world burned so long as they got to go down smiling. But they had tons of time in the future.

She stirred.

A shift in breath. A twitch of her fingers against his chest. Then a quiet sigh, muffled against his skin.

He tilted his head, just enough to glance down at her face. Her hair was rumpled, her expression soft and flushed, her eyelids sleepy.

He couldn't stop the smile that tugged at his lips.

"How's your body feeling?" he asked gently, brushing a curl

from her cheek with the back of his knuckle.

Her eyes cracked open, lashes fluttering.

Then she blinked up at him.

"My body," she said, voice thick with the aftermath of pleasure, "is considering writing you a thank-you note."

Sebastian chuckled. "Should I be flattered or concerned?"

"Both." She nudged him with her knee beneath the blankets. "There may be footnotes."

He grinned and leaned down, pressing a kiss to her bare shoulder. "Footnotes? You wound me. I prefer glowing declarations, possibly carved in stone."

"This will have to do." She shifted closer and tucked herself under his chin like it was the most natural thing in the world.

He chuckled.

"I've rather lost feeling in my thighs."

His brow shot up. "Should we get up? Or was that just a compliment?"

She groaned and buried her face against his chest. "You're impossible."

"And yet, here you are. In my arms. Debauched beyond repair."

"Scandalized," she agreed with a sigh. "Utterly ruined."

He hummed. "Then I'm afraid we shall have to marry."

She lifted her head at that, one brow arching high. "Is this your version of a proposal?"

"No," he said, teasing, even though a part of him was not. "This is my version of a threat."

Her thumb brushed slowly against his skin. Once. Twice. Thoughtful little sweeps, like she was mapping all the lines into her memory.

"I don't know what happens next," she said at last, her voice barely above a whisper. "When we walk out of this lodge. When someone finds us."

"I know I'm not going to walk away from you."

Sebastian exhaled, slow and deep. Relief—unexpected and

unfiltered—settled through him.

He brushed his lips against the crown of her head. "Then it's done."

She tilted her face upward. "You make it sound like a treaty has been signed."

"It's possible I've never been more terrified of losing a war," he murmured.

A small smile curved her lips. "This is not a war."

"Isn't everything in love a war?"

She chuckled. "Sebastian."

"What? I've just battled my way into your bed, your affection, and your future."

She snorted. "Believe whatever you wish."

"What can I say? I take after my mother. She always said one must secure the strategic advantage before someone else makes a claim."

"Oh dear," she sighed dramatically. "I'm bedding a man with battlefield logic."

"Not just bedding," he said, nipping her ear gently, "lounging, entwining, and thoroughly seducing."

"That sounds exhausting," she said, clearly not sounding exhausted at all. "No wonder I can't feel my legs."

"Then you'll simply have to remain in my arms and allow me to carry you around."

"Of course."

She laid her head back against his chest, and her voice, when it came again, was softer.

"What if it's not enough?"

He stilled.

"What if we leave this place," she continued, "and everything changes? What if the world looks at us and decides we don't belong together?"

Sebastian let the question settle between them.

Then, slowly, he lifted her hand and pressed a kiss to her knuckles.

"Then the world can go to… argh," he said. Then he stilled and exhaled. "I love you so much."

"I love you, too," she whispered back.

Sebastian pulled her fully against him, one hand stroking up and down her back with slow, steady strokes.

They lay like that for a long while, no words needed.

"We'll figure it out, won't we?"

He nodded, pressing a kiss to her temple. "Yes. Together."

Chapter Twenty-Five

SEBASTIAN STOOD TALL, despite the ache in his shoulders and the lingering chill in his limbs. His gaze rested on Maddie as she adjusted the blankets around herself, her cheeks still rosy with the remnants of her earlier embarrassment. The corners of his mouth lifted in a smile he didn't bother to hide. She was beautiful, even more so when flustered. Especially when she was his.

"So," Thomas said, breaking Sebastian's thoughts. His boots creaked against the wooden floor as he crossed his arms. "This is serious, then?"

Sebastian didn't hesitate, his voice steady and firm. "Most certainly so."

Thomas studied him for a moment before nodding, a faint smile tugging at his lips as he turned toward the door. Outside, the snow shimmered in the early morning light, the aftermath of the storm sparkling like softened diamonds.

"You've never looked at anyone like that," Thomas said finally. "Not even food when you're starved."

Sebastian's mouth twitched. "Are you comparing my woman to food?"

"I wouldn't dream of it.

"Don't forget you are the one who suggested the use of the

lodge."

"Yes, yes, this is all my fault. You can thank me by naming your firstborn after me."

Sebastian snorted. "Don't hold your breath."

He turned back briefly, his gaze flicking to Maddie as she tucked a lock of hair behind her ear. A firstborn… the word brought a burn to his chest. A good burn. A burn that he refused to let go now that it settled there.

Thomas followed his gaze, then elbowed him lightly. "You're gone."

He didn't argue. "It appears so."

Thomas's voice lowered. "Just… don't break her. And don't let her break you."

"She's not the one I need to worry about."

Don't break her. Don't let her break you.

The words clung to him like mist, seeping into the cracks he hadn't known still existed. He hadn't broken her, in fact, he felt as though she'd been the one to piece him back together.

He hadn't been prepared for that.

Nothing had readied him for Maddie.

And he—saints help him—had fallen for her just as completely.

What if she changed her mind?

What if the world got to her first?

Sebastian exhaled, the thought cutting swift and clean. If she asked him to walk away for her sake, he didn't know if he'd be strong enough to do it.

But he'd never let her face the aftermath alone.

That much, he could promise.

Sebastian stepped into the crisp air while Thomas busied himself with mounting his horse. His attention was immediately drawn to another familiar figure, one that stirred something warm in his chest.

"Swan," he said gently, his voice carrying across the snow-dappled clearing. The horse perked up at the sound of her name, and Sebastian's smile deepened. "I'm glad you got away safely, old friend."

Behind him, Maddie stepped into the doorway, pulling her cloak tighter as she watched the exchange. He turned, catching the faint arch of her brows, her expression curious and just a touch amused.

"Ready?" he asked, brushing her hair from her face as she stepped closer.

Her gaze flicked up to his, uncertain. "Not even slightly."

He leaned in, their faces nearly level. "Then I'll hold on tighter."

A vow.

Without a word, he set a hand lightly on her waist. His touch lingered, warm and deliberate, before he wrapped both hands around her and effortlessly lifted her onto Swan's saddle. It wasn't like before, when he'd been careful, distancing himself from her as much as propriety would allow. There was no reason for pretense now. Not when her safety and trust rested so completely in his hands.

She settled on the saddle, looking down at him with a mix of bewilderment and something he very much hoped was admiration. He mounted behind her, his arms loose but steady as they framed her on either side. Swan shifted under their combined weight, but Sebastian whispered a soft word to the horse, calming her instantly.

She looked straight ahead as they set off, Thomas leading the way at a leisurely pace. Yet, Sebastian couldn't miss the way her back stiffened, her thoughts obvious in the tension she carried. He suspected he knew where her mind had gone.

"Why are you not more concerned?" she asked suddenly, her voice breaking the spell of the silent morning. "The Earl of Linsey caught us. I should..." She trailed off, her words heavy with unspoken consequences. "I should feel embarrassed. Scandal awaits. There's surely some significance to that, but you act as if all were in order."

Sebastian's lips tilted into a faint smirk. "Caught?" His arms tightened slightly around her as Swan picked up a steadier rhythm against the snow. "You aren't caught, Maddie," he said, the warmth of his words brushing against her ear, "unless you believe you are."

"Whatever do you mean?" He had lost his mind. Of course, they were caught. Scandalized. She was compromised most thoroughly.

She shifted within his hold, glancing back at him, her eyes searching for something he couldn't entirely define. But instead of holding her gaze, he simply leaned forward the barest amount, adjusting the way the cloak settled against her shoulders.

"Are you sure you're warm?" he murmured, his tone soft, almost tender.

"Sebastian? What are we going to do?"

"A hot bath, I hope. Fresh clothes. Or perhaps no clothes, and we share the hot bath?"

"Seb—"

But before she could continue, he gave her that smile—the one that melted her heart. She had no chance.

"Maddie, there won't be any scandal if we merely announce our engagement. I need no more than a ride to London to get a special license."

"It has to come from the Archbishop of Canterbury. Surely it's not that easy!"

"His nephew was in my class at Eton. And then at Oxford." Sebastian smiled. "It won't take long if I tell him I found the woman I love, and she agreed to marry me."

The color rose in her cheeks again as she quickly turned away, leaving him with a view of the curve of her neck, her face tipped toward the horizon. His own expression softened as they rode behind Thomas, Maddie resting against him, her warmth melding seamlessly with his. To Sebastian, there was nothing to be concerned with. Nothing at all. Because as far as he was concerned, he already had everything that mattered pressed close against him.

MADDIE'S HEART FLUTTERED as they approached the sprawling silhouette of the castle, its grand spires piercing the grayish-blue sky like sentinels of a world she didn't feel worthy of reentering. It stood proud and unchanging, its stone facade glowing faintly in the morning light. And yet, every clop of Swan's hooves against the gravel path sent a pang of unease through her, pulling her further from the cocoon of warmth she'd felt just minutes ago with Sebastian's arms around her.

At the castle gates, she tried to hold her head high as Thomas and Sebastian flanked her, their presence as steady as it was commanding. They escorted her like she was a princess in some gilded tale, but Maddie couldn't shake the weight settling in her belly. The closer they came to the reality of the grand estate, the smaller, less deserving, she felt. She smoothed her skirts absently, as though wrinkled fabric could undo what had already been done.

"I'll bring the horses to the stables," Thomas declared, drawing his horse to a stop. He looked across to Sebastian. "A beer?"

Sebastian shook his head. "Not now. I want to see to Maddie's comfort."

Thomas tilted his head, the faintest trace of a frown tugging at the corners of his mouth before he dismounted. "Allow me to be clear, then. Ashley will see to her comfort." His tone hardened just slightly, the weight of authority unmistakable. "You and I— we need a word." He gestured toward the stables, his meaning sharp and impossible to argue.

Maddie glanced toward Sebastian, her chest tightening at the tension threading between the two men. She gave him a small, reassuring look, doing her best to convey gratitude and understanding without saying a word. For a moment, his expression softened, the strong planes of his face easing. Then, in a move so gentle it stole her breath, he leaned forward and pressed a small kiss to her cheek. Just a peck.

But to Maddie, it might as well have been the sweep of an orchestra's strings. The joy of it pulsed through her veins, carrying her into the house as though on the wings of a cloud. Over the threshold she floated, past the butler with his polite nod, past the scurrying maids chattering as they rushed toward the dining room. Every step forward wrapped her tightly in the warmth of Sebastian's presence—even as he stayed behind. She barely noticed…

Until she stopped dead.

"Oh no!" she whispered, one gloved hand flying to her mouth.

Her mother's voice rang out like the crack of a pistol. "Darling, there you are, finally!" The cloyingly sweet tone struck dread deeper than any shouted reprimand could. Maddie turned slowly, and there she was, standing framed in the grand entryway of the dining room. Lady Elizabeth Hunt, perfectly coiffed and radiant in a lavender gown, was flanked on either side by her brother and—Maddie swallowed hard—her father.

Ashley, who followed, sent her an apologetic look.

Maddie's heart sank lower with each growing detail of the arrival of her family. Her brother, stoic but quiet, met her gaze first, his assessing eyes flicking over her disheveled state. Her father's gaze lingered on the wrinkled bodice of her gown and the smudge of dirt on her hem. But it was her mother's face that drained Maddie of all joy. It lit with a pleased smile at finding her missing daughter… only to freeze with what could only be called horror.

"Madeleine Sophie Charlotte Hunt!" The full weight of Maddie's name fell with a crushing thud, her mother's voice rising into notes that almost shattered the crystal chandelier above. "Where have you been?!"

"In…" Maddie stumbled over her words, her mouth dry as panic loosened its vines in her chest. "I was… caught in an avalanche."

Her father's brows furrowed, his sharpness cutting through the chaos of her mother's shrill tone. Maddie saw the way his eyes fastened on her wrinkled cloak, the state of her boots, and the streak of mud across the hem of her gown. He said nothing, but the silence was somehow worse.

"You almost died?" her father asked.

"Not almost. But close." Maddie winced as she spoke.

She clutched the folds of her cloak tighter, her cheeks burning as figures began emerging from the nearby halls, lingering just out of direct sight but close enough to witness. Worse still was the silhouette behind her father.

The Duke of Paisley.

"Oh no," Maddie croaked under her breath, the discomfort washing over her like a tidal wave. Her shoulders drew inward as Paisley's familiar, yet detached expression appeared. His dark hair was perfectly groomed, and his polished presence made her feel even more bedraggled. He glanced at her, his gaze flickering briefly to her tangled state before it returned to her father.

Ashley stepped forward just as Maddie felt her knees begin to buckle. Her brother reached for her elbow in a move so swift, she could hardly believe he wasn't chastising her. "If you'll excuse us," Ashley said quickly, her calm voice slicing through their mother's outrage. "Maddie needs rest. She's had an ordeal."

"An ordeal?" Their mother's mouth hung open, aghast, as Ashley began leading Maddie up the grand staircase. "Ashley, what do you mean, an ordeal? We are not finished! Do you know how this looks?"

Maddie caught one last glimpse of her mother's wide, pale face, her father exchanging terse words with Paisley, before she was ushered out of sight and into the quieter upper floors.

She exhaled shakily, attempting to regain a hint of composure, but every inch of her screamed the truth she could no longer bury. The truth her appearance had likely given away without a word. She was well and truly ruined, and no amount of skipping steps on the stairs could lift the horror of it.

Chapter Twenty-Six

S EBASTIAN CLUTCHED THE reins of his horse, helpless as he
watched the scene unfold before him. He wanted to reach for
Maddie, but he couldn't. He could only clutch the reins tighter.

His knuckles blanched beneath his gloves. Swan shifted beside him, sensing his agitation. But he barely registered it. All he saw was Maddie, her shoulders drawn inward, her face going pale, her mother's voice slicing through the winter air like a blade polished in scorn.

Darling, there you are, finally!

It should've been a relief. It sounded like relief. To anyone else, it might have even passed for maternal joy.

But not to him.

Not when he saw Maddie's body jolt, as if struck. Not when her chin dipped the slightest inch and her hand, saints, her hand, flew to her mouth in a gesture of dread so pure it nearly gutted him.

He couldn't move. Couldn't breathe.

Each time she brushed her skirts down with a nervous energy that scraped something raw in his chest.

She didn't look at him. Not once. And Sebastian had the nagging thought that his mother might just be a harridan of the worst sort. Still, he had promised Maddie he would stay, and he would.

He should've blocked her from her family. Should've taken the lash of her mother's tongue himself if it spared Maddie even a second of humiliation. But he knew she wouldn't appreciate that in this moment.

Saints, even the way her mother blasted her name made his skin crawl.

Madeleine Sophie Charlotte Hunt!

A war drum.

Sebastian's jaw locked.

He knew that tone. Had heard it in parlors and ballrooms, dressed in silk and smiles, but no less cruel for the mask it wore. It was the voice of the Ton when a girl stepped out of line. When she didn't behave. When she dared to feel. To want.

And Maddie—his Maddie—stood right in the center of it.

She spoke. Something about an avalanche. Her voice trembled—ah, her voice. But she was trying. He could hear it in every syllable, every shaky breath. Trying to explain and make sense of something senseless to people who would never understand. At least, he saw no understanding on her family's faces.

Should a father not have pulled his daughter into his arms? And her mother? Should she not have cared less about what it looked like and more about the fact that his daughter had survived? Her brother. No words.

Sebastian's grip turned brutal. The leather reins bit into his palm. His horse nickered softly, shifting again, but he didn't loosen his hold.

And Paisley…

Sebastian's breath left him in a quiet, vicious hiss.

The man only worked on his nerves.

He didn't need to see the man's expression to know what it would be. The look of a man who'd already calculated how this moment could serve him.

If Lady Ashley hadn't intervened, he would have stepped up and carried her off, consequences be damned.

It was the first moment Sebastian breathed. Not fully. Not deeply. But enough. Enough to keep him from marching into the hall and dragging Maddie back into his arms like a lunatic. But he could only stare helplessly as Maddie left, leaving her stunned mother and scowling family behind.

And him.

It all happened so fast, as if he entered a dream. But not like at the lodge. A nightmare.

Confound it.

He needed a plan.

Not a fight.

How many years had she spent learning to swallow her voice just to survive?

The reins creaked under his grip again.

He hadn't protected her from this. Hadn't even prepared her for the storm they were riding into. But he would. Starting now. Even if he had to smile through gritted teeth and shake the devil's hand to do it.

She was going to walk out of this house with her head held high. As his. And no one—absolutely *no one*—was going to make her feel unworthy again.

Not if he had breath left in his body.

Because if there was one thing he knew now with unrelenting clarity, it was this: he wasn't leaving this place without her. Not as a memory. Not as a mistake. Not as the girl who slipped through his fingers because he couldn't hold his ground in front of her mother.

He needed to secure her as soon as possible.

Thomas cleared his throat behind them. "A beer?"

Sebastian didn't even glance his way. "Not now. I want to see to Maddie's comfort."

It wasn't a lie. It was just the wrong truth.

What he meant—what he couldn't quite say aloud at the moment—was that he couldn't bear to be apart from her just yet. That every second she stood within arm's reach felt like borrowed grace, and the moment he let her go, the world would snap back into shape and remind him that he was not the one in control.

Thomas's pause was pointed. The words that followed even more so.

"Allow me to do you a favor then and forbid it. Ashley will see to her comfort. You and I need a word."

A thousand things surged behind Sebastian's ribs. Irritation. Defensiveness. Resentment. But also understanding. With a muttered curse, and a nod to her family, he followed Thomas toward the stables.

Thomas shook his head. "Are you mad?"

"Define mad."

"Mad as in unthinking. Reckless. Impulsive. Stupid. Shall I continue? Did you see the look on her mother's face when you said that?"

He hadn't been thinking about her mother. "Sadly, I missed it."

Thomas barked out a note of laughter. "What am I going to do with you?"

Sebastian wondered that himself.

MADDIE COLLAPSED ONTO the plush bed, the familiar silk coverlets cool against her back. She stretched her arms above her head, letting out a long, satisfied sigh as the scent of leather and horse drifted up from her wrinkled cloak. Swan, not Sebastian. A stab of disappointment knifed through her. Still, her smile refused to fade at the memory of Sebastian's body pressed on hers.

And horror.

Still lots of horror.

What was her mother doing here? Her whole family, for that matter? This was not good. Not good at all! Embarrassment aside, she should look like a woman fully loved, right? There was no way her mother missed that?

Ashley crossed the room briskly, her skirts brushing over the polished floor as she rang the small bell near the door. "What, exactly, happened to you?" she asked, her voice sharp with equal parts concern and exasperation.

Maddie pushed thoughts of her mother aside for now and sighed. "Oh, it was wonderful!" She flopped onto her side, her head propped on her palm, and gazed up at her wide-eyed friend. "He's wonderful."

Ashley's brow creased with suspicion. "Have you been hit on the head?" she asked bluntly. "He's not at all wonderful!" Ashley sniffed. "You were in an avalanche, weren't you?"

"Oh yes." Maddie kicked her feet lazily, her boots swinging just above the floor. "It fell right on me. On us. And do you know what he did?" Her voice fell into a dreamy lilt. "He threw himself over me, Ashley. To save my life. To shield me from the snow. Making sure I could breathe. Isn't he marvelous?"

Ashley's lips parted in disbelief, but before she could respond, there was a soft knock at the door. A maid entered, curtsying swiftly before waiting for instructions.

"She needs a hot bath," Ashley ordered, her voice clipped but polite. "And something to eat, please."

The maid nodded and disappeared through the adjoining door that led to the shared bath. Maddie's gaze followed her absently because she still felt as though Sebastian's arms were holding her on top of Swan in a cocoon of love.

"Where are Charlene and Sera?"

"Oh, they are with Rotheworth in town. They don't know yet." Ashley's cool hand pressed against Maddie's forehead, pulling her back to the present. "You sound feverish," Ashley said, frowning. "Are you quite well?"

"I've never been better," Maddie sang, brushing Ashley's hand away. She sat up with enthusiastic energy and clapped her hands like a child anticipating a great treat. Her fingers found the buttons of her cloak, and she fumbled with them, too lightheaded with happiness to bother with her usual grace.

Ashley watched her friend, her expression tight, as if she were examining the edges of a precariously hung painting. "Your mother is settling things downstairs. It's chaos," she said, eyes narrowing. "I don't understand how you can be so calm."

Maddie shrugged, the corners of her mouth twitching upward. "I'm calm because everything will be all right. Even better than all right." So long as she didn't think about her mother bellowing up a storm downstairs.

Ashley folded her arms, clearly unconvinced. "What do you mean?"

"Sebastian went to school with the nephew of the Archbishop of Canterbury," Maddie said, a half-mischievous glint in her eye. "It will take virtually no time at all to get a special license."

Ashley's frown deepened. "For whom?"

Maddie blinked, momentarily thrown by the question, before shaking her head with an indulgent smile. "For us, of course."

Ashley stiffened, confusion plain on her face. "But why? Your wedding is in March. It's all arranged."

"March?" Maddie laughed lightly. "That's two months away."

"Exactly," Ashley said, raising a brow. "The banns need to be read. Richard was very clear about the requirements."

"Not if we have a special license," Maddie countered, her voice lilting with certainty. She leaned forward, her gaze narrowing slightly. "But why March? And how does Mother know?" Why Richard, the Duke of Paisley?

The maid returned, trailing another behind her with a steaming jug of water. Both curtsied quickly as they set about pouring the heated water into the bath, their presence barely registering to Maddie as unease crept into her thoughts, casting doubt over her earlier euphoria. "Why March, Ashley?" she pressed, her voice softer now, almost trembling. Something wasn't right.

Ashley hesitated, an uncharacteristic uncertainty flashing in her eyes before she drew a breath. "Because he accepted the dowry. They've set the date."

Maddie shook her head, confusion clouding her features. "What are you talking about?" The words felt hollow, dread curdling her stomach.

Ashley's voice dropped as she leaned in close enough that only Maddie could hear her. "The Duke of Paisley. He agreed to it, Maddie. Your mother and father finalized everything. The dowry is being transferred... I thought—" she trailed off briefly, swallowing hard. "I thought it was what you wanted. To be the Duchess of Paisley."

Maddie's world narrowed to just her spinning thoughts and the words that seemed to echo too loudly in her ears. The light-headed giddiness she'd been basking in dissipated like smoke, replaced with the sharp, cold sting of reality. Her chest ached, her lungs struggling to draw in air as the full weight of what Ashley had just revealed sank in.

"No." The word was barely audible, a hollow whisper spoken more to herself than her friend. "No, no, no."

Ashley reached out, but Maddie recoiled, sliding quickly off the bed to put the weight on her still-wobbling feet. Her back pressed against the post nearest the bed, her knuckles going white where they clutched it. The warmth Sebastian had wrapped her in earlier was gone now, stolen by the knowledge of what her family had done. What they thought they'd done to secure her future.

What they'd done to ruin her luck.

SEBASTIAN LED THE horses to the stable yard, his grip tight on the reins, each step deliberate as if holding back a storm. The air stung with the bite of leftover frost, and the horses' breath puffed in little clouds as they snorted and tossed their heads. Stableboys rushed forward to take the reins. He handed them over with a brief nod, but the tension pulling at his shoulders didn't ease.

"In there," Thomas commanded abruptly, jerking his head toward the brewery door. His voice carried the unyielding edge of authority, adding weight to an order that wasn't open for debate.

Sebastian followed, the crack of his boots against the stone loud in the cold quiet. Inside, the faint, earthy scent of hops mingled with the woodsmoke from the nearby hearth. Thomas shut the door behind them with more force than necessary before whirling to face him, his face tight with simmering frustration.

"What did you think you were doing?" Thomas snapped, his glare as sharp as flint.

Sebastian straightened, drawing himself up to his full height. His gaze didn't waver. "You hardly have to ask me that, do you?" he replied, his voice even, low, and raw with conviction.

"It's absolutely absurd," Thomas growled as he ran a hand through his disheveled hair. The gesture did little to tame his frustration. "I can't believe you could be so stupid!"

"You've put your entire future at risk," he continued, voice rising. "You interfered with the duke's arrangement. Paisley's not just some spoiled heir—he has ties to Whitehall. Influence that reaches into Parliament. If this blows up, it won't be her reputation that's ruined—it'll be yours."

Sebastian took a step forward, the composure in his expression cracking just enough for a brief flicker of anger to show. "Stupid, you say?" His words rolled out steady but firm, layered with restrained heat. "Why? Because I found the woman who makes me happy? Because I did what needed to be done to save her under that vicious avalanche?"

"That's not what I'm saying!" Thomas snapped, exasperation flaring in his voice.

"Well, what are you saying?" Sebastian demanded, his voice cutting through the air like steel slicing wood. "The avalanche buried us so deep I didn't think we'd come out of it alive. And you have the gall to criticize me now?" He stopped, drawing in a deep breath as the memory clawed at him. "You don't know what it's like until you're under there. You don't know how to crawl out."

Thomas's jaw tightened, but his voice dropped in volume, tinged with a shaky restraint. "Oh, I remember. I was fourteen, not stupid," he said, grabbing a pint glass and filling it from a barrel. He took a long, hard swig, his throat working as he swallowed. "You saved us then, too."

Sebastian's shoulders relaxed a fraction as the memory washed over him. He crossed his arms, his gaze steady on Thomas. "And when I saved you, something changed. I realized you'd be my best friend forever. My brother. My family. It was no different with Maddie." His voice softened—not weak but weighted with something unshakable. "I want her to be my family. My everything."

Thomas lowered his mug, though his hand stayed firm on the handle. "Maddie, hm?" he said, though his tone was quieter now. He took another swig, tilting the pint glass back further than before.

"Yes," Sebastian said. His voice was clear, steady as stone. "I love her. And you should know that." He hesitated, a rare flicker of vulnerability appearing before he continued with a brow raised. "You and Ashley… you didn't wait, either."

At that, Thomas froze. His shoulders squared, though he didn't immediately respond. The words hung in the air until he finally said, "Yes. Ashley and I… before the wedding. Fine. Obviously." He glanced away for a moment, his jaw tightening. "But you shouldn't have!"

"Why not me?" Sebastian shot back. The heat in his voice didn't crest to shouting, but the force behind his words made it clear he wasn't holding himself back. He crossed the room in a few long strides, grabbing his own pint and filling it quickly. "I'll get a special license. We'll be wed." Releasing a sudden breath, he dropped down onto a wooden bench, the worn corner of his pint clinking against the table. "I can't wait. Never thought I'd say that. Never thought I'd be so... eager for a wedding."

Thomas slammed his pint down on the table. It wasn't hard enough to break it, but the impact was sharp enough to make Sebastian's head whip up.

"Well, the problem isn't you or her," Thomas said, his words colder now, as if rehearsed. "The problem is, it's already a done deal."

Sebastian stiffened, the warmth of his thoughts snapping into cold focus. "A done deal?"

Thomas's mouth pressed into a thin line. "Her parents transferred the dowry. They've promised her to Paisley."

The words struck like a blow to the ribs—unexpected and breath-stealing. For a brief moment, he didn't move. The pint sat idle in his hand, forgotten. When he finally moved, it was slow, deliberate. He set the glass down gently, the scrape of it against the table breaking the heavy silence.

"To Paisley," Sebastian repeated, his voice a half-growl of disbelief. He stood, the movement fluid but carrying a weight that seemed to pull the air out of the room. His brows pulled together, and his chest rose as he inhaled deeply, his fists relaxing and clenching in rhythm.

"Yes, to Paisley," Thomas said, equally slow but firm. "That's how these things work."

Sebastian shook his head, his jaw set tight. "Not for us. Not for Maddie," he said, his voice dropping lower, conviction anchoring every syllable. "I don't care about their arrangements. Their dowry." He stepped toward Thomas, no more anger than before, but plenty of unrelenting resolve. "If Paisley thinks she's his, he'll have to go through me."

The corner of his mouth lifted faintly, but there was no humor in it. His next words came like a thunderclap. "And he'll regret it."

"Or you will."

Thomas didn't say it like a threat. Just a truth. And that made it worse.

⤜⟫⟫⟫⟪⟪⟪⤛

"I CANNOT BELIEVE your mother betrothed you to Paisley!"

Sera's outrage exploded through the room, sharp and immediate, making Maddie wince.

She couldn't believe it either. "I think," Maddie said faintly, lowering herself to sit on the edge of the bed, newly changed into warmer clothes, "I am still in shock."

Her sleeves were thick, but her fingers remained stiff and numb. The chill that had left her while wrapped in Sebastian's arms had returned the moment they'd stepped into the castle. Her whole body was cold, in fact. A cold no fire could shake. But even so, "shock" felt too small a word. It was disbelief wrapped in betrayal, wrapped in helpless fury.

"Dear," Charlene said, gliding to her side and taking her hand, "you are more than in shock. You are in a state of emotional ruin. Has anyone brought you sweet milk?"

"I'm not pregnant, Charlene."

"No, but you're promised to Paisley, which is far worse."

"I resent that comment," Ashley muttered from the side.

Charlene shook her head. "You know I didn't mean it that way."

"I'm not promised. I didn't say yes. I will not marry Paisley," Maddie declared, the words low but unshakable—as much for herself as for anyone else. No matter what.

"Well, your mother can't very well engage you to the duke, right? Not without the permission of your father."

Charlene sat back, visibly impressed. "That's... actually rather brilliant, Sera."

Sera preened. "Thank you. I do have moments."

Maddie let the thought settle in her mind. Her father. Right. His mother's word usually held supreme. He rarely raised his voice—rarer still did he raise objections—but he had always, always, wanted Maddie to be happy.

"He'll side with you," Ashley said softly, nodding. "You are his favorite child."

Maddie swallowed around the lump forming in her throat. "He might. If he's not already been flattened beneath Mother's momentum."

"He is a man," Sera said. "He has rights. And opinions. Somewhere. Likely buried beneath a stack of botanical journals, but they're there."

That earned a reluctant curve of Maddie's lips. Just barely, but it counted.

Charlene leaned in, eyes imploring. "You can't let your mother steamroll you into this. Not when your heart—and your body—are already somewhere else."

Her cheeks warmed. "I didn't say it was."

"You didn't need to," Charlene replied knowingly.

Sera waggled her brows. "Speaking of your heart and body's current residence… have you told Sebastian any of this?"

Maddie hesitated.

Sera groaned. "Maddie."

"I haven't left the room yet, and even if I did, what would I say to him? How do I face him?" Her voice caught. Especially after that humiliation when they arrived back at the castle.

"Well, I hate to say it, he might already know."

Maddie's eyes whipped to Ashley. "What?"

"Thomas knows as well, and he might have already warned him."

Oh, no. Even though they'd already confessed their love and intentions, what if he decided it was too much? Too messy? Too public? What if he walked away?

I'll stay.

He'd said that. But still—what if he left?

No. She had to trust him.

She had to trust *them.*

Still, her stomach twisted into a dozen cold little knots.

"What if he doesn't?" Maddie whispered. "What if he thinks

it's all too much? Too messy? He didn't even say anything when we arrived. He was there, right beside me, and he just stood there."

Which was unfair. She hadn't wanted him to speak. Not then. But the silence echoed now in all the worst ways.

"Because he didn't want to make a scene," Ashley said gently. "He was with you, Maddie. That means something."

"He might have been holding back."

Charlene nodded. "Which is exactly what a man like Sebastian does when he's furious and trying to hold himself together. Do you want him to punch Paisley in front of everyone, get entangled in a duel, and maybe die?"

Maddie blinked. Saints! "No. Char, come on. That is rather brutal."

And an image she could have done without.

They all laughed softly.

"Dear," Charlene said, sitting on the bed beside her, "Sebastian is not a rake or a romantic hero in a novel, but he didn't leave when things got uncomfortable. That's his version of shouting."

He didn't leave…

Ashley offered her a faint smile. "He didn't speak, no. But he didn't flinch either. He looked at you. Like you were the only thing keeping him from throttling people."

Maddie's eyes stung. The kind of ache that sat behind the lids and refused to fall.

"Speak to him as soon as you can," Charlene said. "Don't let doubt take root."

"But what if he—"

"No," Ashley interrupted softly, but firmly. "What if he doesn't walk away? What if he fights? What if this is the moment everything changes, and you almost let it slip past you because you were afraid? What if he already has a solution?"

Maddie swallowed the ache rising in her throat. Every word felt like a step toward something she'd tried not to hope for.

They were right.

Sebastian had stood beside her. Now she needed to stand beside him.

"All right."

Sera grinned. "To love. And to not marrying Paisley."

Ashley chuckled. "The world rejoices."

And for the first time all evening, the cold inside Maddie began to thaw.

She didn't feel helpless.

She felt ready.

Ready to fight. Ready to hope.

Ready to choose love, even if it meant choosing it loudly.

Ready to stand by her man no matter what.

ornament

Chapter Twenty-Seven

M ADDIE SMILED AT the note in her hand, the script bold, slanted, and just slightly arrogant.

Meet me at the stables. Bring your appetite.

Signed with a devilishly smug "—S".

Her first note from Sebastian. And it was exactly what she should have expected. Not random. Not careless. Just bold enough to be thrilling.

"A picnic?" she murmured, brow arching. "In the stables?"

An inelegant snort escaped before she could stop it. "Good grief. The man's no better than the Earl of Linsey."

She set the note aside and reached for her coat. Horse men.

Still, she wouldn't pass up the opportunity to meet with him.

At the last second, she paused at her vanity, fingers brushing the small silver etui beside her combs and scent bottle. Habit. Her apothecary instincts never truly went quiet. She slipped it into her pocket—just in case.

She paused by the door, glancing toward the window. The snow had all but vanished, now mere streaks of slush clinging here and there. The road beyond the estate ran clear and open. No longer buried.

Her hand faltered at the latch.

Did Sebastian know? About Paisley?

She pressed her lips together, then straightened her spine. Probably. But she still needed to tell him. Reaffirm her intentions. Her love. Her vow.

She didn't meet any of her friends on her way out—only a few servants, mercifully too busy to tease or question her. But the moment she reached the stables, her steps faltered.

There were no baskets or blankets laid out. No Sebastian leaning handsomely against a post.

Instead, a polished black carriage stood waiting, door ajar, the driver in his seat, ready to take off.

Her heart gave a strange little lurch.

Was he taking her somewhere? A ride beyond the estate?

A thrill ran through her. Without thinking, she stepped toward the carriage and reached for the door.

Her excited smile slipped the moment she met the man's gaze.

She froze.

Inside, seated proudly, was not Sebastian.

"Paisley," she breathed. "My apologies. I thought—"

"No," Paisley said. "You thought right."

Her brows furrowed. "I beg your pardon?"

"I said, you thought right."

The sharp clip of hooves echoed oddly in the still lane—too muffled, too timed. Maddie's slipper paused mid-step.

Something was wrong.

Her foot eased back to the ground, the gravel biting her heel. She turned, just a fraction too late.

A man stepped from the shadow of the carriage, his face half-hidden by the brim of his hat, the edge of a smirk tilting one corner of his mouth. His gloved hand reached for her—not with violence, but with terrifying certainty.

Her breath caught. Her throat tightened.

Before she could scream, his fingers wrapped around her wrist—firm and smooth—and he tugged her forward. Not roughly, but decisively. Possessively.

"What—" she managed, but the word died as the carriage door yawned open and darkness waited inside.

She didn't move. Not yet. Her mind was too stunned to instruct her limbs.

He didn't wait.

She stumbled as he pulled her in. The velvet interior swallowed her whole, and her bonnet knocked askew as the door slammed shut behind them with a sound far louder than it should have been. Final.

She blinked. Tried to see him in the dim light.

The carriage jerked into motion.

She blinked again, her wits returning full force. "What are you doing? Let me out right now!"

"Calm down," Paisley drawled. "If I wished to harm you, it would already be done."

"Oh, forgive me if being kidnapped puts me in a dramatic mood!" she snapped. "How is this not harming me?"

He merely raised an infuriating brow.

"You will not get away with this," Maddie warned. "You must be daft if you think you would."

"I already have."

"You forged a note from Sebastian. That is vile, you mad—"

"Oh, Miss Madeleine," he said her name like a sigh. "Do you really believe he's good enough for you?"

She glared at him. "Yes. I do." How could he not be?

"I don't." His eyes narrowed. "You were supposed to be mine."

"Yours?" She let out a sharp laugh. "I am not a horse, Your Grace. I do not belong in your stable. Or your collection."

A muscle ticked in his jaw. "You would still make me a fine wife."

"Pity for you, I have no intention of making you a fine wife." Maddie crossed her arms and legs, back rigid, chin high.

She had to escape. Some way or another.

He leaned forward slightly, menace cloaked in elegance. "And yet here you are. Alone. With me. There is no other option than for you to be mine now."

There was always another option.

She met his gaze, steel for steel. "You'll return me, Paisley. Because men like you don't understand the power of real friendship. And if you think my friends won't come for me—if you think *he* won't come for me—you are far more foolish than I thought."

His eyes glittered, but she could tell she'd struck something vital.

"Sebastian?" he sneered. "He'll come. And I'll be waiting."

His left eye twitched.

Maddie jerked back. He looked wrong. Too taut. Like a man barely holding his shape.

"By now, Miss,"—he rocked his head back and forth as if bestowing himself a terrible compliment—"your reputation can't be salvaged."

"I know that!"

"You do, of course. And that's why you're mine."

"Never!"

"You are! I have you right here! I claimed you."

He grimaced in a terrifying manner. The mad fox. She remembered it suddenly—her father's story of the one that foamed and snapped and vanished into the woods.

But I won't be his prey.

"You can't claim what's already been—" but she didn't finish.

His eyes glinted. Something in them had cracked.

"What did you say?"

She inhaled sharply. He wanted Sebastian to follow. He wanted Sebastian to see how he'd *won*.

How broken must a man be to call that love?

Her heart pounded—but not from fear.

Not entirely.

Yes, she was scared, but she also knew *he* would come. And Paisley had no idea what kind of trouble he had just invited into his carriage.

Because she wouldn't cooperate.

Already, her mind spun with ways to stall this man.

But first, she needed to find out his plan.

"Where are we going?"

"The church," came his curt answer.

The church? So the man wasn't waiting.

"That would mean you have a special license."

"Correct."

Her jaw nearly dropped. So this had been planned.

"You truly are mad," she whispered. "Do you hear yourself? You think I'll simply walk into a church and say vows with you because you've hauled me into a carriage?"

His eyes gleamed with something dark—hunger, yes, but desperation too. "No. I think you'll marry me because you won't have a choice. By the time anyone finds us, it will be too late."

"You know nothing about me if you think I care about scandal. My mother won't allow a kidnapping to put me in a bad light."

"True. She won't."

Why was he so smug?

He knows something I don't.

Maddie narrowed her eyes.

She was no longer a virtuous lady.

"Oh, I know. You care for your friends. You care for your place in their hearts. And you care for *him*."

He was right on all scores.

"They will never think badly of me, and I would rather be ruined, fully and publicly ruined, than marry a man who tricks and traps his way into a woman's life against her consent."

"You say that now, but once we are wed, and the fury fades, you'll come to see I was right. That we were always meant to be."

"*Always meant to be?*" she repeated, nearly choking on it. "Why don't you turn this carriage straight to Bedlam? That is where you are meant to be!"

His mouth tightened.

She leaned forward, anger blazing now, pressing on, "You don't want me. Not me. You wanted *ownership*. You wanted to win."

"Winning is everything," Paisley said tightly.

Silence stretched taut between them, thick as molasses. Maddie felt her chest rise and fall, breath shallow but steady.

She couldn't talk this man down. But no matter.

He would not win.

And she needed to remain calm for what was to come.

Not that she knew what yet, but she could feel it in her bones.

This kidnapping was just the start.

"Enjoy this moment," she said softly. "Because they are coming, Paisley. And when they do, they won't bring flowers or cheer."

No, they would bring wrath.

If they could find her.

SEBASTIAN STRODE THROUGH the east wing, heart pounding, boots striking hard and fast across the marble. He'd searched every room in this castle—twice. Her bedchamber, all the other chambers, the kitchen, the music room, the parlor, the conservatory, even the bloody linen closet. Maddie was nowhere.

"Have you seen Miss Maddie?" he barked at a footman passing him.

The poor man nearly jerked out of his livery. "No, my lord. Not since breakfast."

Sebastian turned on his heel and strode toward the back of the house.

He'd already questioned half the staff. One maid mentioned

seeing Maddie heading toward the stables. So he'd gone there, calling her name, tearing through the stalls like a man half-mad.

Nothing.

No Maddie. No note. No sign of her.

Just a hollow, echoing silence that clung to the air and whispered of something very, very wrong. He should have found her by now, but it was as though she'd vanished from the estate. As though she'd never been here. As though this entire time had all been a dream.

But it wasn't.

He burst through more doors, more rooms, eyes scanning, breath harsh. This wasn't like her. She wouldn't simply vanish.

He climbed the stairs two at a time, then descended again after sweeping the guest floor once more. Still nothing. The panic clawing up his throat now threatened to choke him.

By the time he stepped into the drawing room, he knew he must have looked half-wild. When Lady Ashley glanced up from her book, alarm flickered across her face. Thomas, beside her, set down his brandy.

"She's not in the house," Sebastian said tightly. "I've checked every room. Twice."

Ashley set aside her book. "You mean Maddie?"

"Of course I mean Maddie! Have you seen her? Did she say anything about going to town?"

It was the only other option that made sense—but his gut rejected it.

Ashley blinked, confused. "No. She would have told me. We were going to walk in the gardens later."

Sebastian scrubbed a hand through his hair. "She's not in the stables either. I thought—I don't know. Someone said they saw her heading there."

Thomas straightened, frowning. "So she left the house, but there's no sign of her in the stables, and no one's seen her since?"

Sebastian's mouth tightened. "Exactly."

Ashley stood. "Are you certain—?"

"Yes!" he snapped, then immediately softened. "Sorry. I didn't mean—just… something's wrong. I know it."

A silence fell, heavy and pulsing with tension.

Then Rotheworth and Lady Charlene stepped into the room, brows raised at the gathering.

"What's happened?" the man asked.

"Maddie's missing," Thomas said. "We're trying to figure out where she's gone."

"How can that be?" Lady Charlene asked. She eyed Sebastian. "Why isn't she with you?"

Sebastian's chest tightened. For a moment, he should've been surprised they knew. But no—he should have expected it. If he weren't so worried, he'd be flattered Maddie had told them. But there was no time for that now.

"If we're all here, where could she have gone?" Ashley pressed.

Rotheworth nodded slowly. "I'm not sure, but I do know Paisley left the estate just under an hour ago. Took a carriage. Bumped my shoulder on the way out—with that air about him."

Thomas made wide eyes and groaned.

Sebastian's head snapped toward him. "What?"

"Yes." Rotheworth crossed to the decanter and poured himself a drink, as if this were any ordinary conversation. "I saw it myself. Polished black carriage. Looked like he was in a rush."

Sebastian took a slow, deliberate step forward. "Did he say anything?"

"Not to me. I didn't think too much of it."

Ashley's eyes widened. "Wait… do you think…?"

Lady Charlene shook her head. "Surely not…"

Thomas turned to Sebastian. "He wouldn't dare."

Sebastian's voice came out low and rough, like gravel ground beneath a boot. "He would. If he thought he had no other chance, if he was desperate enough, he'd find a way to get her alone. To trap her."

Ashley's hand flew to her mouth. Her eyes were wide, shimmering. "Maddie would never meet Paisley alone. And someone would have seen if he carried her off—kicking and screaming—someone would have heard."

Sebastian said nothing. His mind turned the idea over like a knife in his hand.

Not if she went willingly. Not if she didn't know.

"Oh dear," Lady Charlene said softly. "Do you think he forged a note?"

The floor seemed to tilt beneath him. Sebastian froze. His breath stopped.

That was exactly what Maddie would respond to, some cheeky invite…

His voice dropped to a whisper. "He could have. And if she thought it was from me…"

"She'd go," Ashley breathed. Her voice cracked with certainty. "She'd go without question."

"Hold on," Rotheworth said. "Do you truly believe Paisley would do something like this?"

"Yes."

The word dropped like a cannon shot.

Sebastian's jaw tensed. His pulse surged with cold dread. Even if they were wrong, that would be fine. But if they were right—

"Then we haven't a moment to lose."

Thomas was already at the door. "We'll check the route to town."

Sebastian was right behind him, his strides swift and silent.

Maddie, where are you?

He turned to Ashley, every muscle tight with dread. "What does Paisley want with Maddie?"

Ashley's lips parted—but no words came. She looked stricken. When she finally spoke, it was only a whisper. "There's been talk."

She bit her lip hard, as if to keep the rest inside.

Lady Charlene stepped in, her tone low and grim. "There's

been… a jest."

Sebastian's gut dropped. "What jest?" His voice scraped out, hollow with dread.

Charlene winced. "Her mother and his. And the two of them." She sucked her lower lip between her teeth, as though ashamed to say it aloud.

His pulse roared in his ears.

"But Maddie would never take it seriously," Ashley rushed to say, her voice cracking. "Not since…" Her hand moved vaguely, gesturing toward Sebastian. Her eyes shimmered with guilt.

Of course, he thought, jaw clenching. They all knew.

And yet.

Paisley…

Sebastian turned toward Thomas. "He wouldn't—" The rest snagged in his throat. It was too dark a thought, too monstrous.

Thomas rose slowly, his expression carved from stone. He didn't need to speak. The look in his eyes was enough.

Sebastian's stomach knotted as a single, brutal truth slammed into him.

We're already too late.

"We need to save her." Thomas made for the door.

"Now," Sebastian said, voice grim. If Paisley had done this, he wouldn't draw it out. He'd have everything already planned and in place. He wouldn't leave anything to chance again—not after he lost a wager with Linsey when his friend married Lady Ashley. "We check every church first."

Rotheworth stilled. "You think he has a special license?"

"I think the rogue planned this." Sebastian's eyes blazed. "And if he means to make her his by force, he'll have to kill me first. And nothing—and nobody—can help him if he's laid a finger on her."

Ashley's voice trembled. "We must leave immediately!"

Thomas was already issuing orders to a footman in the hall. Rotheworth tossed back his brandy and crossed to the door. "Agreed."

"I'm coming too," Lady Charlene declared, chin lifted in a stubborn fashion.

"Of course," Rotheworth said. "The men will ride ahead, you and Lady Ashley can follow in a carriage."

Sebastian's jaw flexed. He nodded once. "We'll start with the churches within ten miles. One of them will have seen him. If we don't find them by nightfall—"

"We'll keep riding," Rotheworth said grimly. "Church by church, house by house. We'll find them."

Charlene's voice shook with barely restrained fury. "And when we do, I want the first slap."

"No, the first slap is mine," Lady Ashley said. "You can have the second."

Sebastian gave a hard nod. "After I break his skull."

He stormed from the room, rage and dread propelling him faster than reason. Behind him, the household erupted into motion—coats grabbed, boots stamped, doors flung wide.

But in his heart, only one thing mattered.

Maddie was gone.

And he would bring her back—or die trying.

Chapter Twenty-Eight

T HE CHAPEL WAS small, old, and cold. Not in the hallowed, holy sense, but rather in the way of things forgotten. Damp clung to the stone walls. Mildew soured the air. The floor beneath her slippers was uneven, the pews cracked, the cushions flat as parchment. Unlit candles leaned in their sconces like tired old soldiers, and the air was so still it felt like it hadn't moved in years.

Too still. Too quiet.

Only the echo of footsteps disturbed the silence—hers and his.

Paisley's grip around her wrist was unyielding, iron fingers digging into her pulse like a shackle, forcing her forward. At the front of the chapel stood a robed vicar, flanked by a mousy woman in a fur-collared cloak—the witness.

This was happening.

Maddie's breath came fast and shallow, her heart a wild drumbeat inside her chest. She looked around—any object could be a weapon. A candlestick. A book. A loose stone from the floor. Even her own fury.

And then she remembered.

The etui.

Still tucked into the inner pocket of her coat, next to her ribs.

Small, silver, sharp-cornered. And inside: a pinch of cayenne pepper, gifted by Sera as a joke. "Just in case you need to 'spice up a conversation.'"

She hadn't thought she'd actually use it.

But she might.

"Just say the words," Paisley muttered, dragging her toward the altar. "It'll all be done."

"Never."

She twisted her arm. No use. He held on tighter.

"You are mad."

"We've established that already," he said, smiling faintly.

Maddie glared at him. "This will not end the way you think it will."

"Oh, but it will," he said, his tone light. "You'll be my wife, and this whole drama will become a charming story to tell over dinner parties."

"I will never be your wife."

"You will," he said simply. "Because if you don't, your family pays the price. And I have your mother's blessing."

Disgust hit the back of her throat like bile.

"You're lying."

"Am I?"

Even if he wasn't, she didn't care. Not anymore.

"You and my mother have no power over me."

Paisley laughed, a sharp, dry bark. "You're here, aren't you? At my mercy. That's all the power I need."

"I stopped this the moment I opened my mouth," she snapped. "I will not say the words."

"You will. Because your family's name, your friends' reputations, all of it is teetering. And you? You care too much not to give in."

A quiet voice broke the tension.

"Maddie?"

She turned and nearly collapsed.

There, seated primly in the shadows of the chapel, was her

mother. Wrapped in her usual furs, expression unreadable.

"*Mother?*" Maddie whispered. "What are you doing here?"

She half-stepped toward her, disbelief buzzing under her skin. "You know what this is. He's kidnapping me. Forcing me to marry him. And you're just… sitting there?"

Her mother stood, moving toward her slowly. "My darling girl," she said, gently taking Maddie's hands. "Paisley is steady. Responsible. He's willing to pick up the pieces that man dropped."

"No." Maddie's voice cracked. "There were no pieces to pick up."

Her mother frowned slightly. "You're already in love. And ruined. This is… a formality."

"Ruined?" Maddie recoiled. "Mother, I never let Paisley even so much kiss me, or touch me, for that matter, and you know it."

Maddie pulled herself free. "I won't let you sell me off like a spare bonnet."

The chapel swayed slightly as the wind howled outside. Or maybe that was just the storm inside her.

She turned back to Paisley, voice low and sharp. "You may think you have power. But you'll never have *me.*"

"Now, now," her mother said, calm but clipped. "You're confused. Likely feverish."

"I'm furious. That's the heat you feel." Maddie stepped away from both of them. "And I will not be cornered. Not by him. Not by you."

Her mother stiffened. "Your father's orders—"

"I don't care about orders," Maddie said, breath trembling. "I'm in love."

"With me," Paisley said smoothly.

Maddie turned slowly. "*No.* With the Marquess of Cambridge."

"What?" her mother gasped.

"She doesn't know what she wants," Paisley barked. "The girl's dramatic."

Before anyone could speak again, the chapel door creaked open.

A man in clerical robes poked his head in. "Are we ready then?"

"Yes," Paisley said at once.

"No!" Maddie shouted. "We are not having a wedding!"

"You fell in love with a *marquess*?" Her mother's voice was almost a whisper. "Maddie…"

"What's so wrong with a marquess? With even a farmer? I can't demand my heart to follow your desires, mother," Maddie cried out. "I didn't even mean for any of this to happen, but it did. And I'm not ruined, mother. I'm in love."

Her mother's eyes glistened. "How could this be…" she whispered. "How could you… I…"

Paisley stepped in before her mother could finish her sentence, voice cold and final. "She's here. The vicar is here. We begin."

"No," Maddie snapped. "I'll scream. I'll run. I'll claw your eyes out before I say a word to bind me to you!"

"I own every thread holding you together," Paisley snarled. "Say the words, Madeleine. Or watch everything unravel."

Her lip curled. "Then unravel it."

His hand faltered. Barely. But she saw it.

And she smiled.

"Go on," she whispered. "Burn it all down. I'll be the one still standing."

The vicar opened his book.

Then a voice ripped through the chapel like a thunderbolt.

"I would advise you to let her go."

They all swung around.

Standing in the doorway, coat dark with rain, eyes cold as a winter storm, was Prince Alexander von Hohenzoller-Siegmaringen.

Sera's prince.

Maddie's eyes flew wide. What was *he* doing here? Relief

slammed into her the same time as that thought.

Her mother gasped, one hand flying to her throat. The color drained from her face, confusion warring with dawning horror as she looked between them. "Who are you?"

The prince ignored her as his gaze dropped to Maddie's wrist, still locked in Paisley's grasp.

His jaw flexed, eyes flicking back to the duke. "What," he said softly, "are you doing?"

"None of your business, Your Royal Highness," Paisley sneered.

"It becomes my business when you manhandle my wife's friend."

"She's willing."

"She doesn't look willing."

"I'm not here willingly!" Maddie exclaimed.

"No one asked you, pet," Paisley said.

"She just told you," the prince said with a sneer. "Take your hand off her. Now."

Paisley's grip tightened, and Maddie winced.

"You overstep," the duke hissed.

"And you violate every code of decency," the prince said, stepping forward. "Let. Her. Go."

Paisley squared his shoulders. "Going to challenge me to a duel, Your Highness?"

"If it'd work faster, yes. But I'd rather drag you before a magistrate in chains." The prince's voice dropped. "So I'll ask one last time. Unhand the lady."

Paisley hesitated.

Maddie seized the moment. Her fingers slid into her coat pocket, closing over the etched silver edge of her etui. She didn't pull it yet. But braced herself to do so at any moment. "I swear," she hissed, "I'll bite your hand off if you don't release me this instant!"

The prince didn't smile, but his eyes gleamed. "You heard the lady."

Paisley flushed, then slowly let her go. Only to snatch her elbow instead.

Drat this man!

The vicar cleared his throat again.

Maddie's fear was nearly gone now, but not entirely. Paisley could still bolt with her. Still try something reckless. Still force her hand somehow.

But she was ready.

One more second, she thought.

Sebastian, where are you?

He didn't come.

TEN.

They'd searched ten chapels. Nothing. Sebastian clenched his jaw, his fingers tight around the reins as his horse picked its way through the snow-covered road. Dusk was closing in, stretching long, eerie shadows across the countryside. The air had turned bitter, clouds pressing low overhead like a threat.

Beside him, Thomas muttered a curse. "They couldn't have vanished. There aren't that many bloody chapels in the area."

But there were just enough.

"They wouldn't have gone south," Rotheworth added grimly, his eyes scanning the horizon. "Too open. Too exposed."

Sebastian didn't speak. Couldn't. If he opened his mouth now, the fury simmering beneath his ribs would boil over.

Maddie was out there. Somewhere. And that bastard Paisley had her.

He gritted his teeth harder, jaw aching.

Every chapel they'd entered had been emptier than the last. No witnesses. No sounds. Not even a muddy boot print. But still, he felt it.

They were close.

Behind them, carriage wheels creaked on the icy road. The

women followed in silence—each of them holding their breath.

"We're wasting time," Thomas growled. "We should split—"

"No," Sebastian snapped. "Not yet. That's what he would want. If we split, someone misses something."

His voice was low, taut with command.

"He's clever. Clever enough to pick a chapel just remote enough to delay us, but not so far that no vicar would agree to a quiet ceremony." He exhaled sharply. "We stay together."

Rotheworth gave a tight nod.

A gust of wind cut through their coats. Sebastian narrowed his eyes at the bend ahead. Then—he saw it.

A steeple, modest and weatherworn, rising behind a clutch of bare-limbed trees. Half-swallowed by ivy. A chapel no one would visit unless they were desperate.

His gut twisted.

"There."

The horses broke into a faster trot. The chapel came into view—small, crooked, leaning into the hillside as if to hide. And off to the side—

Two carriages. One of them unmistakable.

"That's my coat of arms," Thomas growled. "The blackguard took *my* carriage."

Sebastian was already moving. He vaulted from his horse before it stopped, boots slamming into the frozen ground.

Rotheworth was at his heels, yanking open the chapel's doors without a word. And this time, it wasn't silence that greeted them, but the low, clipped tone of Prince Alexander von Hohenzollern.

"… you really know how to try a man's patience, Paisley."

Sebastian shoved past the threshold, eyes scanning.

There. At the altar.

Maddie.

Pale. Furious. A few curls falling from their pins, her arm caught in Paisley's grimy grip.

"Maddie," Sebastian breathed.

For a moment, dread swamped him. Was he too late? Had he failed her? But her eyes met his, and in that instant, the rigid mask on her face broke. Her body slumped with visible relief.

The vicar flinched as Thomas appeared beside him, likely glaring daggers, while the cloaked woman beside him gasped.

But all Sebastian saw was her.

And the man touching her.

She didn't speak, but she didn't need to.

"Let her go," Sebastian growled, advancing down the aisle, fists already clenching. He was ready to break Paisley in two.

Maddie's voice rose above the tension. *"Sebastian... I knew you would come."* Turning to the duke, she snapped and yanked on her arm, "Let me go! How many times must this be asked of you? I said no. I've said it a hundred times. I'll say it a thousand more. Even if you drag me to a thousand bloody altars, it will be no!"

That's my girl.

Paisley sneered. "You're being hysterical."

Sebastian laughed, low and dangerous. "You've clearly never seen her *truly* hysterical. But please. Continue. Let's see how far your arrogance gets you."

"She's mine by right—"

"She is *herself* by right," Sebastian snapped. "You think dragging her in here like some prize filly to auction proves your worth? It proves you're a coward."

"Agreed," Thomas said, arms folded.

Maddie twisted again. This time, her elbow slammed into Paisley's ribs. He gasped, and she tore herself free.

And ran.

Straight into Sebastian's arms.

He caught her, hands firm at her waist, holding her like a man reattaching a part of his own heart.

"I've got you," he whispered, voice rough. "I've got you."

But Maddie didn't sob. She didn't cling.

She turned, chin lifted, voice clear.

"I told you they would come," she said, staring down Paisley. "That you would not win."

She turned to Sebastian. "I knew *you* would come."

He held her tighter, a fierce, protective hold, as if trying to wipe away the memory of Paisley's grip.

"You're safe," he said. And by all the last straws in the world, he would never let her out of his sight again.

Already, his mind spun. There would be consequences. Paisley would pay.

And then—like justice manifesting at the perfect moment—the chapel doors opened again.

The women burst in.

Charlene. Ashley. Sera.

Maddie didn't flinch.

She stood taller.

Let the reckoning begin.

Chapter Twenty-Nine

MADDIE HAD NEVER been so happy to see her friends pile through the chapel doors.

Charlene, wild-eyed and breathless, was first, her skirts hitched indecorously to her knees, as if she'd sprinted the last few yards. Ashley followed on her heels, stormy and fierce, and Sera swept in last with the composure of a queen surveying a battlefield.

"Oh, thank the stars!" Charlene cried, barreling down the aisle. "Are you hurt?"

"Only my pride," Maddie muttered, still tucked tightly against Sebastian's side. His scent—clean and familiar—steadied her. The moment he'd stepped into the church, she'd known she was safe.

No one would be hurt now.

After all, Paisley was grossly outnumbered.

And that gave her strength.

Ashley stormed up to Paisley, and to Maddie's complete shock, slapped him. Hard. "You filthy rogue!"

Charlene followed suit before Paisley could blink.

The men surged forward, ready to restrain him if necessary, but the duke only staggered back, palm pressed to his cheek.

He let out a curse. "This is ludicrous! How dare you treat me this way!"

"You are the ludicrous one," Sera snapped, her tone laced with disdain.

"Love," the prince murmured, gathering her close.

Maddie smiled faintly. Right—they hadn't seen each other in days.

She stepped forward now, finding her voice.

"He dragged me here," she said, loud enough for everyone to hear. "Lied. Threatened me. Had the gall to plan this entire farce like it was a dinner party!"

"I should've broken his jaw first," Sebastian growled.

Maddie reached for his arm. "No. You'd only get into trouble. Ashley and Charlene won't."

Ashley cracked her knuckles. "Please. I've always wanted to punch a blackguard. This felt like overdue justice."

Charlene nodded solemnly. "He deserved far worse. I daresay I'd like another go." She squared her shoulders, completely unrepentant.

Paisley, red-faced and sputtering, stumbled back. "You women are mad. Every last one of you!"

Sera tilted her head, examining him like a curious but unpleasant insect. "And yet we, in our madness, managed to uncover your scheme and bring it crashing down before the vicar spoke a single word. Remarkable, isn't it?"

Paisley's mouth opened—ready to bluster, or threaten, or lie—but the sight of four furious women halted whatever excuse he'd prepared. His gaze flicked to Maddie.

She didn't flinch.

He sneered. "This is not over. You'll regret humiliating me."

"Oh, you blackguard," Ashley said, folding her arms. "I've been waiting since my engagement for the chance to humiliate you."

"You'll regret everything," he snarled at Maddie, ignoring her.

Sebastian stepped forward. "Say one more word to her and I will break your jaw. I'm not a duke; I'm worse. I have nothing to lose. That makes me a very dangerous man."

Paisley flinched.

Maddie stared at Paisley with a strange sense of detachment—as though the girl who once trembled beneath his threats was someone else entirely. Some pale, frightened ghost in the corner of her mind.

But that girl was gone.

Or perhaps… she had finally woken up.

She stood taller now. Straighter. Not because Sebastian was near, though his presence was balm, but because her friends stood behind her, fierce, furious, and wholly unafraid.

And for the first time in days, Maddie allowed herself to feel something that had been buried beneath fear, shame, and second-guessing: Rage.

Clarifying, righteous rage.

She'd spent too long shrinking herself, walking on eggshells around her mother, trying to survive expectations that weren't hers.

But no more.

This man—this petty tyrant in polished boots—had tried to control her future through threats.

And now he thought she'd regret humiliating him?

No.

She regretted only ever giving him the benefit of the doubt. Her gaze didn't waver as he hissed his final warning. Let him spit threats. Let him stew in shame. She had her voice now. And she had something more dangerous than his title or threats.

She had courage.

It had come quietly at first, like a whisper, but now, it roared. She didn't need rescuing. She had needed the space to rise.

And she just had.

Right here, in front of everyone.

Let Paisley flinch. Let the world watch. Maddie was done playing the part they wrote for her.

Paisley lunged.

Perhaps it was pride, or fury, or one final pathetic attempt to assert control—but he moved, quick and graceless, toward her.

And Maddie was ready.

She calmly slipped her hand into the small etui in her pocket, her fingers closing around the small glass vial of cayenne pepper she'd tucked there that morning on a beautiful, instinctual whim, and flung the powder straight into his face.

Paisley howled. Loud and unholy. His hands flew to his eyes as he stumbled backward, gasping, cursing, red-faced and blinded.

The room froze.

"My eyes!" the man hollered. "What have you done?"

Maddie arched a brow. "A woman must always carry something sharp. Sometimes it's wit. Sometimes it's cayenne."

Ashley and Charlene burst into delighted laughter.

Sebastian's jaw slackened before he broke into a grin so wicked it nearly matched Maddie's.

Charlene murmured, "Oh, she's terrifying. I love it."

The vicar made a strangled noise.

Paisley slumped to the floor, wheezing like a bellows. No one moved to help him. From somewhere in the chapel, Maddie's mother let out a sob. She'd all but forgotten about her presence since the prince's arrival, but Maddie couldn't provide any comfort now, nor did she wish to.

"You didn't need me at all, did you?" Sebastian whispered in her ear.

She smiled at him. "No. But I wanted you."

He kissed her temple. "You're magnificent."

RAGE HAD NEVER felt this liberating.

Not the blind, reckless kind that made men foolish. No, this was the kind that sharpened the senses, that burned behind the eyes with relentless purpose. It was a forge, and Sebastian was steel passing through it. He wanted to strike. Every muscle in his body itched to move. To bury Paisley where he stood.

But Maddie stood beside him. Not hiding. Not cowering.

Her spine was straight, her chin high, her mouth set in a line that dared anyone to try her. The fire in her eyes wasn't borrowed. It was hers. Earned.

And that steadied him more than anything ever could. He'd chosen her peace over his vengeance.

She didn't need saving.

She needed someone ready to battle the world *with* her.

He was more than ready.

His gaze swept the chapel—a pitiful farce of a place. Dried-out flowers wilting in cracked vases. Threadbare pews leaning like old men tired of kneeling. A vicar clutched his book of vows like it was a talisman against disaster. Maddie's mother had slipped out, as far as he could tell. And in the center of it all, a coward in fine boots, undone by the very woman he'd tried to cage.

"This place," Sebastian said, voice low, "feels more like a tomb than a chapel."

Maddie didn't look away from Paisley. But her hand slid into his. Warm. Sure. "Let's go home."

The words landed soft but steady—like a stone tossed into still water.

He nodded once. "Yes. Please."

Ashley, behind them, cracked her knuckles with a mutinous sigh. "I was hoping for one more punch."

"I know," Charlene said, still eyeing Paisley. "He has a very slappable face."

Ashley huffed. "Disappointing."

Prince Alexander cleared his throat. "As delightful as this court of justice has been, I agree with Cambridge. Let's leave this drafty ruin behind. I haven't seen my wife in days, and I'd much rather be with her than among… this."

"I am not cold," Sera said—primly—but nonetheless pressed

subtly closer to him. "But I wouldn't object to a fire. Or wine. And perhaps… lemon cake."

"Cake sounds excellent," Charlene said. "Violence and dessert always pair well."

Maddie turned to Sebastian, her voice softer now. "You truly came for me. Even when you thought I might have agreed to… this ridiculous engagement."

He looked at her then—really looked at her—and let everything he felt pass through his gaze.

"I always will," he said simply.

The vicar stepped forward, still clutching his little book, voice wavering. "My apologies—I didn't know—"

Sebastian silenced him with a single glance. "You can forget this ever happened."

The man nodded so fervently that his wig shifted sideways.

Paisley muttered something unintelligible, slumped in the corner with red eyes and what little remained of his dignity. No one looked at him.

He wasn't worth it.

Sebastian laced his fingers with Maddie's. "Come," he said. "Let's put this place behind us."

She stepped into his side without hesitation.

They walked down the aisle, not as bride and groom—but as partners. Equals. The others fell in around them like a shield wall. Unruly, brilliant, loyal. They were friendship made flesh. Found family. Home.

Outside, the carriages waited.

So did the wind. And the snow. And the world.

Maddie glanced up at him as they stepped through the chapel doors. Her smile was soft and sure, the weight of the day finally shedding from her shoulders.

"Wherever you are," she said quietly, "there is my home."

He squeezed her hand. "And I'll be there. Always."

The door swung shut behind them.

And in its place, came warmth.

And freedom.

✦

Chapter Thirty

Back at the castle

SEBASTIAN ENTERED THE study with a calmness that disguised the fire roaring through his blood. The heavy oak door shut behind him with a final, echoing click, and the hush that followed was sharp enough to cut.

Paisley stood near the hearth, cravat askew, color high, a bead of sweat glinting at his temple. The kind of man who feared scandal more than consequence. Who believed his title would shield him from the weight of his actions.

Not tonight.

Sebastian's boots echoed on the polished floor as he advanced. Behind him, Thomas, Rotheworth, and Prince Alexander formed a quiet, immovable wall. But Sebastian carried the room. His presence. His fury. His control.

He stopped three paces from Paisley.

"You're awfully quiet," he said, voice mild. Too mild.

Paisley attempted a smirk, but it landed crooked. "This is all a misunderstanding."

Sebastian tilted his head, just slightly. "You kidnapped Miss Madeleine. Took her to a chapel under false pretenses. Misled her mother. That's not a misunderstanding. That's a crime."

Paisley paled but lifted his chin. "I was doing what was expected. Everyone knew she was meant to marry well."

"She was never meant for you," Sebastian said softly. And that made it more brutal.

Paisley's eyes flicked toward the others, desperate. "You'd destroy a man's future over a woman? *Her?*"

Sebastian's breath slowed. Measured. "Yes."

"She's not worth it."

He should have struck him then.

Every muscle in Sebastian's body coiled to snap. His hands curled into fists at his sides, his teeth clenched hard enough to ache. He thought of Maddie's voice, steady despite her underlying fear. Her courage. The way she had leaned into him at the chapel, not broken, but burning.

And this man dared call her unworthy?

"Don't," Thomas warned under his breath, stepping forward just enough to anchor him. "He's not worth your knuckles."

Paisley saw the moment. Misread it.

He laughed, a thin, manic sound. "You act like she's worthy to be my duchess. She's nothing! She-she snuck into your room how many times, Cambridge? Everyone knows it."

Sebastian's heart slammed once. The insult didn't wound *him.* But it would wound *her.*

She'll hear of this, he thought darkly. That coward will spread it like rot.

"She's probably ruined already," Paisley went on, sneering. "A little midnight maid, playing nurse. You really think she's untouched?"

Sebastian's jaw flexed.

Then came the crack.

Thomas's fist landed across Paisley's jaw with a vicious snap, sending him reeling into the mantel. The sound rang like a bell. Solid. Satisfying.

Paisley clutched his face, eyes wild. "You-you can't strike me! I'm a bloody duke!"

Thomas stepped back, calm as ice. "And you're a disgrace."

Sebastian's voice dropped to a blade's edge. "She brought me tea. And medicine. When I was ill."

Paisley wheezed. "Like a maid?"

"No." Sebastian stepped forward, voice like steel. "Like a friend. Like someone decent. Something you wouldn't recognize if it spat in your face."

Paisley's face contorted. "You think you're better than me?"

Sebastian didn't blink. "I *know* I am."

Prince Alexander stepped forward at last, his voice a velvet blade. "Your name will carry no weight in Vienna. Nor Budapest. Nor Paris."

Paisley's head snapped toward him. "You—you wouldn't—"

"I already have," Alex said coolly.

Then Rotheworth stepped in. "And you may look forward to hearing from my mother. She'll be delighted to speak with yours. It will be the end of your Season. And likely… of your standing."

Sebastian watched the color drain from Paisley's face like ink from a blotter.

"Your name," he said softly, "will be a punchline."

Paisley choked out something unintelligible.

Sebastian stepped in, close enough that the duke could see every inch of rage in his eyes. The promise of what would come next, should he ever dare again.

"You will never speak of Miss Madeleine again," he said. "Not to me. Not to anyone. Or I will not hold back."

Paisley trembled. "You've ruined me."

"No," Sebastian said. "*You* did that."

Then he turned.

He left the room without looking back, and when the door opened, the cold air that rushed in felt like clarity.

He didn't need to see Paisley crumble to know it was done.

He had won.

Not just the confrontation.

But *her*.

And that meant something more. It meant *everything*.

He made it ten paces down the corridor before his breath

caught and the fury drained from his limbs like rain from a storm-wracked roof. The tension that had held him upright, steady, now bled away.

Thomas caught up to him first. "You didn't hit him," he said, like he almost didn't believe it.

Sebastian gave a sharp breath of laughter. "*You* did."

"I couldn't let him insult her. Not after…" He stopped, jaw tight. "He deserved worse."

Rotheworth joined them, rubbing his brow. "Paisley may try to salvage what's left. Cowards don't go quietly."

"He'll stay quiet if he values what's left of his spine," Sebastian said. His tone didn't leave room for interpretation.

They paused at the corridor's end, beside a tall window glazed with frost. Outside, snow covered the grounds in untouched silver.

Sebastian stared out, jaw tight.

"She'll hear about it," he said, low. "The things he said."

"She'll know they're lies," Thomas said.

"She shouldn't have to endure them at all."

No one disagreed. And that silence said everything.

Then Alex appeared behind them. "Let's ensure she doesn't."

Sebastian turned. The prince's voice was steady. Cold. "Word will go to the papers tonight. The official story will be… *sympathetic* to the lady."

Sebastian's shoulders eased slightly. "Thank you."

Alex gave a slight shrug. "Don't thank me. I like her."

Sebastian turned back to the snow, a soft breath escaping his chest.

"She's mine," he whispered.

Not a declaration of ownership.

But of belonging.

THE DOOR CREAKED open, and Maddie looked up from her perch near the hearth, shawl slipping from her shoulders like shed armor. Sebastian stood in the doorway, silhouetted against the snow-dusted corridor, coat unbuttoned, dark curls damp from the cold. He looked tired. Bone-deep tired. But it was him.

Her heart stuttered. It was really him. Whole. Here. Not a memory to cradle in the dark.

He looked like home.

She rose slowly.

"You came," she said, her voice softer than the hush of air in the firelit room.

His eyes found hers. "As soon as I could."

They didn't rush to meet in the middle. They didn't have to. The gravity between them was quiet and sure. Each step carried weight. Every breath was the first one after nearly drowning. When she reached him, he lifted a hand and brushed his knuckles down her cheek. She leaned into it without hesitation.

"I thought I'd never see you again," she whispered.

His voice hitched. "Every second I was away felt like a year. I would've torn the world apart to find you."

Her breath caught. "You did find me."

"I should've seen it sooner. I should've known what Paisley was planning—"

"You stopped him," she said firmly. "That's what matters now."

He looked away, jaw tight. "He tried to humiliate you."

"I know, and my mother helped him."

"How *is* your family?"

"They've accepted my choice." And perhaps some bonds weren't meant to be mended, only released.

He chuckled, then shook his head. "He said vile things." His shoulders tensed again. "And I didn't hit him. Thomas did."

A shaky laugh escaped her. "Of course he did."

Sebastian's smile flickered, then faded. "I wanted to. Every part of me wanted to. But I thought… you wouldn't want me to lose my honor over him."

She shook her head slowly. "You kept it—for both of us."

"And it cuts deeper for him to be struck by an earl. Twice."

He stepped closer. The firelight reflected in his eyes.

"I would've fought every man in that chapel if it meant you never had to feel afraid."

She pressed her palm to his chest, over the beat of his heart.

"You did enough," she whispered. "You always do."

He covered her hand with his. "Do you know what he said? That you were ruined… for bringing me tea and medicine."

He looked at her, truly looked, and she felt seen—utterly and wholly.

"What he called disgrace, I saw as grace."

"You came to me when I was ill. You stayed when you didn't have to."

"I wanted to," she whispered, trembling. Because she had. Every time she went to him, it had been a choice. A quiet act of devotion. A whispered hope.

His fingers threaded gently into hers. "Why?"

"Because…" Her throat tightened. "Because I think I loved you before I understood what love meant."

Sebastian's breath caught.

He looked at her like the world had just shifted and put itself right.

"You… you love me?"

"I think I've been falling in love with you since the night you made that egg-flip."

He laughed—sharp, disbelieving. She laughed too, giddy and teary, her fear chased out by something brighter.

Then he kissed her.

Not tentative. Not testing. This was a vow.

Her fingers clutched the front of his coat, his arms wrapped around her like a promise. When they parted, their foreheads touched, breaths mingling.

"I nearly lost you," he murmured.

"But you didn't."

He cupped her face in both hands. "I love you."

"I know," she whispered, grinning against his mouth. "You just said so. But say it again."

"I love you," he repeated, more certain. "Maddie, I love you with everything I am."

She kissed him again, slower this time. Sweeter. Anchored.

"I love you too."

They laughed softly, still tangled together.

She brushed her thumb along his cheek. "Are you always this poetic?"

"Only with you."

She grinned. "I rather like it."

"I rather love you."

Her smile wobbled, shimmering with tears. "What happens now?"

Sebastian's expression softened, turned reverent. "Now, I ask you to be my wife."

Her breath caught. "I already sort of agreed."

He didn't kneel. He didn't need to.

"I want you beside me for the rest of my life," he said. "I want to wake up to your tea, your laughter, your brutally honest fashion critiques—"

"They're not critiques. They're cries for help."

"—and your fierce, fearless heart. Marry me."

She blinked through the mist in her eyes. Then smiled—a radiant, reckless smile. "Yes."

His arms wrapped around her again, laughter warm in her hair. The fire behind them crackled, as if the very air exhaled relief.

They kissed again.

And this time, it felt like the beginning.

Not the end of a storm, but the start of something bright and boundless. Perhaps she'd been waiting all along, not to be saved, not to *find* love, but to step into her own story. And now she had.

Chapter Thirty-One

MADDIE'S HEART BEAT far too quickly for how slowly they were walking. Sebastian's hand was warm around hers, steady as ever, and yet her fingertips trembled. Her ring—still unfamiliar, still a miracle—glinted in the morning light. It felt like a promise wrapped around her finger.

They crossed the threshold into the east drawing room, and she had only a breath to take in the familiar scene before the moment shifted.

Ashley sat on the settee, a book forgotten in her lap. Charlene sipped tea from an oversized porcelain cup, her brow arched in its usual pose of amused detachment. Sera stood at the window, chin lifted, as if soaking strength from the pale winter sun.

They looked up.

And then they saw.

Sebastian cleared his throat, but Maddie could feel the smile rising in his chest through the hand she held.

"We've something to tell you," he said.

Ashley blinked. Once. Then again.

Charlene froze mid-sip.

Sera's eyes widened.

Maddie glanced up at him, nerves bubbling like champagne in her chest. But then he squeezed her hand once—sure and steady—and she felt them quiet.

"She said yes," Sebastian said simply. "Miss Madeleine will be my wife."

The words landed like snow—soft, silent, and then—

Ashley shrieked.

"Oh, Maddie!" she cried, flying across the room, arms flung wide, laughter and tears pouring out in one joyous mess. "I knew it! I told you you'd be next!"

Before Maddie could reply, Sera barreled into her from the other side, handkerchief pressed to her cheek, shoulders shaking with happy sobs.

"It's happening again! Another one—it's happening again!"

Charlene stood slowly, placing her tea down with deliberate grace.

"Well," she said, smoothing her skirts, "the final domino falls." She stepped forward and, with a rare and elegant smile, added, "It's about time."

Maddie laughed, breathless, her heart near bursting.

Ashley caught her hands. "Let me see it—show me the ring!"

Maddie held it out, blushing furiously.

Charlene leaned in. "Understated. Elegant. Naturally."

Sera sniffled louder. "We all thought you'd be the sensible one, and now look—you've caught the worst case of it of all."

Maddie blinked. "Caught what?"

Ashley beamed. "Wedding fever."

That set off a round of giggles—Sera dabbing at her eyes, Charlene smirking, Ashley already planning a thousand details aloud—and Maddie stood at the center of it all, wrapped in their joy, her chest so full she thought it might crack open from the light inside her.

This was it.

This was her life now.

Then came the sound of footfalls in the corridor.

The men arrived—Thomas, Rotheworth, and Prince Alex— greeted with grins and teasing as they entered. Sebastian remained at her side, and she reached for him instinctively.

"Careful," Thomas called out with a grin. "Don't get too close. It's contagious."

"It is wedding fever," Ashley said with great seriousness, still dabbing her cheeks.

"Please," Rotheworth scoffed. "You say it like we're trout. We weren't caught."

Thomas groaned. "Speak for yourself. I was the victim of a plot." He took Ashley's hand, kissed it, and added, "A successful one."

Sebastian leaned close to Maddie, lips brushing her temple. "I walked right into the net. Willingly."

"And gladly," Maddie whispered back.

The room buzzed with laughter, with lightness and love. But when the women turned to each other—Charlene brushing Sera's cheek, Ashley clutching Maddie's hand—something deeper stirred beneath the surface.

"This isn't fever," Maddie said softly. "This is love."

"A wild, reckless, wonderful love," Ashley added, grinning.

Charlene gave a rare, genuine smile. "And thank goodness we all have it now."

Sera, tear-streaked and glowing, threw her arms around all of them.

"Let's never be sensible again."

They laughed—the four of them—wrapped in each other's arms. Maddie closed her eyes for just a second and breathed in the moment.

This. This was what forever felt like.

She turned, just slightly, and there he was.

Sebastian.

Watching her with that quiet, ruinous smile.

She held his gaze for a long beat.

He winked.

And Maddie knew, without a single doubt, that the rest of her life would begin just like this—

Surrounded by love.

Warmed by laughter.

And cherished beyond reason.

SEBASTIAN WATCHED AS the laughter of four women turned into something brighter—a radiant joy that filled the entire room.

He had seen many things in his life. He had seen greed. He had seen malice. He had seen Maddie's eyes when she feared he might not come for her.

But this?

This was the kind of sight a man carried in his soul until his final breath.

Maddie's eyes found his across the room.

They shimmered, still dancing with joy, still catching light like snowflakes kissed by sun.

He winked.

Because he couldn't help it.

Because she looked like a secret only he knew. Like a life he'd almost lost and now could finally hold.

And her smile bloomed in answer.

Private. Bright. Meant only for him.

He took a step forward. Then another. Their ring—his ring, their future—shone on her finger like a vow already made. He reached for her hand. She gave it without hesitation. "You all right?" he murmured. He didn't know why he asked—but he needed to.

She nodded, even as her lashes shimmered. "I think I'm floating."

A pointed cough came from behind them—probably Thomas. Sebastian ignored it. Maddie tugged him gently toward the window, just far enough to steal a moment for themselves.

"It feels like my soul might leave my body."

Sebastian inhaled slowly, letting it settle.

"Me too." His voice softened. "I've never felt anything like this. Not even close."

Maddie tilted her head, watching him with a gaze that saw everything.

"This feeling that something is finally… right. Like I'm exactly where I'm meant to be."

Her fingers tightened around his.

"I used to think love had to be wild," he said. "Tragic. That it came with pain, or sacrifice, or fire."

"And it didn't?" she teased, gently.

He smiled. "Well… there was no fire. Not much pain. And no sacrifice at all."

She stepped in close, rising on tiptoe to kiss his cheek. It was soft. Not urgent. Just *true.*

And something inside him unraveled—again.

He caught her hand. "Come."

"Where are we going?"

"Somewhere private."

More laughter and teasing followed them as they slipped from the room, but he didn't care.

"I want to kiss you madly," he said.

Maddie blinked. "You do?"

"Why do you look surprised?"

"Because no one's ever dragged me away in front of an audience to be kissed."

"Get used to it."

Then he kissed her. Cupped her face in both hands. Claimed her lips like a man starved of sunlight. Not gently. Not sweetly.

Madly.

"I've wanted to do this since you smiled at me across that drawing room," he said between breaths.

She rose to meet him, hands fisting his coat, kissing him back with such fire she stole his breath. She *set fire to his mouth*—and if that was love, he wanted to burn.

His hands slid into her hair and a groan tore from his chest as she melted against him. When they broke apart, she was breathless, her fingers still clutching his lapels.

"I think you've ruined me again," she whispered.

He smiled against her lips. "Then we're even."

"You really do like kissing me," she said.

"You make it impossible not to."

"You're terrible at restraint."

"Correction. I'm excellent at restraint. I'm just not using it right now."

She arched a brow. "Have you always been this cocky after a kiss?"

"Yes."

"You wouldn't be if you saw your hair right now."

He grinned. "Disheveled in the name of love."

"A noble sacrifice."

"So are my good intentions."

"Were they ever good?"

He leaned in, brushing his nose against hers. "They never stood a chance around you."

She laughed, breath warm on his lips. "I like you like this."

"Disheveled?"

"Carefree. And not sneezing."

He groaned. "Will I *ever* live that down?" He kissed her forehead. "Let it be known, you make me forget every reason I ever built walls."

"Good. I can't imagine what I look like right now."

He stepped back, just far enough to see her whole face. The curve of her lips. The fire in her eyes. She wore her love like she wore her skin. Boldly. Unapologetically. "You look like forever," he said.

She blinked, then smiled. "Is that a vow?"

"It is."

Her expression softened. "Say it again."

"Forever."

She reached up, fingers brushing his jaw. "I never thought someone would love me like this. Fiercely. Freely."

"Neither did I." His voice dropped. "Shall we go back?"

"To knowing smiles and smirks?"

"Or… stay here for a tryst?"

"Absolutely not!"

"Are you sure I can't tempt you?"

She tilted her head. "I mean…"

He grinned and kissed her again. "Still no?" he asked.

"That's not fair."

"I'm not aiming for fair. I'm aiming for *irresistible.*"

"You're incorrigible."

"And you're not saying no."

"I'm *thinking* about saying no."

He leaned in again, his lips brushing the shell of her ear. "That's practically a yes."

"I have to preserve *some* reputation."

He nuzzled her neck, shameless.

"Darling, that ship sailed the moment you brought me tea in bed."

She laughed, shoving his chest. "That was *medicinal!* And I wasn't sneaking, I was *healing* you."

He caught her wrist, lifted it to his lips, and kissed her knuckles.

"Come away with me. Sneak into my chamber again. Just ten more minutes."

She stared at him. "Ten minutes?"

"Ten minutes of you. Then I'll shield you from all their smug grins."

She shook her head, but her smile said otherwise.

"Ten minutes. And don't think I don't know you can't shield me from anything."

His grin was full and shameless.

"I knew I could tempt you."

Chapter Thirty-Two

THE LIGHT STREAMING through the lace curtains cast a soft, golden glow across the room where Ashley stood, her wedding gown cascading around her like a shimmering cloud. Maddie was at her side, fastening the last delicate button at the back of the dress, Sera nitpicking with her hair, while Charlene lazed cross-legged on the plush ottoman, a mischievous glint in her eye while her friends did all the work.

"So you'll marry the man that sneezed on you," Charlene piped up. "What did she call him again? The Earl of Glowering?"

Maddie laughed and tilted her head to warn Charlene. "Behave! Would you, please?"

Sera arched a brow in the mirror, her fingers still deft in Ashley's hair. "Well, she's not wrong."

"So shall I call your husband to remove you?" Maddie said in jest. "I doubt he'll have a problem with that. I shall *cross* you from this wedding."

Sera laughed.

"Oh, please! Yes, his name is Adam Cross and there isn't a pun you've missed to tease me with."

"And you are the Duchess of *Rotheworth*, then? Very *cross* even for you!" Ashley chuckled. "But I don't think we'll need this anymore."

On the vanity before them rested the small, weathered handbook, its edges frayed from countless moments spent in their hands, guiding them through the seasons of their lives. Charlene picked it up, her fingers brushing over the cover as though it carried a weight far beyond its size. The handbook.

Ashley looked toward the reflection of her friends in the mirror, her lips curving into a tender smile. "Do you remember when we first opened that silly little book? I thought it would solve everything."

Maddie chuckled softly, smoothing a soft fold in Ashley's sleeve. "It did solve some things. Other times, it only reminded us how clueless we were."

"Agreed," Sera said. "I was perhaps the most clueless of us all!"

"Hah! Speak for yourselves," Charlene quipped, but her teasing was soft, her smile a little uneven. "It wasn't all bad advice, you know. It got us here, didn't it?"

Ashley turned to face them, her eyes already glistening. She reached for the handbook, wrapping her hands around Charlene's as they both held it. "It didn't just get us here. Its awful advice carried us. Through every mistake, every victory, every plan that went so wonderfully, miserably awry."

Maddie stepped closer, resting a hand on Ashley's arm, her expression one of quiet reflection. "Season by season," she said, her voice lighter than her brimming emotion, "we made it through. We found love, and yes, we caught the wedding fever."

"But only Maddie thought there'd be an ointment to cure it, didn't she?" Ashley laughed, putting her hand on her stomach. It was still flat, but not for much longer, Maddie reckoned.

"Well…" Maddie said. Her concoction, not so much ointment, had gotten Ashley in a spot of trouble in the past.

"I, for one, enjoy a good ointment," Sera said.

Ashley laughed tearfully, shaking her head. "Imagine that. Us—notorious cynics about happily-ever-afters, reduced to wedding squabbles and banter about giving away our flowers."

"And look at you now," Charlene added, her grin a little wobbly. "Marrying the love of your life in a dress that looks like it came from a storybook. Honestly, Ashley, you've gone full fever and passed it on to all of us. There's no hope for you now."

They all burst into laughter, though the sound trembled with the weight of the moment. Ashley drew them all into her arms, her voice soft with love. "I don't think we need this little book anymore, do we? Awful or not. We've made it through, just the four of us." She looked to Maddie, Sera, then Charlene, holding their gazes. "And we're just fine."

Maddie nodded, her voice thick as she added, "Better than fine."

Charlene held the handbook up, glancing at it one last time before setting it on the vanity. "We wrote our own rules in the end. And besides, if we've caught the wedding fever, well... I can't think of anyone better to catch it with." She brushed a tear from her cheek, her wink breaking the sentiment even as her heart vied to hold onto it.

"To us," Ashley said, raising her hand in a pretend toast.

Maddie smiled, pressing her hand over Ashley's. "And to love."

Charlene joined in, her voice warm, her eyes shining. "And steamy bedchambers."

Sera grinned. "And to catching the wedding fever!"

Chapter Thirty-Three

T HE CHAPEL WAS aglow with flickering candlelight, their flames dancing gently against the cool hush of winter morning air. Red winter flowers, vibrant and velvety, lined the pews in garlands that twisted with greenery, their petals a striking contrast to the season's pale stillness outside. The sweet, earthy scent of pine and floral notes mingled faintly in the air, warming the space as it filled with soft whispers and rustling fabric. High above, the stained-glass windows caught the slanted rays of morning light, splashing hues of crimson, gold, and sapphire across the stone floor in a kaleidoscope of color. The light breathed life into the shadows, turning the chapel into something almost otherworldly, a cocoon of warmth and beauty against the frost-laden world outside.

The soft murmur of voices faded as the chapel doors creaked open, the sound cutting through the stillness like the hush before falling snow. Maddie's fingers fidgeted with the hem of her gloves, her chest tight as she sat between Sebastian and Charlene. Her ice-blue gown rustled faintly when she shifted, the fitted lace around her bodice an almost-too-tight reminder of the storm swirling inside her. Quiet gasps drew her gaze forward, where everyone had turned toward the bride.

"You look beautiful," Sebastian mouthed.

Would she ever stop blushing under his attention?

Then the organ started to play and the doors at the back of the chapel opened.

Ashley stood silhouetted against the soft glow of the snow-dusted day outside, her arm looped through her father's. Her blonde curls tumbled in soft waves over her shoulders, catching the light like spun silk, and the palest blue of her gown shimmered faintly beneath the white ermine draped over her. Maddie's chest tightened, and her fingers involuntarily stilled. Ashley was a vision, so effortlessly radiant that Maddie could do nothing but stare, her hands frozen in a knot of nerves.

She wasn't sure if it was the beauty of the moment or the weight of everything she felt pressing into her chest. Maybe both.

Ashley's father led her forward, a vision. Maddie's eyes drifted to Thomas at the altar, his expression filled with trepidation and delight as they fixed on his bride. His love for Ashley was there in every line of his face, so open that it felt too intimate to watch.

But it wasn't the groom who held her attention for long. It was Ashley's gaze, skimming across the aisle before it stopped on Maddie. A small smile danced at her lips, blooming like the first brave petals of spring. There was no mistaking the warmth there, the unspoken words carried in that look alone: Be brave. Have faith. You deserve this.

Maddie's throat tightened as her vision blurred. The tears came before she could stop them, slipping hot over her cheeks. She blinked quickly, but there was no stopping the tremble in her breath. Then she felt it. Fingers brushing over hers, warm and steady.

Without looking, Maddie curled her hand around Sebastian's. His palm was firm, grounding, and when he gently squeezed her fingers, she turned her face toward him. He didn't say anything at first, just looked at her in that way he had, like he knew every thought tumbling in her head without needing her to voice it. The curve of his lips softened as his thumb traced a small circle into her palm.

"You'll ruin your gloves," he teased, his voice pitched low, meant just for her. His mouth twitched faintly at the corner as if holding back a grin, but his eyes never wavered, intent and unshakable.

Maddie bit her lip to keep herself steady, shaking her head. "I can't help it," she whispered. "It's all too much."

"It's supposed to be," Sebastian said simply, his voice easing into her like warmth by the fire. "Some things are meant to feel this way."

The certainty in his tone, the way he said it as though it was the simplest truth in the world, left her breathless. For a moment, her grip on his hand tightened. She wanted to say something, to tell him he was the reason tears spilled so freely now, but the words tangled somewhere beneath the weight in her chest.

Ashley and her father reached the altar, and the ceremony began, the vicar's words ringing low and sure through the candlelit space. Maddie tried to listen, her gaze flitting between Ashley and Thomas, but everything blurred at the edges. Her focus drifted back to the quiet warmth next to her. It was Sebastian's presence, his hand still holding hers, that softened the sharp ache of emotion inside her.

Charlene leaned closer from her other side, nudging Maddie lightly with her shoulder. "Breathe, you goose," she whispered, her smile wry but kind. "It's a wedding, not a tragedy."

Maddie blinked rapidly, a nervous laugh escaping her. "I wasn't prepared, that's all."

Charlene's grin widened, and she nodded toward Sebastian. Maddie felt the weight of Charlene's amusement before she even spoke. "I think someone else was."

Maddie's cheeks warmed, and she dropped her gaze to their entwined hands. Sebastian didn't seem to notice Charlene's teasing, or if he did, he didn't care. His thumb continued its steady motion against her knuckles, grounding her in a way she didn't realize she needed.

The archbishop's voice rose, drawing her attention back just as Thomas reached for Ashley's hand. The vows unfolded like poetry, each line drawing a thread of light through the quiet of the chapel. Maddie could feel the stillness pressed around them, the quiet awe from every guest as Ashley and Thomas sealed their promises with words that seemed to hover like frost-kissed breaths.

When it ended, and the vicar declared them husband and wife, the room erupted into applause. Ashley and Thomas turned together, their hands clasped as they began the walk back down the aisle. Ashley's expression was luminous, her joy infectious as she passed Maddie's row, her smile stretching into something beautifully familiar.

"Thank you," Maddie whispered, though she knew Ashley couldn't hear it. The words fell into the space between her and Sebastian instead, and she realized with startling clarity that they were meant for him too.

When the guests began to rise, Maddie moved to stand, but Sebastian didn't release her hand. His grip firmed for just a moment, holding her back when she turned to face him. His gaze caught hers, steady and unyielding.

"You don't have to say it yet," he murmured, his voice so quiet she wondered if she had imagined it. "But I need you to know—I'm staying. Whatever it takes, whatever it means. I'm here."

Maddie breathed in sharply, emotions cresting inside her like a tide she had no way to stop. He looked at her like there was nothing else in the world that mattered, nothing except her. She squeezed his hand, her voice barely more than a whisper. "You don't have to stay, Sebastian. You already are."

He smiled then, a small, knowing smile that carried more weight than words could. The press of his lips to her knuckles was soft, fleeting, but it left her trembling.

And with that, Maddie realized that this moment wasn't about the wedding or the vows ringing through her thoughts. It was about him. It was about them. Snow swirled softly outside the chapel, but she had never felt warmer.

❦

Epilogue

The Morning Gazette
August 14th, 1816

DUKE OF PAISLEY ARRAIGNED—TRIAL OF A PEER FOR VILE OFFENSES

It is with no small sense of public relief that we report the conclusion of proceedings against Richard, Duke of Paisley, whose name has long been whispered in connection with certain lamentable scandals which have, for some years past, shocked the sensibilities of polite society.

The present charge—of the forcible abduction of a gentlewoman of high rank—was brought after a series of accusations had been quietly suppressed by powerful friends. Many will recall that, some seasons ago, the duke was rumored to have been implicated in the ruin of a young debutante, the matter being hushed at the time for the sake of her family. It seems, however, that such leniency emboldened rather than reformed him.

The recent affair began when the lady in question (whose name we forbear to print) was discovered to be missing from her family's seat under mysterious circumstances. Within a week, she was recovered—shaken, but mercifully unharmed—through the prompt and resolute action of her betrothed, aided by several gentlemen of unimpeachable honor. The duke, apprehended in the act of conveying her to a remote location, was conveyed under guard to London.

At the trial, evidence was produced not only of this most recent outrage, but of a pattern of behavior so infamous that the assembled peers could scarcely bring themselves to hear it recounted. After deliberation, the duke was found guilty and sentenced to perpetual exile from the realm, his remaining estates placed in trust, and his titles suspended.

It is said that His Grace departed under escort, showing no contrition for his actions, and vowing to "return in triumph." Society may rest assured that His Majesty's ministers have made such a return impossible.

In happier news, we are pleased to add that Lord S——, whose courage in the matter has been widely commended, is now enjoying domestic felicity with his wife, the former Miss M——, who is shortly to present him with an heir. Those who saw the couple at a recent gathering observed that his lordship kept her so close at his side that one might suppose he feared she might vanish should he so much as release her hand.

Maddie set the Morning Gazette aside, the pages crackling faintly in her hands. The bold headline about the Duke of Paisley's exile stared up at her like a final line drawn through his name. She let the satisfaction bloom fully this time, no reason to hide it.

"Well," she said, smoothing her skirts with deliberate calm, "that serves him right."

Sebastian, lounging at her side with a watchfulness that hadn't diminished since the day they'd kissed, arched a brow. "Not worth another thought now," he murmured, though the way his thumb brushed over her knuckles made her suspect he'd been keeping one eye on her reaction since the moment she opened the paper.

Across the room, sunlight streamed over Ashley, who had her son balanced on her lap. The baby gurgled—a happy, bubbling sound—and clapped his little hands, the picture of innocent delight. Maddie watched as Thomas leaned in, his expression softened to something utterly unguarded and made a face that had the child shrieking with laughter. It was hard to say which of them he adored more—Ashley or their boy—but if Maddie were forced to guess, she might call it an even match.

They were already debating which new foal in the stables should be gentled for their son—Ashley naming the sweet-tempered bay filly, Thomas insisting the spirited gray colt would build character.

In the far corner, Sera sat close beside Prince Alex, their heads bent together over a book spread wide between them. Maddie caught the low murmur of Sera's voice, her lips shaping careful syllables in Romanian. Alex corrected her pronunciation with a quiet patience that spoke volumes of his devotion to her, his hand resting over hers on the page. "By the next time we're in Transylvania," Sera said with a little lift to her chin, "I'll be able to greet everyone in their own tongue." Maddie smiled, certain that the next visit to Bran Castle would be for the baptism of their first child—Sera had that luminous look about her.

By the hearth, Charlene and Rotheworth were in the midst of an animated discussion over a map of Spain spread across the table.

"Do we have to bring your mother?" Charlene asked, one brow raised in mock challenge. Maddie laughed at the faint horror on Rotheworth's face before he tried for diplomacy.

"You and she are on better terms now," he said, with the air of a man hoping to keep the peace. "A few grandchildren and she'll be singing your praises to the skies." Charlene snorted softly, but there was a glint of affection in her eyes when she looked at him.

Sebastian leaned toward Maddie, close enough that his breath stirred a wisp of hair at her temple. "Is the baby kicking again?" he asked, his voice gentled to something meant for her alone.

She caught his hand and drew it to her belly, covering it with her own. A moment later, the tiny thump came—a firm, certain little movement—and his breath hitched. His eyes softened, the corners crinkling in a way that melted her right down to her bones.

"That," he said quietly, "is the sound of our forever beginning."

Her heart clenched, full and unguarded. She thought of Paisley's smugness, now half a world away, powerless and forgotten. Instead, she focused on the man beside her—one who would stand between her and every storm, without hesitation, without condition.

As long as there were men like Sebastian in the world, she would never—could never—understand someone like Paisley. If fate hadn't brought her to him, she'd have chosen spinsterhood a hundred times over.

She leaned into his side, letting herself savor the warm hum of voices, the soft gurgle of Ashley's baby, the rustle of Sera's turning pages, the low chuckle from Rotheworth. Love, laughter, and a future stretching bright before them all.

And when Sebastian's fingers tightened just slightly over hers, as if he meant to hold on for a lifetime, Maddie knew she would let him.

Thank you for reading the Wedding Fever series. Did you know that the apothecary whom Maddie got her medicines from is Alfie Collins from *The Scent of Intuition*, Book 2 in the *Miracles on Harley Street* series? For more books by Sara Adrien, please visit www.SaraAdrien.com.

RECIPE FOR SEBASTIAN'S BEER-BASED EGG-FLIP

If you'd like to whip up some delicious beer-based egg-flip for a nightcap like Sebastian did, follow these easy steps:

Ingredients:

2 egg yolks

2 tablespoons of sugar (or brown sugar)

1/4 teaspoon of nutmeg (or less)

1 cup of dark beer (such as stout or porter)

Whipped cream (optional)

Extra nutmeg (for garnish)

Grated lemon rind or chocolate for garnish (optional)

Instructions:

Combine the egg yolks, sugar, and nutmeg in a cocktail shaker or blender. Shake or blend until the mixture is smooth and the sugar has dissolved. To avoid the risks from consuming raw eggs, consider giving the egg yolks a boil and adding the whipping cream at this stage in the blender; the mixture will be even creamier.

Slowly pour in the beer while continuing to blend/shake until the mixture is well combined.

Pour the egg-flip into a heat-resistant glass or mug and top with whipped cream (if desired) and a sprinkle of nutmeg, chocolate shavings, or a rind of lemon on the corner of the glass.

Enjoy this delicious beer-based egg-flip nightcap, perfect for warming up on a chilly evening.

AUTHOR'S NOTES

Dear Readers,

Thank you for reading *Ways to Kiss a Marquess This Winter*, the final installment in the *Wedding Fever Series*! I hope you've enjoyed this seasonal journey of love, laughter, and a touch of mischief.

If you've been wondering why Paisley is the bad guy in Ashley's story, you might want to revisit *Dare to Tempt an Earl This Spring* (Wedding Fever Book 1). Paisley gets his turn to meddle here, but don't worry—each book in the series can be read as a standalone, so feel free to jump in wherever you like!

A special note on Maddie's delightful concoctions, which come from none other than Alfie Collins, the charming apothecary on 87 Harley Street. Alfie is one of the heroes in Sara Adrien's *Miracles on Harley Street* series, who gets his love story in *The Sound of Seduction*. If you haven't read it yet, it's out now and waiting for you!

And speaking of the *Miracles on Harley Street* series, don't forget that Prince Alex has a brother and a sister with their own captivating stories. Princess Thea's tale unfolds in *A Touch of Charm*, while Prince Stan's journey is told in *The Sound of Seduction*. Both are available now, so be sure to check them out!

Finally, I want to express my heartfelt gratitude to you, my readers. This story came straight from the heart, and your support means the world to me. If you enjoyed this book, the best way to show your appreciation is by leaving a review and sharing it with others. And don't you think a 4-book bundle with a story for every season makes the perfect gift?

Thank you for being part of this journey. Here's to more love, laughter, and happily-ever-afters!

Warmest wishes,
Sara Adrien

Dearest Reader,

Every love story is brighter when shared, so thank you for sharing ours! Your support, your laughter (I hope!), and your willingness to fall in love with these characters as we have means the world. Though the curtain falls on this collaboration and its cast, countless new adventures await just beyond the wings.

I hope to catch you in those others.

Much Love,
Tanya

ABOUT THE AUTHORS

SARA ADRIEN

#1 Bestselling author Sara Adrien writes hot and heart-melting Regency romance with a Jewish twist. As a law professor-turned-author, she writes about clandestine identities, whims of fate, and sizzling seduction. If you like unique and intelligent characters, deliciously sexy scenes, and the nostalgia of afternoon tea, then you'll adore Sara Adrien's tender tear-jerkers.

For more information and exclusive sneak peeks, new releases, and more books, sign up for Sara Adrien's newsletter at www.SaraAdrien.com.

TANYA WILDE

Award-Winning and International Bestselling author Tanya Wilde developed a passion for reading when she had nothing better to do than lurk in the library during her lunch breaks. Her love affair with pen and paper soon followed, after she devoured all their historical romance books! When she's not meddling in the lives of her characters or pondering names for her imaginary big, white greyhound, she's off on adventures with her partner in crime.

Wilde lives in a town at the foot of the Outeniqua Mountains, South Africa. You can read a bit more about her at www.authortanyawilde.com.

9 781969 349768